The Message

Eight Stories of One Misunderstood Text

Andrew Allen
Brian Grall
Robert Jacques
Michelle Johnston
Matthew J. Kolell
Marcus Maichle
Catalino Tolejano, II
Patrick A. Waldoch

Published by Authors Rising, LLC

Published by
Authors Rising, LLC
Milwaukee, WI
www.authorsrising.com

Cover photo, layout, and interior design by A. Weisensel

ISBN-10: 0-9830746-2-3
ISBN-13: 978-0-9830746-2-5

This book is dedicated to all aspiring writers everywhere. If you want to be published, and are willing to work hard, listen to honest feedback, and help others, come see us.

-Authors Rising

Thanks to family and friends for their support and understanding, and my wife for believing in me. Thanks also to all the authors who have inspired me with their stories, writing blogs, and hard work – from Jim Butcher, to the others in this book, and all the rest at AuthorsRising.com.

-Andrew Allen

The Id of Brian Grall would like to thank the Nobel Laureates, the board of directors, the…oh, sorry; wrong dedication.

-Brian Grall

To Derick. Thank you for always believing.

-Michelle Johnston

Thank you to Sara for her love and support. Also to Andrew for making me write a real story.

-Matthew J. Kolell

For Mom, my light and life. I miss you already, and I'll think of you always. May your next journey be only joyful.

-Marcus Maichle

To my friends and family who convinced me to continue writing, and to the Tarantino's, Easton Ellis', Koushun Takami's, and Stephen King's of the world who had the bravery to tell the stories they wanted to tell. Thank you.

-Robert Jacques

Thank you to Authors Rising, the Authors involved in this work, Andrew for driving us to success, and all those who have inspired us to create the stories herein. I'd especially like to thank my family for understanding this need and accommodating my writing affliction! Thank you all!

-Catalino Tolejano, II

I dedicate this story to all my math teachers and tutors from grade school through college that got me to and though calculus. Little did I think I'd be using calc again just to write a short story's space travel correctly.

-Patrick A. Waldoch

CONTENTS

Dangerous Directive

Michelle Johnston

I looked around the table at the grim faces. No one was happy and my report, or lack of one, was the reason. At least I wasn't at the head of the table, I thought wryly. Not everyone had a direct line of sight to me, and I could pretend there were a few friendly faces. The mayor shook his head and said the same thing he'd been saying for the past hour.

"Without other major cities resisting, it's only a matter of time before the Unified World Union takes over. Los Angeles can't stand and fight alone."

Frustration threatened to boil over as I leaned forward and explained for what felt like the thousandth time. "The rebel movement is still in its infancy. Los Angeles was our first victory, and it has only been a month since we ousted the UWU. The net has started to call 3/31 Independence Day. They are calling us "The Freedom Fighters". That bodes well....people are being inspired and patriot fighters are springing up all across the world. We have support, and it's growing as word gets out."

No one made eye contact. "Sympathy and support are all well and good, Ms. Wakefeld, but we need successes. We've heard no news from your contacts in the resistance. When will you hear back from them?" This was directed at me from the police chief. He had the decency to look slightly embarrassed for asking. I acknowledged the question with a brief hand motion.

"They are putting their lives at risk by defying the edict for all subjects to display loyalty to the Unified World Union. The UWU solidified its control of the major communication companies. Now that we've made our stand, there's a good chance that all channels are being monitored. With the risk of discovery they will limit all communication to essential information. I'll hear from them when they have important news."

An unhappy silence descended upon the table. It was not what they wanted to hear. Not that I could blame them.

"They'll do anything they can to help further the cause. But they have to be careful not to put each other, or us, in jeopardy. Being too easy with communication could backfire. We're rebels. We do what we must. And now, we must wait." It was a phrase borrowed from a fellow fighter, but it fit well. I closed my notebook pointedly.

"What should we do in the meantime?" asked the mayor's aide. Now we were getting somewhere. I gave her a quick smile.

"We need to show the world that Los Angeles stands strong. Keep "business as usual" going all across the city. Pretend we're not in the middle of resisting a hostile world takeover. Give the rebellion some time to get on its feet."

"In that case," the mayor said as he rose, "let's break for lunch. Afterward, we can reconvene and discuss how to keep the city supplied with necessities in light of the trade siege." He looked pointedly at me, "We won't be needing you this afternoon."

Nodding, I made my goodbyes. It would take time for their fears to numb. For the time being, I was a constant reminder of their precarious stand. Only the police chief nodded encouragingly at me as I made my way out, heading back to my apartment.

. . .

Closing the door behind me, I breathed a sigh. Regardless of the obstacles, Los Angeles still stood. The trade siege was creating only a minor inconvenience so far, and the general public seemed to have high spirits. The comments in the meeting worried me, though. People needed to see consistent progress. If we didn't have success in another city soon, the rebellion would flounder. Los Angeles would fall and the UWU would control the entire USA. It already controlled China and Europe. From there, it would be a matter of months before the entire world was under its shadow.

Across the room the indicator on my smartphone flashed. I picked it up and entered my password. There was a text from one of the main leaders of the resistance, Alex. I hoped it was good news.

PJW-
Remember 3/31? Need help desperately, not much time left. Please, you're the only one! 2713311869101001 You know what to do.
- Alex

I sat back in my chair and consulted a sheet of paper with numbers and names written in two columns. When the UWU had started to take over, we devised a set of codes to denote various cities and provinces throughout the world. 2713311869101001 was the code for Hong Kong, which also happened to be the UWU headquarters.

Mixed emotions and a myriad of thoughts flooded through me. What did he mean I was the only one? When the rebels left Los Angeles, I stayed behind to act as the base for the movement. I wasn't a fighter: my strengths were communication and technology.

The urgency in his message worried me. If Alex wanted me to go to Hong Kong, it could mean only one thing. They had a chance at taking out the UWU from the inside, but things had gone horribly wrong. What worried me most was that Alex hadn't given me rendezvous coordinates. If the resistance had been compromised, or worse, the leaders had been caught, it would be the end of the rebellion.

I wasn't sure what I could do, but I trusted Alex and if he needed me there then I had to go. He'd saved my life in the initial assault on LA. If for nothing more than that, I owed him.

I went to grab the phone and call the city council, and decided against it. No point in telling them. It would only demoralize them more than they already were. Chances were that they wouldn't come looking for me for a few days. If I wasn't back by then, all would be lost anyway. I started stuffing necessities into my duffel bag.

. . .

Due to the UWU siege, LAX was no longer in service. I'd have to make it to San Diego International Airport to catch a flight to Hong Kong. Getting out of Los Angeles was going to be risky. There were checkpoints and blockades around the entire city. Luckily, I had an ace up my sleeve.

I walked up to a dingy apartment and knocked, making sure no one was around. I surveyed the cracked paint and dirty windows and chuckled to myself. Few would believe that one of the best smugglers in the world lived in such a hovel. The door cracked open.

"It's me, Arnie. Open up before someone sees me."

The door flew open and I was engulfed in a crushing hug.

"Penny! Last time you came to visit, we became legends!"

Closing the door behind me, I walked into the living room. On the wall hung photos of UWU officers being forced from the city. He noticed my gaze.

"A man likes to celebrate his victories! What brings you here now? More fun?"

"I need you to get me out of the city, past the blockade."

He nodded thoughtfully. "With you, it's always a challenge. But there isn't anything Arnie can't do. What's the time frame?"

I gave him my sweetest smile. "Today. I need to be in San Diego to catch a flight this evening."

The thing I loved about Arnie was his ability to instantly take a job. He feigned scorn and shook his head, but I knew better. I flashed a roll of cash.

"Well it just so happens I have a few fake IDs lying around. We'll smuggle you through the checkpoint as Amy Townsend."

He tossed me a bottle of bleach and a pair of glasses. "We've got some work to do. Amy is a blond with terrible eyes."

. . .

Flashing lights signaled the checkpoint just up ahead. My hand shook as I adjusted the wig, and gave myself a quick look in the rear-view mirror. Arnie patted my arm reassuringly as he stopped the car.

"Relax. I've brought people in and out many times since the blockade went up."

A uniformed officer walked up and peered inside the window. "I'll need to see ID's for both of you."

I fumbled and dropped my ID on the floor of the car. Arnie picked it up and handed both IDs to the officer.

"Lovely day, isn't it Officer? Say, any news on when you folks will take back the city? It's getting mighty tight in there, resource wise. Those rebels promised freedom, but the way I see it, freedom means no food and a whole lotta hassle."

The officer barely spared him a glance as he ran the ID's through his system.

"Does it always take this long?" I whispered nervously.

Before Arnie could respond, a gun pointed into the car.

"I'm going to need *Amy* to step out with her hands up." The emphasis he put on the name told me we'd been caught.

I slowly got out of the car, hands raised. He pushed me onto the hood and cuffed me. My heart sunk. I knew I could handle the interrogation (and likely torture) I would receive. I would die before giving any information on the resistance. But I had no way to get in touch with Alex, and no way to send anyone in my place.

"Well, well, Amy. Turns out you've been dead for six months. So either you're a ghost, or you're in enough trouble with the law to hide your identity. Either way, you're going to be valuable to me." He looked pointedly at Arnie. "Do you know what the punishment is for harboring?"

"Just how valuable is a fugitive? This one is a real piece of work...grand theft auto, armed robbery, the works." Arnie lowered his voice conspiratorially. "She paid me fifty grand to smuggle her out. Guess the local cops were hot on her trail. Tell you what, I'll go 50-50 on it with you."

The officer considered. He looked me over. "Well, she sure isn't a rebel. Just a common criminal. I'm a merciful man myself. Believe in second chances, as long as treason isn't involved. 80-20, and we'll call it justice."

. . .

The rest of the way to San Diego was open road. It gave me plenty of time to berate Arnie, albeit mostly to cover how fried my nerves were.

"You paid him forty grand!"

Arnie smiled. "I know you're good for it, sugar. Honestly, I figured you'd be mad I didn't think you were worth more!"

"I told you never to call me that. I'm deducting 5% from your bill," I growled.

In typical Arnie smile, he just laughed and reveled in the victory.

As we pulled up to the airport he turned to me. "Be careful in there. If you don't come back, I'm out forty grand."

I laughed and gave him a quick hug, then headed towards the terminal. I had no time to procure a new ID, so I'd just have to use my own. As far as I knew, no ties had been made between myself and the rebellion. It should be clean. Unfortunately, that would leave a trail. It couldn't be avoided. Scanning the ticket counters, I picked the friendliest face I could. In a matter of moments I'd purchased a ticket on the 5:45 flight to Hong Kong and headed towards security.

"ID and ticket, please." The security officer seemed pleasant. I handed them over and held my breath.

"Oh, dear. Reggie, come take a look." Her manager came over and squinted at the screen. His eyes widened.

"Ma'am, I'm going to have to take you aside for additional screening. Please come with me."

He led me to a small room with a table and a few chairs. "Have a seat, I just have some questions I need to ask you."

I tried not to look nervous. "Is there a problem, sir?"

He sat down across from me and leaned over onto the table. "You haven't filed for citizenship of the UWU. In fact, your ID is listed in the system as missing and unaccounted for."

Licking my lips, I thought furiously for an explanation. If I didn't come up with one, he'd likely haul me to the nearest UWU correction center. "Did the deadline pass for registering?"

He said nothing. His stare seemed to say, 'try again'. I could tell I wasn't going to be able to bribe my way out of this one, and I had never been much good at bluffing.

"Ok, let me be honest. I'm from LA. I was caught up in the sensationalist propaganda of the so-called "Freedom Fighters". By the time I came to my senses, the deadline had passed and I was considered a traitor. I didn't know what to do. I've heard that if you present yourself to the UWU headquarters with information on rebels, you can be pardoned. My plan is to show up there, with some knowledge of the inner workings I gleaned while living in LA." I tried to put as much truth into it as I could. Maybe the small bits of truth would stop him from catching the lies. As if any of us rebels would ever turn each other in for amnesty.

"You realize I'm going to have to inform the flight crew of your situation. They will get in contact with headquarters, and a UWU officer will escort you there for processing."

One problem at a time. I'd deal with the officer when I got to Hong Kong. It was always amazing to me that people believed what they wanted to hear, no matter how unlikely. "That sounds wonderful," I lied. "I don't want there to be further confusion. I'd like to get my *situation* cleared up immediately."

He held out his hand. "Ok, Ms. Wakefeld. Enjoy your flight. And welcome to the Union."

. . .

I stepped off the plane to a bright, sunny day. The flight attendant escorting me looked around, then headed towards two men in full uniform. I did a double take; one of them was Alex. She shook hands with them both.

"Good afternoon, gentlemen. This is Ms. Wakefeld. Is there anything else I need to do?"

Alex took the lead. "No, now that we have Ms. Wakefeld you are released from liability. Thank you, and have a nice day."

The flight attended barely spared me a glance as she hurried away. Things couldn't have gone better, I thought to myself. Alex must have hacked the UWU communications. Now we could deal with whatever crisis he was in. All my worries and fruitless planning on the flight over vanished. I went to speak, but the other officer cut me off.

"Penny J. Wakefeld, you are under arrest for treason." He slapped handcuffs on me and started to lead me out.

"What? Alex..."

"You are advised to use your right of silence, Ms. Wakefeld," Alex interrupted coldly. "You're to be transported to headquarters, and immediately face a tribunal."

. . .

The tribunal was quick and heart wrenching. Multiple rebels appeared to testify against me. It seemed Alex wasn't the only one to turn, although his testimony was the most painful. His testimony had sounded more like the speech of a loving but disappointed father than a condemnation.

With all the evidence against me, the judge didn't even need to deliberate to come to a decision. Guilty. Sentence: hanging. I was escorted to a cell to await the carrying out of my punishment. I lay alone for hours, shock numbing any emotion.

Eventually, a key turned in the lock and my cell door opened. I spat at the figure standing in the doorway.

"You have a lot of nerve, Alex."

He smiled and wiped his face. "I'm sorry I had to put you through this. I knew you'd be upset at first. "

"You traitors. What did they offer you?"

Leaning up against a wall, a look of confusion clouded his face. "Don't you understand? Penny, we're on the inside! We're safe. "

I rushed at him, but the chains stopped me from getting into striking range. "I understand you turned traitor. What did they offer you, money? Power?"

He started to laugh. "Do you honestly believe we could do that? With all we've been through? Our only chance to succeed is to take the UWU down from the inside. Well, we're on the inside now! Your capture proved our loyalty. I'm sorry we had to use you. It was the only way."

I stared blankly. What was he saying?

"Now we can begin to undermine their operations." He leaned forward and gently touched my face. "When this is all over, you will be a hero."

"I'd rather be alive."

His face turned hard, and the moment of gentleness was gone. "Your life for the freedom of the world. I would be honored to be in your position."

I laughed bitterly. "Easy to say from where you're standing. And I'd be ashamed to be in yours."

"I will see to it that the world knows of your *willing* sacrifice." With that, he was gone.

The lights clicked off, and I was left to my thoughts.

That was Alex for you, all business. Like he'd always told me: We're rebels. We do what we must.

Michelle Johnston *has been reading non stop since she turned 4. Eventually, inevitably, she ended up writing. Michelle is also a hiker, loves bicycling, cooks obsessively, and constantly daydreams. She lives with her husband, cat, and dog in the Pacific Northwest.*

The Message

Andrew Allen

"You will find enlightenment when you finally reveal your true self to others."

"-- in bed" Deuce automatically added, "Heh. Nice one, Jack." The two of us were just finishing our Chinese take-out in the car. The meeting at the restaurant had come to an abrupt end when Arthur Koning, one of my biggest rivals, angrily walked out shortly after we'd all ordered. We had quickly asked for our food 'to go,' and gotten out of there as well. Deuce and I were now parked in a mostly-empty lot overlooking Lake Michigan, with snow still piled up around the edges even after a few above-freezing days. The engine was running to keep us warm in the cold, late-March evening.

"Here, open yours..." I handed him the cookie. "What'd you get?"

"Uh... this is weird, man..." Deuce frowned as he read the little slip of paper, "Um... in bed? Yeah, that don't work at all ... this is the weirdest fortune I've ever gotten. Aren't these your initials?" He handed me the paper.

JAC-Remember 3/31? Need help desperately, not much time left. Please, you're the only one! 2713311869101001 You know what to do. - Alex

I read it aloud, trying to make sense of it. Those *were* my initials... but it had to just be a coincidence. How would they end up inside a fortune cookie with such a strange message?

"You're messing with me, to get back at me for all the long days we've been putting in meeting with the other bosses," I accused. "How'd you manage to pull it off?"

"Jack, I don't know nothin' bout this. I been with you the whole day, and we didn't even know what restaurant we'd be at until we got Koning's call." Deuce seemed pretty sincere. I gave him a sideways look, and read through it again.

"Alex... Alex... hmmm... do we know anyone named Alex?" I asked, half to Deuce, half to myself. I looked out over the lake as I thought about it, and glanced around the parking lot. It was mostly empty, but there were a few other cars: two down at the other end near the entrance, and one not too far away. Something caught my attention about the nearer vehicle... light reflecting off something inside that was occasionally visible even through the darkened windows.

"Deuce... is there someone watching us from that car over there?" His eyes were better than mine.

"Which one, Jack? That mini-van? Why would they be ... well ... hmm ... maybe so?" He studied the car with a sudden concern, and searched for signs of trouble. "Looks like whoever it is has a camera."

I decided to be bold on this one, and set down the remnants of the Chinese food. "Be right back" I told Deuce, as I stepped out of the car. I didn't take cameras lightly. I wasn't quite a 'Crime Boss,' but the Organization was questionable enough that some people would probably think I was pretty close. And I didn't need anybody nosing around in my business these days, as I tried to consolidate support among the high-ranking Organization members. The last thing I wanted was someone with a bunch of pictures showing me going around to all the others, outing them in the process. No, cameras were not something I could tolerate these days – and Koning had just been arguing earlier tonight that a boss needed to take a tougher hand in things, and let people see who was in charge.

The night had gotten colder since we left the restaurant -- but I could still hear the voices of children out enjoying the last of the snow. I looked back towards the voices as I prepared to go confront our stalker in the mini-van... and saw kids playing on the huge pile of snow a plow had made just beyond where we were parked. They were sledding down the pile and had added a jump at the bottom. I·shook my head, and got back in the car.

"What was that all about, Jack?" asked Deuce.

"Nothing." I pointed to the kids outside, "It's just some dad taking pictures of his kids going over that jump. I must be getting paranoid. Maybe we should call it a night?" Deuce put the car in gear, and pulled out of the parking lot. I felt better once we were moving. With those kids and their parents, the almost empty parking lot had felt oddly crowded. "What were we talking about?"

"The message you got in the cookie." Deuce's reply seemed like it ought to be comical, but the reminder of the weird fortune made me concerned more than anything. I read it again, and thought about it as we drove. They were my initials – JAC, Jonathan Anthony Cassanova – as if the note were addressed to me. The "not much time left" kinda made sense, if you took the 3/31 as a date -- that would be tomorrow. But someone with an urgent message wouldn't take the time to put it into a cookie; that would take forever. And no one knew we were going to be at that restaurant, anyway ... wait a minute.

"Deuce, did you pick the Chinese place to meet at, or did Koning?"

"Well, we were talking about food, and there were a couple places we both suggested..." Deuce thought out loud, "But in the end I guess he did."

It could have been him, then. Must have been, nothing else would explain it. But why go to the trouble? Koning and I had a borderline-hostile relationship, that had actually crossed over that line earlier tonight, as it did fairly often. He'd been furious with me a couple months back. I had upset his takeover of a high-profile project in the Organization, managing the release of a new designer drug I'd named True Love. That fury turned to hatred when our boss was shot under questionable circumstances only a few months later, and I'd become the acting head of the Organization in the Midwest. I had more to do with those questionable circumstances than anyone knew. The drug had turned out to be far more dangerous than any of us realized, but the boss was solely focused on the potential profit. I had to be in charge in order to keep True Love off the streets, but the drug's danger, and the way the boss had died, both needed to stay unknown if I was going to have any chance of making this "acting" leadership position into a permanent one.

There was no question Koning thought he was better-suited to be the one on top... But how did this fortune cookie thing help him?

"It had to be Koning," I said to Deuce, "but I've got no clue why or what he has to gain."

"Maybe this Alex is a friend of his," suggested Deuce, "but he can't ask for your help openly, 'cause he knows it would make him look weak?"

"Or, he wants me to waste time on a wild goose chase," I replied, "while he tries to convince others to support him."

"Maybe he's got to tell you about the situation, since you're acting Boss -- but this way you'll ignore it, until it's too late? Then he can say he told you, but you didn't do anything?" Even Deuce seemed to realize that was a bit far fetched. "Do you want to ask him about it?"

"No," I replied, "not if I can help it. If it wasn't Koning that sent it, asking him about secret messages in fortune cookies would just give him more ammunition to use against me." I rubbed my eyes, and flipped down the visor to see if I looked as stressed-out as I imagined these days. My eyes were a bit red, and I definitely hadn't been getting enough sleep. I squinted my eyes against the bright lights that flashed in the mirror as a car followed us around the turn onto my street. There was very little on my street, other than the building I lived in, a couple businesses that were closed at this time of night, a bar called the High Tide, and an empty lot across the way. The street dead ended into the river, so there was no where else to go. "Deuce... how long has that sedan been behind us?

"Not sure," he checked the mirror, "but at least a couple minutes since I first noticed it. Think we should be concerned?"

"I don't know.... pull over and let's see what he does." Deuce slowed down and pulled the car over to the curb, but left the engine running. We watched as the sedan drove past us and pulled into the empty lot... and sat there. With the engine running.

"Did you see how many people were inside when they drove by?" I asked, "I thought there were at least two, but it was hard to tell."

"Sorry Jack, I have no idea." Deuce looked up and down the street. "What do you suppose they're waiting for?"

"Maybe to get a clean shot, as I get out and start walking towards the building." We hadn't really stopped in front of my building's entrance when Deuce pulled over, and I didn't look forward to the half-block between me and the doors. "They're definitely watching us."

"What do you wanna do?" Deuce got out his phone, "I'm sure a couple of our club boys are nearby -- should I give Johnny and his friend with the spikey hair a call?"

"No, I have a feeling if something's going to happen, it will go down before they'd get here. Besides, we've got to show I can handle this kind of thing." I opened the glove box, and took out the guns, handing Deuce his. It hadn't been that long ago that he'd been surprised to find I even owned a gun, since I so seldom carried it. Lately, though, we'd both been regulars at the range, practicing to the point of being really comfortable with our weapons. I think Deuce still didn't believe he'd actually have to use his -- he'd opted for style over function, and had a long-barreled Smith & Wesson 626 revolver. It was stainless, and chambered for .357 Magnum, but all we had along for it were .38 special wad-cutters for use on paper targets at the range. The intimidation factor would hopefully be enough to keep us from having to use it anyway. I put the clip in my 1911, and "cocked and locked" – chambering a round, and putting the safety on – being careful to keep the gun out of sight for now.

"Drive over and see what's going on?" Deuce looked at me expectantly.

"Do it." He pulled the car back out into the road, and we headed slowly toward the lot. Just then the driver of the sedan opened his door and got out, talking animatedly on a cell phone. "Hold on, Deuce." He pulled back over, in front of my entrance this time. The passenger had also stepped out, and as soon as he shut the door, the driver beeped the auto-lock button on his keys, and they headed across the street towards the High Tide. The passenger seemed to have a little video camera that he was filming the driver with, who seemed kind of annoyed with the whole thing. He stayed on his phone the entire way into the bar. Neither of them ever so much as glanced our way.

I let out a breath I hadn't realized I'd been holding. "Good grief, Deuce -- what's wrong with us tonight?"

"I dunno, Jack." he replied, handing me back the revolver, "I blame Koning and his hysterics at the restaurant. Together with the weird fortune cookie, it put me on edge." I put his gun back in the glove box, and tucked mine away.

"Yeah, me too. Good night, Deuce." I opened the door and got out.

"What was it that fortune said again?" he asked.

I read it to him.

"I don't think I know anyone named Alex" said Deuce.

"We'll figure it out in the morning." I replied, and headed up the steps.

He waited until I was inside. I looked back at the fortune as he pulled away. Then it hit me: I did know an Alex, sort of -- and he'd been warning me about dire events pretty much every time he saw me. But he'd died over the True Love thing the same night as the Boss had. Alexander Giorna, a name I'd thought was safely in the past. The message couldn't have come from him, but it could just be to link it to True Love. Maybe this was Koning's way of showing he knew more about what had happened than I thought he did.

* * *

We sat at Alterra the next day, drinking coffee. We'd been there all morning, laptop open on the table, as we tried to puzzle out what the message was asking us to do.

"The key has got to be in the numbers." I insisted.

Deuce shook his head to clear it. "I'm going to go get a refill."

"You just want an excuse to go talk to the brunette behind the counter again," I joked. He just smiled and wandered off. This kind of task -- figuring out what the message might be hiding -- wasn't really his kind of thing at all. I was still trying different versions of the message on Google when he came back and set a couple pastries on the table. I pushed the laptop his way and grabbed one of the pastries. "You just couldn't resist buying something more from her, eh? I think she's got the upper hand here."

"You think so?" Deuce said haughtily, as he dropped the receipt on the table. In bold but beautiful script, it had 'Eve -- 273-2123' written on it. "I got her digits."

I looked back at my search query, and then again at the receipt. Hmm... it could fit.

"Deuce, give me your phone for a minute." I reached a hand over, and he looked at it skeptically, but then took out his phone, unlocked it, and handed it my way. I punched in the first 7 digits of the number from the message: 271-3311. It rang.

"Thank you for calling the Oriental Theater. For a list of show times, please press 2 now." A theater? Could that be right? *"Join us for a special event today, March 31st, at 1pm, when we kick off the newest Sinclair reality TV phenomenon with a live guest panel and premier showing of the first episode. Everyone will be here... shouldn't you?"*

"Deuce, that first part is a *phone number*. Look up the Oriental on the laptop." Wow. A special event at the theater. Emotions will be running high as the excitement builds at a first screening. That would be a perfect venue for unleashing an emotion-enhancing drug like True Love -- but the combination of amplified emotion and almost total suggestibility was very unpredictable. It could turn ugly fast.

There'd been an incident once before, a gang fight that was unbelievably vicious, and left 19 people dead. True Love was behind it. That was when I had decided I had to get it under control back then. I couldn't let Koning or whoever was behind this use True Love that way again.

"Looks like the site's all focused on some mystery event they've got going on." Deuce said as he scanned the page he'd opened up. "Starts in a few hours. Do you think the rest of those numbers have something to do with it?" He plugged the string of numbers into Google one more time. "869101001... well, it's a prime number? Does that mean anything?"

"I don't know, but we don't have time left to figure it out. We'd better get over there now, and try to see if we can stop this."

* * *

As we pulled up to the theater, I could tell this was going to be a problem. There were lots of cars, even more people, and police and reporters everywhere.

"Deuce, let me out here, and find a place to park where we can get away quickly if necessary. Text me when you're set." He stopped the car to let me out, and I headed into the crowd.

I scanned faces, bodies, jackets, purses. I looked for water bottles that were being shared, looked for anything that hinted at True Love being deliberately spread.

I checked out the police -- they were mainly keeping people organized in line. They'd have no idea what to do once the people turned into an ugly mob. I had a feeling I was being drawn inexorably towards my own personal doom. If only I could figure out what was going to happen, I might be able to keep it from getting totally out of control. I made my way closer to the front doors, avoiding the camera crews that were watching the arrivals, or doing interviews with the people who hadn't been able to get inside. One camera seemed to be pointed at me, and I shielded my face, and turned away.

Wait a minute! I looked back, and caught the eye of the operator. It was the camera guy from last night, the passenger from the car that had been tailing us. The camera he had pointed at me was different, but the guy was definitely the same. When our eyes met, I saw a sudden look of fear on his face as he realized he'd been recognized. He lowered the camera, and the look became a strange smile that filled me with dread. He turned and started pushing quickly through the crowd to get away. He'd been following me, he was in on whatever it was that was going to happen, and that smile made me more worried than ever that I was too late. It almost seemed as if the shock of being recognized had given way to a satisfaction that whatever plan he was in on was happening, whether I'd seen him across the crowd or not. I quickly started dodging through the people -- I couldn't let him get away. As I neared the edge of the people, he ducked around the corner to the back of the theater. I broke into a run, wishing I hadn't left my gun in the car. He had the heavy camera, and I knew I could catch him. I bolted around the corner just in time to see one of the theater exit doors swinging shut. These were the emergency exit doors that only opened from the inside -- if it closed all the way, it would lock and I'd have lost him. I reached the door just in time to get my fingers around the edge before it closed, flung it open, and ran inside after him.

A blaze of light hit my eyes, and I stumbled to a stop, thinking he'd blinded me on purpose. I put an arm up to shield my eyes, and ducked out of the way of the blow I knew would be coming.

It didn't.

I looked out from behind my arm. The cameraman was there and had the camera pointed at me again -- but so was another guy I vaguely recognized from TV, and he was holding a microphone. I was at the bottom of one of the theaters, in front of the screen -- and it was full of people... all looking at me. I straightened up, and noticed a few chairs had been set up on the stage. The first three had people in them.

"Welcome!" said the guy with the microphone, looking at me, "To our final contestant and member of today's panel, Jack Casanova! I'm Alex Sinclair, and you've made it successfully through the first stage of "Mystery Message!" The crowd cheered, and my head spun. As Alex Sinclair – I knew I'd seen him before – showed me to my seat, I saw a collage of images playing on the screen, involving the people sitting in those three other chairs on the stage, and occasionally Deuce and me. There we were in the parking lot last night, there we were at Alterra, there I was chasing the cameraman around the building. As I watched the loop, I even saw the argument at the Chinese place. Koning must have hoped I'd get caught on camera doing something wrong, and have to distance myself from the leadership of the Organization as the police came investigating.

Even if he didn't have the rest of the Organization watching this, there was no doubt they were going to see it all once word got out. I didn't look that bad in the pictures, but my mind was racing as I thought back over how close I'd come to disaster. If I'd listened to Koning in the restaurant, and taken a tough approach with the people in the mini-van last night... If Deuce and I had gone for the cameraman outside my building with our guns, or called in a couple enforcers on them. Or, worse yet, I'd just been wishing for my 1911 as I chased the cameraman – what if I'd run in here after him and pointed it at everyone? That sort of display of power was Koning's style, and he must have thought I'd do the same.

Luckily, that's not how Deuce and I rolled. We didn't jump to our guns at the first sign of trouble, and I didn't lead the Organization like a heavy-handed crime boss, over-reacting to any possible challenge to my authority. Koning was right that I needed to learn how to be a better boss – but I wanted this to be a business, and I was learning to be a businessman, instead of a thug like him.

Alex was talking to one of the other contestants, and as I took the moment to look out at the audience, my mind began racing again. This time I was thinking of all the ways to turn this unexpected publicity to my advantage. I could work with this turn of events.

But really, reality TV? Koning, I was going get you back for this.

The Message

A student of martial arts, and a multi-sport enthusiast, **Andrew Allen** has realized that you don't have to be good at your hobbies to enjoy them immensely. He has two incredible daughters who love to read, and the greatest wife in the world.

The Quest for the Holy Grail

Brian Grall

PROLOGUE:

The Amazing Adventures of Captain Clutch # 36: The Reprint

Page 51:

NARRATOR-*Meanwhile, at the Hall of Integrity! The evil Baron Von Blitzkrieg has our hero wrapped in chains and dangling upside-down above a vat of sulfuric acid surrounded by a moat of his hungry, genetically engineered Croco-Bears!*

BARON VON BLITZKRIEG-"MWAH HA HA!!! I have you now Capi-tan Clutch!!! You shall never escape this most fiendish of traps, even in your own hideout!"

NARRATOR-*Clutch is working feverishly to undo the chains that bind him, just enough that he can get his hands to his invisible back-up utility belt that the evil Baron Von Blitzkrieg didn't know about, when he removed the visible belt.*

CAPTAIN CLUTCH-"Why would you do this to me?!?! We used to be friends! We still can but you have to let me go to save the kids from your rampaging Cyclo-Vultures at the school!" Buying time while he still fidgets to get his hands loose.

Page 52:

BARON VON BLITZKRIEG-" WHY, you ask??" As the Baron steps closer to the dangling Captain. "We are arch-enemies, sworn to battle again and again forever throughout time! Ying and Yang! Black versus white! Dark versus light! Positive versus negative!"....He grabs the Captain by his collar pulling him closer, looks down into his ingenious trap then back at the Captain and darkly says; "Matter versus anti-matter, which is what you'll be in thirty seconds! MWA-HAHAHAAHAHAHAHAAHAHAAA!!!!"

NARRATOR-*At this moment, the Captain spits in the evil Baron's eye, who shoves the Captain away from him as he recoils. Blitzkrieg then grabs the chain switch pushing the button as he says; "Auf wiedersehen Capi-tan, enjoy your dip!" The chain gives and begins to plummet towards the vat with the Captain in tow.*

Could this be the end of Captain Clutch?!? Will he survive the acid just to meet his demise in the jaws of the Croco-Bears?!?! Find out next month in THE AMAZING ADVENTURES OF CAPTAIN CLUTCH!

PART I:

The Quest Begins

"That's It!?! Oh my God, did that *suck!* See Alex?!?! That's why the book was canceled in forty-two because of the horrible writing! 'Croco-Bears,' really!?" exclaims Jimmy 'The Grip' Pearson, an eight year old child trapped in a thirty-five year old rotund man's body, with the brain capacity of a 'Slushee.' He's known as 'The Grip' due to his incredible ability to keep hold of something no matter what it may be. As soon as he gets it into his hands, it's as good as his; no power in the Universe can make him let go – but he says it's due to his extensive martial arts training (a.k.a ninja movies). He's 5'8", has bright red curly hair, small devilish green eyes, and more freckles than a sandy beach has sand. He is happily unemployed and he likes wearing all the 'geek' tee-shirts he can, whether or not he knows the reference - though he almost always does; he is a geek after all. Oh and he still lives with his parents in the basement, or what Jimmy likes to call his "Inner Sanctum."

"Oh come on, man that was the final issue, and what do you expect from the Forties! Most of the stories of that time were overly simplistic and that's the way I like the old heroes: simple!" retorts Alex to his best friend. Alex is thirty-four years old, 5' 11", dark hair, decent shape, some scruff on the face, blue eyes, wears a lot of DC Comic superhero shirts, and has a simplistic view of the world as well as his heroes. He's been Jimmy's best friend since the third grade, when Jimmy saved him from the local bully, not so much thanks to his fighting style but rather his exuberantly psychotic behavior that scared the bully away. Alex, unlike his best friend, has a steady job and his own apartment that Jimmy happens to have a key to, even though Alex doesn't remember giving him a copy.

"You knew exactly who the good guys and bad guys were, no jumping around going back and forth when the situation called for it. Though," confesses Alex, "I still like the modern books with their modern story elements - but I always like to go back to the Golden Age, just for a break."

"Give me *Plastic Man* any day. At least he can be serious and comedic at the same time," Jimmy responds. "Besides, at least with *Plas* you know what you're gonna get."

"You mean to tell me that you'd rather have a dimwit like *Eel O'Brien* saving people in red tights, looking like a bad love-child of a seventies porn star, Tom Selleck and *Mr. Fantastic* than a true hero like Captain Clutch?!? I guess nobody cares about the 'original' super heroes anymore or what they stood for. Today it's all about sex, blood and guts, rape and murder." Alex responds a little roughly.

"Give me sex anytime," says Jimmy with a grin.

"Talk to your hand then," says Alex sharply. They look at each other for a few seconds then they both laugh heartily.

"Speaking of sex, how's your mom?" retorts Jimmy, ending that with a playful cat's meow and a claw hand gesture.

"Oh shut up and pass me the remote!" says Alex still chuckling.

"Here," as Jimmy tosses it at Alex, he asks "I'm going upstairs to get some more Mountain Dew and Fun-Yuns and to call Domino's Pizza to get them to bring back the 'Dominator.' Want anything else?"

Alex shakes his head 'no' but says, "tell your sister I still have her underwear!" to which Jimmy just stomps up the wood plank steps saying "yeah, yeah, eat me!"

"That's what she said!!" blurts Alex as Jimmy grumbles under his breath and finishes stomping up the steps.

"Heh, the 'Dominator'; I haven't had the 'runs' in a long time...."Alex says to himself as he turns the remote around and switches the TV on to the *G4 Network*. He catches the last bit of 'ATTACK OF THE SHOW' where he finds out that Edward Gamlin will be attending the C2E2 comic book convention on March 19th in Chicago, IL. Alex jumps up out of his seat and shouts, "WHOO-HOO – YEAH, BABY!"

Upon hearing the cry, Jimmy comes flying down the stairs (literally) performing a nice barrel-roll on the steps on the way down. Miraculously, the bag of Fun-Yuns doesn't break, nor Jimmy for that matter, but they're going to have to wait for the 'Dew' to settle. Alex watches the badly choreographed stunt in shock and awe, mouth gaping.

"Aw, DUDE!! What the Hell!!!! I thought you were getting attacked by ninjas or something! I came racing down the steps to take those frackers out with my karate-jiu-jitsu-acrobatic-hyperbole-nuclear kick!" thunders Jimmy after he painfully gets up from the bottom step, where he was sprawled out against the cinder block basement wall. "What happened?"

"Edward Gamlin is attending C2E2 in March!" says Alex in a panicky tone.

"Who?" questions Jimmy, out of breath.

"What do you mean 'who', its Edward Gamlin, the creator of CAPTAIN CLUTCH!" shouts Alex, tightly grabbing Jimmy's round, ginger head.

"OW! Alright, alright; I was just playing with you man! Back off!" groans Jimmy.

"Oh, sorry pal. I just got excited and didn't know my own strength I guess," apologizes Alex. "Wait, did you say 'hyperbole'?"

"Yeah………..Yeah you're like a retarded Chewbacca strong, man," Jimmy says mockingly trying to quickly segue. They both chuckle again, but Alex is too focused on the inner workings of his feverish brain at the moment. "What are you thinking? Oh God, you're thinking about meeting this guy, aren't you? Tell me you're not thinking that? The dude's not even gonna know what you're saying man, he looks as old as my great-grandpa and he's been dead for fifteen years!"

"Yeah... yeah that's what I'm going to do. Come on, where's your laptop, we gotta buy tickets to the con!" barks Alex like a Marine Corps Drill Instructor with a mission to kill. "I'm gonna find one of the hardest comics to find, period. The final issue of THE AMAZING ADVENTURES OF CAPTAIN CLUTCH, number thirty-six," standing with his hands on his hips, speaking like he's the narrator of his favorite eighties superhero cartoon, Alex says, "and if that doesn't work, I can always get this reprint signed."

"Ahhh, man!" complains Jimmy but then just as quickly shouts "ALRIIII-GHT!!!" just now realizing that they're going to a comic book convention. "LET'S DO THIS!! Wait a minute. We have a month before C2E2 and there's a local con down by the airport going on this weekend. Wanna go?" asks Jimmy. "Who knows, maybe you'll find it there?"

"That's highly improbable. But let's go anyway and we can also hit 'The Perv's' shop tomorrow for the weekly books and maybe we can get some info from him too," suggests Alex. "I gotta text 'The Perv' quick so he knows what I need." Alex reaches for his phone and types: "MJW-Remember 3/31? Need help desperately, not much time left. Please, you're the only one! 271-3311 869101001. You know what to do. - Alex"

"Yeah and if he still has that 50% off and roll the dice sale, I'm gonna squeal the 'Perv' and pick up that first appearance of *Guy Gardner* off his wall!" retorts Jimmy the Grip.

PART II:
The Scoundrel

The boys make the weekly trek to their favorite comic shop on Wednesday or "new comic book day" as it's known in the vernacular. They walk inside the door with the familiar cowbell **dung** sound it makes, followed sharply by the **CLANK!** on the glass as the door closes behind.

"I need more cowbell!!" Jimmy shouts as the door closes and sniffs the air thrice, turning slightly to his back left shoulder to Alex, stopping him in his tracks. "Aaahh......that, my friend, is the sweet smell of fantasy comic ambrosia!" he exclaims as he turns back and nearly trips on old boxes of comics that 'The Perv' is still sorting through from years before, near where the nastiest couch in the world resides and slowly decays.

"Oh, come on Mark! When are you going to finish this!" shouts Jimmy in the general direction of the office, for one can never be sure of just where 'The Perv' will pop up.

"SORRY!" is heard bouncing off the walls of the shop, but they just can't pinpoint the source.

Sniffing the air again, Jimmy says, "You smell that? 'The Perv' just opened a new box of freshly minted twenty-one pages of awesomeness!"

"Alright, calm down before you have another accident. And this time I'm not covering for you," Alex says quickly but seriously enough.

"Yeah but come on, 'The Perv' had the uber-rare, retailer incentive *Wolverine/Deadpool* variant cover for me; you were drooling too!"

"Maybe, but I didn't have to go home right away just to spend some 'alone time' with it..." states Alex, beginning to re-examine his friendship with 'The Grip.' Alex is also wondering if there's a different reason he got that nickname. He shudders at the thought, trying to shake it out of his mind, and steers himself to the left side of the store where the action figures are, telling Jimmy to "play nice."

"Hey Mark! Do you still have the roll the dice sale going on?!" shouts Jimmy again.

And from every corner of the shop, a voice echoes "Yep!"

"Outstanding!" exclaims Jimmy.

As they move further into the overabundance of comic back stock that sits in the middle of the store, which is where they spend most of their time, they see 'The Perv's' assistant Brodie, slightly hunched over and facing the right perimeter wall of the store where all the new issues are placed. He is putting up the new *Fantastic Four* "Death of the Human Torch" issues, cursing under his breath "frickin' marketing ploys! Book's not good enough to sell anymore so they gotta kill him off! Bunch'a fascists is what they are!" Even Jimmy <u>tries</u> to keep his distance from Brodie. "Something's just not screwed on tight about that guy" he thinks while giving Brodie the 'stink eye'- he just can't help himself.

Above the new comics racks and the blustering Brodie, are all the older, more valuable comics lining the wall, waiting to be taken home and that is what Jimmy comes here for today. In the dimly lit corner of the store is the *Green Lantern #59* comic that Jimmy has been mulling over for the past few months: the first appearance of *Guy Gardner* as *Green Lantern*. He just stares up with a glimmer in his eyes and within a few seconds, a pool of saliva begins to form in the rounded corners of his open mouth.

On the other side of the store, Alex looks up from sifting through a long box of old *Batman* books, though not in time to see 'The Perv' jump out of nowhere. "AHH! Oh Mark, I hate it when you do that!" shouts a startled Alex, now looking over at Jimmy, waiting to see if he'd save him for real; but to no avail. "The place could be on fire and he'd still be in a comic coma," he thinks to himself.

"Ha, ha! Hi'ya Alex, whatcha lookin' fer taday?" inquires the grungy shop owner.

"I'm just looking for the first print of '*Y: The Last Man*' number one and do you have any old issues of 'The Amazing Adventures of Captain Clutch' running around? Specifically number thirty-six?" asks Alex with such hope in his voice. From the darkened back corner, there's a loud 'bang' and some commotion, but neither Alex nor Mark moves a muscle to look in that direction; though Alex does slightly wince.

'The Perv' thinks for a moment with a raised right eyebrow, an arched right upper lip and a semi-contorted face; looking like he just got kicked in the nads by a flying monkey. "Well, I got your text yesterday and I gotta tell ya, that was quite a doosie. I haven't had anyone ask me about that in a long time," Mark says. "I wish I did, but sorry, no I don't have it, that's a tough one ta find."

"Well thanks anyway man. Any idea where I could find it? I'm going to C2E2 next month and I'm hoping to score it there, though I know I'll be paying through the nose for it."

Mark replies, "other than your typical auction houses and *eBay* where most of the copies are graded, there's really no place else that I know of." Rubbing his left eyebrow for a few seconds, Mark says, "Wait a minute.......waiiiit a minute. I do remember a guy in California who claims to have dozens of all of the Clutch books, but that was years ago."

"Well, I'm not going to the houses or 'feebay,' and I didn't come here to knit, so do you still have that guy's number?" questions Alex eagerly.

"I got it somewhere in the bureau. Give me a few minutes and maybe I'll find it." And 'the Perv' disappears into the office. Alex is so giddy that he can barely contain his pent up frustration and hope, so much so that he almost doesn't see the ruckus in the back of the store between Jimmy and Brodie.

"Oh, you're so full of shit it makes me sick!" screams Jimmy with a 'death grip' around Brodie's leg, both grown men rolling on the filthy, comic-strewn floor.

"That's because you know I'm right!" shouts Brodie back at Jimmy, while grasping his auburn locks. Alex swings around the graphic novel section, just in time to get caught up in the melee himself.

"OW! OW! Jimmy, that's me you idiot!" hollers Alex as Jimmy has him in a grip of the 'titty-twister' kind. Jimmy lets go immediately and the scuffle breaks for a moment.

Panting and massaging his throbbing left breast, Alex interrogates Jimmy, and says "what the Hell was that all about?!? What could he have done to get you guys fighting again this time?!?!"

Jimmy sternly reports that "this douchebag says 'Greedo shot first' and you know it's a lie! Everyone in the world does, even the ones who haven't been born yet know Han shot first!"

"I swear this happens every time you guys see each other and you can't act this way at the con, or they'll throw us out and I'll miss my opportunity to find that book!" yells Alex at his friend, grasping him around the head and walking him away from Brodie.

"You're right, you're right, but he just pisses me off. I mean, come on, really? Greedo shot first and they digitally move Han's head to the side while the rest of him just stays perfectly still? That's not cool looking man, that's retarded! Even George Lucas admitted he was wrong to change that!"

"I know, I know," agrees Alex with his psychotic friend. "George Lucas is old and senile and ruined all that history with three crappy prequel movies."

Then, all of a sudden, Jimmy spins around, straightens his "Han Shot First" t-shirt, cocks his head and heads back to the darkened corner where Brodie is cleaning up the mess. He grabs a step ladder, maneuvering Brodie out of the way, climbs up and pulls out the *Green Lantern #59* that he drooled over not-so-long-ago. As he walks past Brodie, he says, "I suppose this time you're going to say Anakin Skywalker wasn't a whiny bitch? It runs in the family DNA, you know." Getting glared at by Brodie, he just keeps walking proudly to the register.

Meanwhile, Mark comes out of his office and hands Alex a slip of paper with a name and number on it. "What happened back there this time? Wait, wait, don't tell me, I don't wanna know." Waving his hands in between them and continues. "Keep a good eye on this. Don't tell him where you got the information, for there is one 'creature' out there that will make your search near impossible – and that's the Scoundrel," says Mark in a worrisome tone.

"The Scoundrel?" Alex says in disbelief.

"SHHH! Yes, the Scoundrel." His head darts up looking around as if he's being watched by the CIA, 'The Perv' continues. "Rumor has it he's as old as *Captain America* and that he attends all the major cons he can, just to randomly choose someone out of the crowd, stalk them throughout their time there, find out what they're looking for and snatch it right before they do. Which leaves you with only two options, to either buy a more expensive one or try again some other time. It's what he does and if he finds you, he'll grab that 'ish' so fast you'd think you got accosted by a group of rabid Ewoks!"

Alex could see the fear pumping through the veins in his forehead.

"He moves so fast and stealthily that no one can ever decide what he looks like. He wears a black hood and cloak. They say he has unlimited resources! They say he can read minds! They say he's a mirage, a puff of smoke, a fart in the wind! No one knows anything about the guy! Some even think he's not a guy at all, but a disgruntled comic book creator who's wreaking vengeance from the grave on the 'true-believers.'"

Alex scoffs and tells Mark, "You're a grown man, how can you believe this crap?!"

Mark's voice is now beginning to tremble. "I saw it with my own eyes when I went to the San Diego Comic-Con in 1982, but it was only for a second! I could feel the gaze of a demon on my back all day, and when I turned around, I saw a whisk of black move faster than the crowd in front of him or behind him moved! I swear to you man, that's why I haven't gone back to a con since!"

Alex is really captivated by Mark's story, when Jimmy storms up and slams his hand on the counter, scaring the holy 'doonkle-shtoomp' out of Mark and Alex.

"Here you go Mark, let's roll the dice and ring it up. I'm gonna make you squeal!" declares Jimmy triumphantly.

PART III:
The Waitress

"Ha, ha, ha, ha, haaaa! Hello? Hello operator? I'm afraid my party's been... disconnected! HuhuHAHAHAAHHHEEHEHE" declares Alex's favorite ringtone of Mark Hamill as 'The Joker', from *Batman: The Animated Series*. This also happens to be Jimmy's ringtone whenever he calls.

"Dude, do you know what time it is?" questions the groggy Alex.

"Of course I do. Why does everyone keep asking me that?" replies Jimmy in a bewildered tone.

"Wait," Alex mumbles with his cottony tongue. "What do you mean, 'everyone'?"

"Well, I called Henry about the con today and he wasn't too thrilled to talk, so I called 'The Perv' and I ended up irritating him, so I figured I'd call Brodie just to call him a 'dick licker' when he answered, just to piss him off, before I called you. Why what's the matter?" says Jimmy.

"What's the matter? It's five-thirty in the morning! That's what's the matter!" blurts the enraged Alex.

There's a slight pause on the other end of Alex's phone; Alex is praying to God that he just hung up or lost the signal, but then Jimmy courteously says, "Well, at least I didn't stop by your apartment this time. That's good, right?"

"Yeah, yeah it is," Alex says with a sleepy chuckle. "So, where's the fire?" he asks with a little clarity.

Jimmy gets all serious and tosses his query quickly. "What if Mark is really the Scoundrel? Huh? Huh? What do you think? It's possible, right? I mean he knows all this stuff about him and what better way to spread your own legend than telling everyone yourself?"

"Aw, I don't know man, that's a bit of a stretch, even for you. I saw his eyes man, he was freaked out!" Alex says much more awake now.

Jimmy says excitedly, because he knows he has Alex's full attention, "Come on man, **think** about it! It's perfect! It's just like in the movie *The Usual Suspects* where there really was a Keyser Soze when everyone thought he didn't exist - but he really did exist; like he was just a rumor or a bad guy boogieman!" Then Jimmy yanks the greatest *Usual Suspects* movie quote right out of thin air: "That was his power. The greatest trick the Devil ever pulled was convincing the world he didn't exist. And like that", Jimmy blows air into the phone and whispers, "he's gone."

There is a sudden, long pause on Alex's side of the phone, which doesn't happen very often to Jimmy, mostly because he's the one who's always doing the talking; silence makes him uncomfortable. Alex does come back on the phone and says with a yawn; "Alright. Come pick me up and we can get some early breakfast before the mini-con. I'll be ready when you get here," thinking that he can sleep for an extra half-hour before he has to go downstairs.

Chuckling, Jimmy responds, "Oh, I don't know about that…"

Nails on chalkboards, the buzzing alarm clock, high-pitched squeaky voices, White Sox fans at Wrigley, people talking in the movie theater, babies crying on an airplane, yappy ankle-biting dogs, Lady Gaga; you can just hear all the annoying sounds going through Alex's mind in a millisecond; "you're already here, aren't you?" he says with a disgruntled sigh.

"Yyyy-ep. I'm in the parking lot," Jimmy proudly states.

Alex responds with a little more disgust and a rather big sigh; "O-kay, I'll be down in a few."

The bright, but cool day is Sunday, a month until C2E2 in Chicago, and the boys are on their way to the local, every-other-month Burnham Bowl Comic-Con. This is a nice little con that people can pay two dollars to get in and rummage around to see what's available; which, depending on the month, could be good or bad. They stop off and grab some grub at the nearby 'Greek' restaurant, where breakfast is served around the clock.

The boys walk in noticing that there really isn't a large crowd for the morning and sit down in a window booth. Alex takes a gander at the menu; Jimmy doesn't even pick his up.

"Well, what do you think?" says Jimmy trying to help Alex wake up.

With a rather long pause, Alex replies, "I think I'll have the eggs Benedict this time".

Flustered, Jimmy stabs, "No, I mean about 'The Perv' being 'The Scoundrel'!"

"I don't know, man. I'm trying not to think about anything at the moment, because I should STILL BE SLEEPING!" shouts the angered Alex, rising in decibels.

Surprised at his outburst, Jimmy shakes his head ever so slightly and thoughtlessly and says; "Alright, alright. Jeesh, SOME-body got out the wrong side of the bed this morning huh?" If looks could kill, Jimmy would be ground meat right about now.

Lucky for Jimmy and the rest of the six a.m. breakfast crowd, the waitress comes by to take their order. "Good morning Alex, what'll you have today?" She says, happy to see him.

Alex returns the greeting with a sudden change of mood and says, "Hi Doris. I'll have the eggs Benedict with white toast, a large glass of milk and a side of bacon, please."

"You got it hun," says Doris with a little longing twinkle in her eyes.

She then says in a tone that is only reserved for Jimmy - thankfully it was Jimmy she said it to. "What do you want!"

Putting on his happiest happy face, Jimmy tells Doris, "I'll have my usual please" and adds a wink at the end.

"Ugh….; so Alex, you want the eggs Benedict with white toast, a large glass of milk and a side of bacon. And HE wants the children's pancake meal, cut in the shape of Batman's head, blueberries for his eyes, bacon for his ears and a single piece of toast cut like the bat symbol and a large Mountain Dew. Is that all?" she repeats the order to the boys.

"Um, it's a cowl, actually," corrects Jimmy snottily.

"Whatever!" retorts Doris as she turns to walk away, shooting Alex a quick happy glance before she bobs off to put the order in.

"Uaaaua….are you gonna ask her out or what, man? I mean you've been eyeing her up for the last couple years! She's hot and all <u>over</u> you dude!" Jimmy tells Alex as if he didn't know, snapping his fingers and pounding the table for added measure.

"I know, I know. But I don't even really know her. We never went to school or anything like that so, I don't know. I don't even know her last name or her likes and dislikes. What do I say to her?" Asking the advice of the one person he knows he shouldn't, but does anyway.

"Tell her you like how she puts the food on the table. You know, when she leans a little too far in your direction so you can see her 'pillows'?" He says with the "finger quotes," where Alex interrupts and says "No she doesn't, does she? She probably does that to everyone." Jimmy continues with, "Oh no she doesn't…trust me. I've been waiting for her to do that for me since we've been coming here! Or you can tell her you like watching her walk away, just ask her to do it slower. Or you can tell her you dream abo…OW!" He's cut off quickly with a kick to the shin by Alex, as Doris comes back without their food.

"So, what are you boys doing today?" she asks as she sits down next to, and steering her question towards Alex.

"We…ahem…are going to Burnham Bowl today." Alex sheepishly says.

Surprised, Doris says, "Oh, I didn't know you guys bowl?"

"Oh we don't. Ahh, we're going to the mini-con there today." Alex responds by turning slightly in his seat, like he's going to get shot by a firing squad.

"I forgot that was today. How long does it go for? Think anybody has any *Silver Age* books there?" questions Doris, surprising the heck out of Alex and Jimmy who respond only by his pupils hitting the top eyelid and opening his mouth, though forming no words.

Alex stutters a bit and replies, "um, ah, til four this afternoon." From out of nowhere, he works up the willpower to say, "Would you like to meet us there?" If he had a *Green Lantern* Power Ring right now, it'd be brighter than the Sun.

"Yeah, I'd love to. I get off at two and I can be there around two-fifteen or so. Is that okay?" She says excitedly.

"Y-Yeah, that'll be great. We'll see you then." Alex replies equally excited, though still nervous.

The familiar DING! is heard from the kitchen and a cook shouts, "Order up, Doris!"

"Well, there's your food. I'll be right back." And Doris gets up from the booth and goes to get their order.

"Whew…can you believe that? Hahahaha! I just asked her out!" shouts the disbelieving Alex; Jimmy looks as if his brain just broke. "Hey, did you see that? I actually asked her to do something that I'd never thought I would, and then it turns out she likes comics just the same! Talk about luck, huh? The only thing that could make today the best day ever, would be finding Captain Clutch!" Jimmy continues his catatonic state for a few extra minutes.

Doris brings out their order, and that happens to be the only thing that snaps Jimmy back into the land of the living – the smell of his Batman-styled pancakes. Alex is still riding high from only a few minutes earlier; when she places his food in front, she does lean in a little too far and that's when he actually notices the 'pillows' that Jimmy commented on earlier.

Jimmy grabs his plate, holds it up next to his face and says in a thick, gravelly voice, "I'm Batman!" This actually gets a small chuckle out of Doris and Alex just rolls his eyes with a smile. As Doris hands Alex a slip of paper, she says, "Here's my number.

What's yours, so I can call you when I'm done with work and we can meet up." Hurriedly and excitedly Alex tears off a small piece of the paper place mat and scribbles down his number, then hands it to Doris with a smile.

"That's great, I'll call you when I'm done then," says Doris.

"I'll be looking forward to it," responds Alex, thinking he's now just as suave as James Bond. Jimmy is oblivious during this whole exchange and just scarfs down his food like *Galactus* gobbling a planet. Alex watches as Doris bobs away again and turns to look at Jimmy, who's already finished with his Bat-breakfast.

Alex downs his breakfast and now they're getting ready to pay at the register, when Jimmy says, "Dude, can you cover for me? I don't have any cash on me yet. I gotta hit the Tyme machine." Alex is not shocked by this and pays for the entire meal, shaking his head and repeating "typical," while Jimmy is trying to count the jellybeans in the jar to have a meal named after the winner.

Part IV:
The Mini-Con

The boys kill some time between breakfast and the con, by going back to Alex's place and watching some episodes of the live-action series of *The Tick* on DVD; one of their favorite comic book shows, for which both share the sentiment that it's a shame it was only nine episodes long.

On the way to the con, Alex asks Jimmy, "Do you think they'll have anything good today?"

"Highly improbable," responds Jimmy.

As they pull into the parking lot and walk down the few steps into the main hallway, they spot Henry at the door, who organizes this con.

"Hi guys!" says Henry, performing his patented one stiff handshake to each. "It's two bucks today."

"Hey, Henry. Anything new--,"Alex is interrupted by Jimmy who interjects, "or good!" before Alex finishes with, "--today?"

"Well, we got a few new dealers in. But not much in what you guys are always looking for. Alex, there is a guy here who has a bunch of old 'Super Powers' figures and play sets here. He's down the third aisle at the end," reports Henry.

"Yeah, thanks pal. I'll hit that guy up," says Alex as he pays for himself and Jimmy; again.

"Please, 'By the Power of Grayskull,' don't say 'hit'!" snaps Jimmy as he disappears.

Just after they leave Henry at the door, Alex's phone rings and he struggles to find which pocket it's in; for he knows who's calling and he's still nervous.

"Hello?"

"Hi Alex, it's me, Doris. I'm just getting into the parking lot. Are you guys still here?"

Quickly, but calmly Alex replies, "Yep, yep we just got here actually."

"Great! I'll be in in a minute. Anything good today?"

"Well, Henry did tell me that there are a few new dealers here and one has a bunch of 'Super Powers' stuff that I'm looking at right now."

"Oh, yeah. I remember those. My brother had some when we were kids. Those were awesome! Oh here's the door...." And the phone goes dead.

Alex looks at his phone like a monkey doing a math problem, then realizes that Doris just hung up. He spins around to see Doris putting her wallet in her purse and walking towards him with a smile, which he returns.

As the new couple look at the toys of yesteryear, Jimmy is on the adjacent aisle rummaging through a bunch of old *Playboys*. "Augh....I didn't know they could do that!?" he says softly, referring to a centerfold picture. He then snaps out of it, looks around and catches up with Doris and Alex, who is buying the *Plastic Man* Super Powers figure; "See? I told you, you wanted *Plas* yesterday! Not as dumb as you thought, huh?" Jimmy adds. The trio then moves over to a dealer with some old Silver Age comic books on the display rack leaning against the wall.

"How much for the three *Wonder Woman* books?" asks Doris.

The dealer turns around to refresh his memory and tells Doris, "$120 for the three of them."

Doris then gets into her 'barter' mode and comes back with "In that condition, how about $90? No one's going to buy them other than myself, and I'm eager to do it right now." The dealer then makes a painful face, but then agrees, because he knows she's right and he needs to dump them. They make the monetary exchange and Doris walks away happy, putting the books in her bag.

"I just got schooled! This chick knows how to 'wheel and deal!'" Jimmy bellows in amazement. Alex stands there, proud as can be that the girl he's been pining over, and she him, is comic geek to the core and will do anything she can to get the books she wants.

Then for the second time today, Alex pops a difficult question; "Hey, Doris. Would you marry me?" She spins and shyly says, "Not yet. But if you play your games right…"

"Well then, would you like to go to C2E2 with me next month in the meantime?"

"Why Alex, I never thought you'd ask."

"I now pronounce you geek and geek-ette. You may now look at each other's comic books!" Jimmy pipes in. "Now can we please get the hell out of here? My 'Herbie' is growling." Grabbing his stomach and squeezing it together. The other two just laugh and make their way to the door, when Jimmy sees Brodie sneak in past Henry, without paying.

"Hey, dickhead! You gotta pay Henry, you know! See, this guy right here?" Jimmy yells, to get everyone's attention; making himself look great but more importantly, a free chance to embarrass Brodie and get him riled up to the point of exploding at the same time.

Brodie glares at Jimmy, who's smiling ear-to-ear with his arms crossed, and he looks around at the folks who all paid to get in, giving him some stern glances. He then skulks his way back to Henry, saying "Sorry. I didn't see you there" and passes the Washingtons to Henry's hands. Henry, being the gentleman he is, shrugged his shoulders and lets it go without passing judgment.

The trio turns to leave and Alex hangs back a second, telling his best friend, "Boy, you really always gotta go after that guy, don't you? I love it!"

"That was awesome, Jimmy. I don't like that guy either. He's always trying to sneak a peek down my shirt or up my skirt or to get me to touch my elbows behind my back. He's just a pig of a man!

Maybe <u>he</u> should be the one you call 'The Perv'!" exclaims Doris.

Alex and Jimmy look at each other for a moment, seeming to be in a courtroom that only resides in their brains. But the ruling comes back swiftly and assuredly: "Nope. We're sticking with Mark. Alex says he's seen midget porn scattered about in the front store area and upstairs in the overstock, right?" says Jimmy.

"It's true, I swear it! I saw a DVD box behind the glass case in front of the statues and the other mixed upstairs in the old *DC Direct* action figures!" confesses Alex. "Next time we all go there, I'll show you!"

"Alright, boys. Let's go get some lunch," says Doris who's pushing them outside.

Part V:
The Snatch & Grab

Ka-CHUNK!!

Wakes a startled Doris from a restful sleep in Alex's apartment. Alex doesn't even hear anything until she pushes on him to go check it out; he snorts himself awake.

"Alex, Alex wake up! I think someone's in your apartment! Should I call the cops?" whispers the scared girlfriend.

"No, not yet. I'll go check it out first, but be ready, just in case." The also-scared boyfriend responds.

Alex makes his way out of bed, grabbing the closest weapon he can, which happens to be a Master Replica of Luke Skywalker's green Lightsaber from *Return of the Jedi*. "It has two functions," Alex thinks to himself, "it's five feet long, solid and it lights up, so I'll be able to see what I'm hitting and I'll be alright...I hope."

He hasn't turned the saber 'on' yet, just so he can get as close as he can before he needs to catch the intruder.

He walks out of his bedroom and into the short hallway that's lined with some of his most cherished comic books, all framed and matted under UV protective glass that leads to the kitchen, when he hears the noise for himself. **Ka-CHUNK!!**

He knows now that there is someone in his apartment. He starts walking a little more slowly, even though his heart is ready to leap through his chest like the 'Alien chestburster.'

As Alex nears the corner of the hall that turns into the kitchen, he sees a subtle light and smells the familiar aroma of peanut butter and jelly waffles. He thinks "Is this guy making himself breakfast, too?"

Alex stands next to the corner for what feels an eternity, brings his 'saber' to attack position in front of his face, musters up his courage then swings around the corner, hitting the saber's button simultaneously with the familiar sound, and charges into the kitchen with a battle-cry:

"AAAAAAAAAAAHHHH!"

Doris screams thinking that there's an all-out battle going on for life and death and her new boy-toy is to come out the loser. She jumps out of bed with her phone and also grabs the first thing she finds, though this is even less scary; it's her homemade, laser-printed *Wonder Woman* comic book canvas bag.

She walks down the same hall that Alex did mere moments before, although a little quicker. She still hears some wrestling and struggling sounds.

She nears the corner where Alex was earlier gathering his manhood. She peeks first and, seeing and hearing nothing but the blood pumping through her brain, she jumps around the corner, purse raised, only to find the most disturbing of pictures: Alex and Jimmy, lying next to each other, one leg over the other's, out of breath and covered in jelly, eggs and Mountain Dew, with the rest of the two-liter bottle spilling onto the kitchen floor that is being translucently lit by the Lightsaber.

"Ugh...you idiot! How did you get in here?!" screams the hysterical Doris at Jimmy.

Still out of breath from the epic battle, Jimmy responds "Well...you guys have been....dating a while...., I just....couldn't wait and I do have a....a key." Then Doris turns her gaze to Alex, who just sits there and nods 'yes' with his eyebrows going up and making wrinkles on his forehead. Doris then reaches into her bag and pulls out the deadliest of weapons – a camera – and quickly snaps a few to remember this fine moment. A few seconds pass and they all get a good laugh out of it as they look at each other.

***

Now that they've all cleaned up, eaten a great waffle breakfast, showered (Jimmy's wearing his "I had friends on that Death Star" shirt, Alex has his usual con attire "I Killed Jason Todd And All I Got Was This Lousy T-Shirt" shirt, while Doris is sporting her "Marvel Girls Do It Better" low-cut shirt), it's time to get on their way to C2E2 in Chicago, whose doors open at ten. Doris is riding 'shotgun,' Jimmy's in the back seat, and Alex is driving because he won't trust Jimmy driving in Chicago traffic.

They're all talking while they cross the state line, and Doris asks Alex what's first on his agenda. Alex replies, "Well, the only thing I'm buying today is going to be a copy of one of the hardest Golden Age books to find: The Amazing Adventures of Captain Clutch, number thirty-six. It's going to cost me a couple grand and that's all I can afford to blow on that; even though it's only graded around a five. I just can't go any higher. Hope I find it for cheaper though."

All Doris can say is "Huh. Wow, I'm dating a high-roller!" Alex chuckles.

Jimmy adds, "Yeah, good luck man…but I'll be keeping my eyes out for this 'Scoundrel' dude. I'll just also look for some broken down, creepy guy who resembles the proprietor of my favorite comic shop and I'll prove it to you it's 'The Perv'!" Doris just looks strangely at Alex, who then explains who Jimmy's talking about and his theory.

"I know that guy, he seems alright to me," says the always optimistic Doris. "I raid his dollar bins a lot, he almost always has cool stuff in there and generally in good shape, most are better than reader copies."

"You know it's strange we've never seen you in there, because we're there every Wednesday when he opens for the new books," puzzles Alex.

"Well, I only get in there once a month. I have a box Mark puts my books into and I get them when I can. He's pretty cool if I slide on a few too," Doris replies.

"She said 'box,' he..he..he," chimes the uncouth Jimmy, mimicking

Butthead's speech and laugh.

"Well, I only use my box for the variants; otherwise everything is already waiting for me. We pretty much get first picks since we're there so early," Alex says a little cocky.

The trio pulls into the McCormick Center parking structure in Chicago, grabs their gear and follows the other lemmings into the con. As they get up the elevator and walk what feels to be miles to get to the entrance, Alex is beginning to get overly anxious and Jimmy is ready to run on top of the people's heads in front of him; only Doris keeps them both contained, and barely at that.

They make the last turn onto the main hallway and there it sits, the official C2E2 sign. Doris grabs her camera for some pics before they go inside. A picture with Alex, then Alex and Jimmy together, then the three of them together, then Jimmy gets an impromptu one with Doris with the camera in her face and he over her shoulder; she's showing her 'patience is wearing thin' face.

Doris keeps the camera ready and hanging around her neck so she can capture all the 'fan-iacs' in their homemade costumes; most are really well done but then there are some that should never wear skin-tight costumes, and those you can erase from your camera but never erase from your mind.

As soon as they enter the exhibition hall, all that can be seen from one side to the other is comic-themed toys, comic book paraphernalia; books from dozens of companies; creators and artists; video game companies; retailers and dealers galore; an overabundance of geeks in the Artist Alley area, where Edward Gamlin is supposed to make his appearance today.

Before Alex can turn around to confab with his team, Jimmy's already M.I.A. and Doris is standing in place, not knowing what to do next.

"Where'd Jimmy go?" asks Doris, who seems to rather have him around than all these other geeks. "Oh, I have a pretty good idea," replies Alex. "Are you alright?"

"I've never been to a con this big before….it's pretty overwhelming!" says the dumbfounded Doris.

"Yes it is." As Alex chuckles and grabs her hand, he says, "I've been to a bunch of these and you get used to it after a few times. But that first one will always stay with you. Oh, yeah. Expect to run past a few people that have an 'odor' to them…the trick is, when you first get the scent, hold your breath and move as fast as you can. It's a good thing Jimmy's not here now, he'd be much more descriptive! What do you wanna do first?"

"I'll just follow you for a while, I gotta take this all in," the bewildered Doris says. Alex smiles, holds her hand tightly but gently and the two disappear into the throng.

Jimmy on the other hand, make a beeline to the 'adult-ish' area of the con. That's where all the Pin-Ups and wannabe adult film girls appear; though in much more clothing than they're known for. Jimmy has died and gone to heaven and may not be seen again.

As the time passes and the miles of back-and-forth walking are rubbing their shoes onto the floor, Doris is feeling much better and back in her element. She's shopping for some *Wonder Woman* books that'll complete her *Silver Age* collection and she's getting the best deals she can. Alex begins to wonder where she gets the money from; "must be some tips!" he thinks to himself.

"So, how are you doing in your search?" asks Doris. Just then, a lot of people pass through and someone bumps into Doris, pauses for a second then continues. Doris shrugs it off as most people do in crowded areas.

"Pretty good, I guess. I'm finding most of the stuff on my list, so it's knocked down to about 125 books on it now, but just as I thought, most of the dealers here are charging top dollar for *Clutch* and there are only a couple dealers that have them. They won't even take trades either and I have some great *Silver* books, but nothing to cover the difference," replies a somewhat disgruntled Alex.

"Well, why don't we take a break. Wanna get something to drink?"

Doris asks.

"(Sigh)…Yeah sure, let's go grab something real quick. Maybe we'll find Jimmy on the way."

As the couple makes their way through the crowd to the food stations, Alex bumps into someone while he was utilizing his best stare-walking skills. He turns to apologize and -- "Oh my God! I can't believe it! You're Edward Gamlin! Sir, I am a <u>big</u> fan!" he screams at Edward.

"Why, thank you young man," says Edward as he turns down his hearing aid. "It's nice to know that those old rags are still being read by today's fans," Edward humbly says. Just then, Doris finds her way back to Alex, takes his arm and tries to lead him to the food station; that's' when Alex pulls her back so she can meet Edward.

"Oh…! Hi, Grampa!" says Doris as she hugs Edward in front of the stunned Alex. "I'd like you to meet my boyfriend, Alex."

"It seems we already have, my dear," replies Edward as he shakes Alex's hand to make it official. "Alex here was just saying how much he's enjoyed reading my old books."

"Oh, he's been going on and on about finding *Clutch* number thirty-six, meeting you today and getting your autograph. I just didn't have the heart to tell him that you're my Grampa. I wanted it to be a surprise," giggles Doris.

"Well, it certainly is a surprise…I…I don't know what to say," says Alex.

"Say you two will come over some time for dinner and entertain an old man," Edward says.

Alex looks at Doris, who nods her head, and responds faster than *Billy Batson* can say *'SHAZAM!'*; "We'd love to."

"I'll even show you some of my old artwork and scripts that never made it to print. You'll be one of the first people to read those in over sixty years!" Alex opens his mouth to speak, but plays a flabbergasted mime. "He doesn't talk much, does he 'Punky'?" Edward continues.

"That's one of the reasons I love him!" exclaims Doris, squeezing Alex around the waist, as he blushes a bit.

"Well, I do have to be off. I'm in the autograph booth in ten minutes and I have to go to the little boy's room before, so if you'll excuse me…" as he grabs another hug from Doris and takes his Sharpie out, motioning to sign something for Alex. Alex reaches into his bag and pulls out the *Clutch* thirty-six reprint.

"Ahh, number thirty-six. Boy have I got a story for you when you come over," Edward says as he signs the reprint. "To Alex, 'Always Be True to Yourself' Edward Gamlin." Edward then shakes his hand once more and walks away.

"Well, what do you think? Surprised?"

"I…I….I…can't believe it! You're his granddaughter and you never even mentioned it to me?!?! Well played babe; well played." Alex says with a huge smile. "If I can't buy the actual book, then I don't need to! I just had the best day ever!" And Alex gives her a great big hug. "What's 'Punky' refer to?"

"That was my favorite TV show when I was little and it's what he's called me since then," says Doris straightaway and without embarrassment.

Just then, another pile of people pass by bumping and shoving as crowds do, as well as Jimmy, who struts up like he's a billionaire hanging out in the Red Light District; he even has lipstick on his cheeks, with glazed eyes and a huge smile to prove it. "Hey, who's that old dude you were just talking to?"

"That's just my Grandfather," Doris tells Jimmy, with a nod from Alex.

Jimmy responds, "Whoa, that guy's gotta have a crap-ton of old comic books if he's still running around with this crowd!"

"Oh, you have no idea…" Alex finishes.

"Al-right. Okay, what's next? I did most of what I wanted to do, now I just gotta find 'The Scoundrel-slash-Perv' and some comic books," Jimmy blurts out as he sees he has no clue what's going on.

"Well, I think I'm going to get back into it to find my *Clutch*. Anyone care to join me?" asks Alex.

"I'll come with. You're going where I'm going anyways," says Jimmy.

Doris says, "I'll see you later. I'm going to meet up with my Grampa," as she kisses Alex bye.

"O-kay, I would like to go alone now," complains Jimmy.

The boys hop back into the river of fans and ride the currents until they reach one of the few dealers that have *Clutch* number thirty-six, though only in a graded/protected slab. While Alex waits his turn for the dealer, Jimmy keeps watch like a Secret Service agent, mimicking Alex's every move. He's like a lion staking out his perfect prey, watching all manner of people walk past, like a chaotic symphony that makes these conventions memorable. It's during one of the breaks in the concert, that Jimmy's 'Spider-sense' goes off and he notices someone that's not like the others... "There's something not screwed on right about that guy" he thinks to himself and continues to keep vigil.

Finally, Alex gets the attention of the dealer and asks about the *Clutch* book. The dealer hands it to him telling him the information that he already knows; it's a 9.6 grade near-mint condition book, with bright crisp covers and white interior pages. This is one of those books that seem too good to be true, but here it is just the same. He hands it back to the dealer and asks the price for this book graded as it is. The dealer responds with the digits Alex already knew: $45,500.00. That price tag is a bit out of Alex's reach, so he thanks the dealer, taps Jimmy the guard and continues onto the next dealer.

"What does the other dealer have it priced at?" asks Jimmy.

"What!? Oh, uh, five-thousand, but something doesn't seem right about it, why?" responds Alex.

"Just trying to figure out how many old ladies you'll have to finger-bang to get your money back!" retorts the belligerent Jimmy.

"Nice…" says a disgusted Alex.

Alex leads the way, with Jimmy close behind, scouring the crowd for any persons deemed 'scoundrel-ish.' Jimmy's 'Spider-sense' is starting to go off again, as they approach the only other dealer with *Clutch* for sale; he's looking around much more frantically, trying to hone the signal in. Jimmy spots a 'scoundrel-ish' looking guy, kind of hunched over and already speaking with the dealer at the end of the other side of the table. Jimmy immediately steps in front of his principal target, blocking Alex from the would-be perp.

As the perp leaves the dealer's table, Jimmy relaxes a bit then turns his attention towards Alex and the dealer.

"What can I get for you?" asks the cheery dealer, who's currently making a killing.

"Yeah, what happened to your copy of *Clutch* thirty-six? It was just here a half-hour ago," puzzles the perplexed Alex.

The dealer responds, "I just sold it a minute ago, sorry. Is there anything else I can get you?"

Flustered and depressed, Alex says, "No, thanks," and turns to face the highly aggravated visage of Jimmy.

"Dude, I am so pissed off right now! I can't even stand up straight!" yells Jimmy. "What are we gonna do now?"

"I don't know, I guess I'll have to try some other time. Let's go find Doris and see if she's ready to go home," replies the beleaguered Alex.

They turn from the dealer and it's at this time that Jimmy and Alex both see 'The Scoundrel' as described. Slightly hunched over, wearing a black hood and cloak, standing perfectly still like the rumor he is, a mere twenty feet away. The boys are entranced and don't know what to do; not even Jimmy's extensive martial arts training can save them this time. They stand there frozen for what could be thousands of years in a few seconds. Then, like the whisper he is, 'The Scoundrel' raises his head, only revealing a demented grin, holding the previously purchased *Captain Clutch* number thirty-six next to his shadowed face and vanishes in the passing crowd, the tail of his cloak whipping away, exactly as 'The Perv' has said.

A few minutes pass and the boys collectively blink, glance at each other and get themselves reacquainted with the waves of people almost knocking them over.

"Dude, 'the Perv' was right….you were right. That was him, 'The Scoundrel'," says the awe-inspired Jimmy. "We just saw the biggest, baddest, geekiest and scariest being in the universe and we were helpless in his grasp! Now THAT's power; you gotta respect that!"

"I'm so overloaded right now, I can't even think. What with Doris' grandpa being the creator of *Captain Clutch*, and 'The Scoundrel' who happens to have snatched my copy, I've had a pretty big day and I think I need to sit down."

Jimmy snaps back into it with, "wait, that old dude you were talking to is Doris' granddad AND the creator of *Clutch*? Dude, you lucky S.O.B., you're the man!"

"Yeah, can you believe it?" says the hushed Alex. "He also signed my *Clutch* reprint for me, just before you showed up."

"Ah, now see? That makes this whole trip worth the pain and agony!" Jimmy says with a chuckle.

Alex nods in agreement and says, "well, there's always the next con." Alex and Jimmy find Doris over in the Artist Alley, still sitting with her grandfather, and tell them about their encounter.

"He's still around? I remember that guy from when I worked at *Cool Comics* in the fifties, and he was a rumor then too! That guy's at least as old as I am!" exclaims the comic legend. "We didn't have the types of conventions like we do today, but I heard stories of him going around and buying all the comics off the racks, all over the country. I was glad I worked for the company and I got my books for free. Sometimes we had to give them away, nobody would buy them."

"Well, if he is the real thing, then he moves as fast as lightning!" says Alex.

Jimmy segues back to Edward's books by saying, "do you still have all your books that you created?"

"I sure do. As a matter of fact, I have four or five of each book I ever did. I had more, but I had kids to put through college and the money was much better used for that. Even back then, I couldn't get anywhere near what I can today. I remember you could buy *Action Comics* number one for a few hundred dollars back in the sixties and seventies! Today, well, that book is extremely rare and worth hundreds of thousands of dollars to millions!" tells the elderly gentleman. "Who'd think that was going to happen to those old flimsy pieces of paper?"

Jimmy interrupts and says, "Do you have one of those, too?" To that, Edward only answers with a sly smile.

"Shut up! DUDE! You're sitting on a gold mine! Can I have a few?!" Jimmy begs greedily.

Edward just chuckles and says, "no, those are for my family; sorry Jimmy."

"Ah, that's okay. It was a long shot anyways," replies Jimmy as he waves his right hand as if he was swatting a fly. Then he moves closer to the open-mouthed and big-eyed Alex and whispers to him; "Do **NOT** let her get away! Do whatever she says and smile as you're doing it! Wear an apron or an 'I'm her bitch' t-shirt if you have to!" Alex just shrugs him off, though with a sly smile as well.

The rest of the con strolls on, with a few fans and admirers stopping by Edward's table for a tale and an autograph. The trio stays with Edward for a couple hours, just soaking up the history and the stories, all the while appreciating the pioneers of the 'Geek Industry.'

Part VI:
The Holy Grail

A few months pass since C2E2, and Alex and Doris have had dinner with her grandfather a dozen times. Both relish their time with him and his stories; not to mention a chance for both of them to see his extensive collection from over the last seventy-five years.

While finishing cleaning up the dinner table, Doris turns the TV on to the *G4 Network*: "*…That's right folks! You heard it right here….the only copy of Captain Clutch number thirty-six that was sold at C2E2, back in March, was a fake! The person that bought the phony funny book for a reported $5,000.00 is named Brodie Jensen…*" "Wait, turn that up!" says Alex. "*..And, (chuckle) get this, he works at a comic book shop in Milwaukee, WI! Now you may wonder, 'How in the Hall of Justice, did this guy make that kind of mistake?' Well it turns out that he only bought it to get back at some patrons of his shop, because he hates them! I'm sure that's one expensive lesson on hate that won't soon be forgotten…*" Doris turns the TV off.

"HAHAHAHAHA!! Can you believe that! Brodie's 'The Scoundrel'!!! He HAS to be!! The dealer said some guy bought it like a minute before I got back and that has to be him…ah, this is just too good!" exclaims the newly weight-off-his-shoulders Alex. Just then, his phone vibrates with a text from Jimmy declaring the same sentiment, though more colorful: "WTF?!?! BJ is 'Scoundrel'??!?! Gonna nut-kick him nxt time I c him!!! Holy MoFoSht..need drink!"

"Wow, that's ridiculous! I can't believe your luck! I didn't like Brodie before, but that just tears it! Now aren't you glad you didn't waste your money on that book?"

"Oh, God, yes…I feel great; nothing can top this! I knew something wasn't right about that book!"

Doris and Edward smile heartily, for they know tonight's not over yet.

"That's enough of the cleaning for now, I'd like to get back to the fun. Now tonight, I'm going to show you the prizes of my collection." Edward leads them downstairs to the basement where he keeps all his geek stuff. "You mean I haven't seen all of it yet?" asks Alex.

"No, not yet. They're in this room here that's separate from the rest, for they hold a special place in my heart." Edward leads them into a side basement office that's been converted to a temperature-controlled environment, that he calls "The Swamp." As they pass through the doorway, the first thing that Alex sees in the middle of the main wall is Edward's near-mint copies and all are sealed in a comic graded case for protection. *Superman*'s first appearance: *Action Comics* number one. To the right of that is a near-mint copy of *Superman* number one. Underneath on the next row, is the first appearance of *Batman*; *Detective Comics* number twenty-seven, and just to the right of that, is *Batman* number one, forming a square.

ACTION COMICS #1	*SUPERMAN #1*
DETECTIVE COMICS #27	*BATMAN #1*

These four books by themselves are valued at $3.6 Million!

Right above that, Alex sees all thirty-six *Captain Clutch* issues graded, framed and spaced out evenly across the length of the wall, next to a copy of his first commission check. Every part of every wall is covered in over seventy-five years of comic book history; from old books to new, including quite a few action figures based on his characters as well as other mainstays in the business, on display and very organized; it's truly a sight to behold, even if you're not a 'True Believer.'

"Oh wow! Edward, I've never seen anything like this before…this is amazing!" says Alex, excitedly but softly, as if he's in a museum – which in a way, he is.

"You can talk louder if you'd like; you won't break them," adds Edward, trying to make Alex feel at home. I've had these all of my life and I've been their proud protector and keeper. But I can't take them with me, so Alex; I've decided to give you one of my *Captain Clutch* books; number thirty-six, the one you called your 'Holy Grail.' Well, here it is."

The stunned Alex just looks at Edward, then at Doris, with his mouth wide open.

Knowing he's giving this comic to the right person, Edward says; "remember when I said I got them for free when I worked there? Well, it so happens that back then there weren't a lot of checks and balances, so you could just take as many as you wanted. What you did with them after that was up to you. I loved working in the comics industry and was very proud of the work we did all the way through; so, as you can see, I was very careful with all of these books I've had. And I know you will take great care of them, too. That's not to say I never read them; I sure did. I love comic books, the stories they deliver, and the places they can take you. Those reader copies are stored with the rest of my collection you saw last time. I'm also giving you a copy of a rejected script of *Clutch* thirty-six, that my editor didn't like, though I thought it'd take him in a more realistic direction. I never liked those 'Croco-Bears'."

"I don't know what to say…I mean I don't deserve this….what I mean to say is, thank you," says a most humble Alex.

While Doris continues to look through the room, Edward takes Alex aside, tosses an arm over his shoulder and around his neck and quietly says, "you're welcome. Let's just say that I took a liking to you instantly and it didn't hurt that Doris liked you too. I don't just do this for every guy she's dated; just you. She's been on and on about you for a couple years now and I was tickled pink to find out things have worked out so well between you both – it seems you both got everything you wanted."

"Well, I did. Long before what you've given me, too," Alex glances over at Doris,. "This book is just awesome icing on a really big cake!" he replies.

EPILOUGE

The next day, the couple drives to 'The Perv's' shop to mock Brodie, though they're missing a crucial piece of their trifecta.

As that old familiar **dung** of the door with the sharply followed **CLANK!** is heard walking into the shop, Brodie is nowhere to be seen; which although satisfying is also a little unnerving for that's not like him. Instead they see a clerk with a chubbier build putting books into the back issue bins. A clerk that looks strangely like…

"Jimmy!?!? Did you get a job here?" exclaims the shocked Alex.

"Y-yep! I got it on the Monday after G4 broke the fake Clutch story. I still haven't found any midget porn though… I just walked in and told Mark what I can do for him that that douchebag couldn't."

"And what's that?" asks Doris.

"Not Frak up like that idiot did!" retorts Jimmy. "Besides, I get half-off everything in the shop and I can extend that discount to you guys too!"

"What happened to Brodie?" questions Alex, as if missing him.

"After pulling that stunt with you at the con and on TV, I told him he's bad for business and to piss off!" comments Mark 'The Perv' from out of nowhere; this time, it happens to be his office. "Jimmy told me all about the entire day when he came in on Monday and basically took the job from Brodie, same day. It didn't help that Brodie was late anyway, or being 'The Scoundrel.'"

"Well, did you ask him about why he became 'The Scoundrel'?"

"No, I just wanted him out of here so I didn't lose any business; it's hard enough as it is!" replies The Perv. "Though now, I wish I did…I have a few bones to pick with him and whoever the jerk was at that San Diego con all those years ago!"

Then, Mark quickly changes topics. "Say, Doris. Jimmy tells me that your grandfather is the creator of *Captain Clutch?* Well, I or 'we' actually, were wondering if he'd like to come in for a signing and meet some fans. This whole con fiasco got *Clutch* back in the public's eye again, so why not use it to everyone's advantage?"

Astonished, Doris says, "Sure, I'll ask him for you. I'm sure he'll want to give you a call or come in to meet you. He may even bring some of his stuff to show you."

"What do you mean, 'we'?" ponders Alex.

"Well, we're partners now!" Jimmy proudly tells. "I figured its time I put my considerable intellect to work and I have some great ideas to get this shop back on top too."

"Well that's great buddy, I'm happy you finally found your calling. No need to worry, I think business will pick up soon, for even negative publicity is still good publicity, right?" 'The Perv' just nods in agreement.

"Now, what were you saying about a discount?" questions Alex.

(dedication continued)

    Ahem…his beautiful and wonderfully understanding wife Debbie; his daughter Emma for keeping him young and being his greatest creation; his dog Indy ("we named the dog, Indiana!"); his parents for buying him so many toys to help his imagination soar with no siblings to break them or get in the way; his friends that still dare to be called his friends; his cousins Tom and Bob for continuing to act as they did when they were kids; alternate universes; the third person narrative; his favorite non-picture book author Douglas Adams; flannel; Escanaba and da U.P eh?; MARCO!; Scribbles; his ability to draw and customize action figures; POLO!; The Guild of Calamitous Intent; time travel; Captain James Tiberius Kirk (for obvious reasons); the Big Bang (which is widely considered a bad move); movies; the BTC; cows; waffles; Sir Arthur Guinness for the greatest beverage in the known universe (outside of the Pan Galactic Gargle Blaster); the U.S. Postal Service; Fuddruckers; Nicolas Cage for not portraying Superman; Matt Stone and Trey Parker; riding lawnmowers; building snow forts; baseball; the Green Bay Packers; Walt Disney; Joe Shuster/Jerry Siegel and Superman; Bob Kane and Batman; William Moulton Marston and Wonder Woman; Ben Edlund and the Tick; Stan Lee and your friendly neighborhood Spider-Man as well as the thousands of other comic books he's read over the years and Matt Damon – "Maaatt Daaamon".

Days Without Sun

Robert Jacques

"It's a dangerous business going out your front door."

-J.R.R. Tolkien

CHAPTER1:
Landing on Burning Sunshine

"I'm never going back," stated the young American man sitting on the plane next to me. Like me, he was contracted to teach English in the rural coastal prefecture of Shimane, Japan in the summer of 2003. He wore a baggy suit that didn't hide the fact that he was obese, even by American standards, and was clearly in need of a shave. His words reeked of bad coffee and animosity.

"Excuse me," I replied, as I popped an aspirin from my carry-on satchel and tried to get past his foul breath. I was still recovering from the Japanese heat, and jet lag of the 15 hour flight from Chicago O'Hare to Tokyo Japan just 3 days before, mixed with the Karaoke drinking parties I attended the past 2 nights in the seedy district of Shibuya.

I had flown in to Narita Airport for an arrival conference to prepare me for my new life in Japan as a 9th grade English Assistant at a local junior high school. However, I remembered little information from this two day event, as I had been going out late with fellow ex-pats from various countries who wanted to enjoy our new found land as much as I did. The heat and humidity coinciding with my lack of sleep had caught up with me. *God*, I thought, *it can't always be this hot and humid? Can it?*

"I'm never going back," he repeated. "To America you know. Hey your name's Alex, right? I saw you at *Go Go Karaoke* last night. You were doing shots with that blonde surfer guy from Hawaii, and you guys were talking to those Japanese girls at the bar." He paused as if to visualize something that pleased him, "How'd that turn out?" He smirked at me as I tried to will away the headache that was slowly moving its way to different parts of my head like an out of control jackhammer on hot summer's pavement. He ended with the side comment, "I like your suit by the way."

"Thanks," I replied looking at my black suit that was way too warm for a Japanese summer day. "Yeah, I suppose that was me. I'm Alex, Alex Jones. So you're headed to Shimane too, huh?" I commented, unaffected by his jovial attitude towards the events of last night. I rubbed my head and tried to close my eyes but he continued with his interrogation. No respite was to be given as we flew towards Izumo Airport, near the Japan Sea in central Shimane. We shared the typical background information, as we awaited our fates as newly christened English teachers in rural Japan. He had been from some southern university that I never heard of and he obviously had no intentions of returning to America. I told him that I had studied at the Writer's Workshop at the University of Iowa and was going to teach English in Japan as a way to do research for a novel I was writing. It was a re-imagining of Bram Stoker's *Dracula* that would take place in feudal Japan, based on the Christian Martyrs of Tsuwano during the Tokugawa Shogunate. Tsuwano was a small town just a few hours' drive from where I'd be living.

After an hour-long, sleepless flight we arrived at our destination. I was greeted by lovely 100-degree humid summer weather and two friendly men with a sign with my name on it. One man was a skinny Japanese gentleman in a white dress shirt, black slacks, and black tie. He introduced himself as Masuda as he shook my hand and bowed. The man to his right was a muscular Caucasian gentleman wearing gym shorts, a sleeveless T-Shirt and a grin a mile wide. His name was Sam Jensen. Sam had become famous around the rural community, I later found out, for having an unmatched energy for teaching English, so he was better known as Super Sam. He was from Perth, Australia and would turn out to be my main source on everything about life in rural Japan, as he had been working at pre-schools and elementary schools throughout the territory for the last five years.

After the typical introductions we drove down the Japanese coast, picturesque even on an incredibly hot and humid mid-summer's day. Stopping at a famous shrine we discussed the many duties I would be expected to complete during my time in Japan. The first were a meeting with the Mayor of the town I would be staying at, and writing an introductory article for the local newspaper. Since I studied at the Writer's Workshop it seemed as if they believed me to be some famous writer. I was humored by this but also felt a bid of confidence flee from my body. The paper would feature an article on World War II, since a local veteran Miharu Kenta would be turning 77, and commemorate the bombing of Hiroshima, a bordering prefecture about an hour drive from where were located. My article seemed insignificant in comparison to its accompanying topics. It turned out the veteran was a neighbor of mine and his wife was a very nice lady who was the vice principal at an elementary school I would be teaching at twice a month.

My mind was racing with amazement and confusion as we drove towards my new home in the very rural and picturesque coastal town of Nima. I was quickly observing that my Japanese skills were amateur at best despite my prior training. As each building and sign passed me by I was reminded how foreign this land was to me. The security of the last few days of spending time with other Americans fled from my body like a foreboding wave crashing into the jagged rocks of the Japan Sea.

So began my time in rural Japan. I would be living in a nice-sized one-story traditional Japanese house in a very quiet and secluded fishing neighborhood with many older Japanese citizens. I would often awake to temple bells that rang at 6 a.m. every morning, and would bike to my nearby school even though this required an uphill scale of two mountain valleys. As time would pass, so would the feelings of confusion and alienation as I set into my regular routine, teaching at almost a dozen junior and elementary schools. They ranged from small mountain schools to larger junior high schools with multiple homerooms for each grade. For those first few months I will never forget the feelings of confusion and isolation that accompanied me at that time. However, these emotions pale in comparison to the mystery that would haunt and accompany me for the duration of my 3 year long stay and beyond.

Robert Jacques

CHAPTER 2:
Mystery Boxes and the Rainy Season

It was exactly 8 months and 16 days into my stay in rural Japan that I began receiving the traditional business sized Japanese envelopes --that opened horizontally on the smaller end as opposed to western ones that open vertically-- filled with 10 newly pressed 10,000 yen notes (approximately $1,000 USD). No note or letter was attached and there were no distinctive marks on the envelope that would set it apart from any other that could be purchased at any Japanese convenience store. I remember this day very clearly, as it is not every day that a person receives an unmarked envelope filled with cash, and a rather large sum of cash at that. At first I felt elation and surprise. But soon my feelings turned to trepidation and apprehension. I analyzed the envelope some more, fingering every seam and crease to make sure I didn't miss anything. Nothing was found except more questions for me to ask.

I ran out my door to examine the mail box only to be met with heavy rain drops as powerful gusts of wind blew rain into my face. My mailbox was an old fashioned slot in the door, with a box on the inside to catch the mail. "Psssh," I spit out the rain that slapped my face as I realized my stupidity in checking the outside slot of my mailbox, with its interior design. It was the now the rainy season in Japan, called "tsuyu," meaning "plum rain" because of the plum season it coincides with. I should have known better than to go outside with such haste, as it had been raining non-stop the past few days. However, this was my first experience of a true rainy season. Unfortunately it would not be my last. I stood in the rain examining my neighborhood streets. No one seemed to be out in the rain and not even lights seemed to be on. It seems weird now thinking back to it as I had checked my mail in the afternoon when I had returned home from school. No clues would be ascertained by me at that time.

I returned inside wet and disappointed. Questions quickly filled my head. *Who sent this to me and why did they send it? Was I receiving my key money I had paid as a security deposit on the house I was renting? Did the town's Board of Education reward me with a bonus for my extra work tutoring students for the prefecture-wide English speech contest? One of my pupils did take first place.* But I soon disregarded my delusions of grandeur and I thought *no way, the budget is tight right now and I doubt my extra hours of work these past 2 months would validate such a bonus, maybe I should just chalk this up to another of the many misunderstandings I encountered as a young American living in rural Japan. It must be the key money I deposited,* I concluded. I mean I had refurbished my wood floors all myself and paid for them to fix my AC unit, and I did dig a nice garden in the small area next to my house that used to be a weed patch. *Not all that bad accomplishments for a 24 year old that had been on his own for the first time in his life,* I thought to myself, trying to justify this odd gift I had been presented with.

I remember using a little of the money later that day at the super market as I had forgotten to take out cash before I left. I returned home feeling guilty over what I had spent, and drove directly to the bank to replenish the money I had used. Something didn't sit right with me; call it the Catholic guilt that had been ingrained in me during my 12 years of parochial schooling. I returned the whole amount to the envelope and hid it in a cupboard in an old green tea can above my refrigerator. This is where I stored all the money I ever received. I never spent a single yen of it. Over two years like clockwork the mysterious envelopes would come monthly, never at the same time, or day. All the envelopes piled up, and I remember having to get additional tea cans to hold the money. I often wonder what I could have bought with these riches, however I know the reward this money brought me is worth more than any penny could buy.

CHAPTER 3:
Men without Sun in the Year of the Rooster (1945)

In the winter 1945, in the waning years of World War II, the American 503rd Parachute Regimental Combat Team *assaulted the Japanese-occupied Island of Corregidor located in central Philippines. Their orders were to recapture the Japanese stronghold on Manila Bay. This would be a daunting task as many Japanese soldiers were encamped in elaborate tunnels and subterranean passages. Among the Parachute Regiment's difficulties were precise landing locations, parachute malfunctions, and heavy Japanese fire. Causalities were high, and many went missing in action.*

Alex Jones had felt he had been preparing for this his whole life. He was 23 but the war had been long and seemed as if it was a completely different life than one he had left behind in Bangor, Maine. However, his preparations never covered the situation he was now faced with. He had found himself coming under heavy fire, with what he only hoped was a broken leg. His heart was racing in excruciating pain; he feared what lay hidden under his left pant leg. He had missed the landing target completely as his parachute malfunctioned on his perilous descent, his ragdoll body caught the western face of a jagged mountain edge at alarming speeds, exploding his left femur like an elephant stomp snaps a twig.

He sat in shock. He tried to think back to his preparation, his time in parachute camp. But his mind could not ignore the pain that was shooting up his left side like a freight train late for its arrival. He rolled to center himself and tried to avoid putting pressure on his destroyed left leg. This only caused him more pain as his movement loosened the earth beneath him. Then the ground gave way completely, his body descending and sliding below into a cavern of darkness. Rubble and dirt accompanied him on his fall. His mind found a new level of fear. A tunnel of darkness lay ahead of him. He tried to catch his breath, but he found the air in this tunnel stale and damp. He thought of all the M.I.A.s he always heard of, all the casualties of war the men try not to talk about. *This is what will become of me,* he accepted. He took a deep breath, and welcomed the darkness as he closed his eyes.

Alex went in and out of consciousness. When he would awaken, he would have no idea how long he had been out for. It felt like days, even years, in the darkness. The endless black made him see things. A vision of a small girl no older than six that reminded him of his cousin Virginia, who died of polio the previous fall, appeared before him. Her eyes cried tears of blood that created red pools on the homemade white church dress she wore every Sunday. She faded as another vision approached him. This time, the apparition of his younger brother- armless, pale, and dressed in fatigues- smiled, offered him a lucky strike, and laughed as he had no hand to lend. Alex shook his head as it throbbed in anguish. He had regained some consciousness as the hallucinations had rattled his disorientation further. Then he heard something.

Voices, yes, voices, Alex opened his eyes wide, unable to see, but convinced he had heard something up ahead. He worried it was another vision, another fever dream sent to torture him. They were so disturbing and real he feared for his sanity. In all honesty he had no idea how long he had been out for or how long he had been stuck in this black version of hell. It felt like days, even years in the darkness. But he rationalized it couldn't have been more than a day since the pain in his leg was still real as ever. A black shape moved towards him like a well-uniformed phantom ready to carry him to another existence. Alex laid still, held his breath, and abandoned all hope.

The Japanese soldier stopped within ten feet of Alex's motionless body. He spoke to himself about the current state of the war in a language strange and foreign to Alex, as he nearly missed Alex's battered body. If not for the rocks Alex' had jarred loose in his decent to the gallows the young soldier, Miharu Kenta, would not have noticed the change in the subterranean landscape that he had made his home for the past year. However, a larger rock that the young soldier often released his bladder on was not in the same location it had usually been in. He eyed it with curiosity and then the shine of Alex's boot caught his eye. He yelled in shock at his discovery and drew his weapon.

CHAPTER 4:
Mushrooms and Red Demons

I mulled over the different ways I could catch my mysterious benefactor but ultimately thought the money would stop coming and my life would go on as normal. However, as the months continued, so did the envelopes. I had finally had enough. I wanted to know why this was happening and I decided to conduct a little detective work. It was spring time now and the Japanese school year would be ending. I would have a few weeks off to plan my case. First I asked friends and colleagues about the different reasons people would give money in Japan. I received the customary answers of weddings and funerals, basically for celebrity purposes. But one answer I got intrigued me. Super Sam, who I met upon my arrival to Shimane, said something of great interest.

"Well, I find that the Japanese like to throw money at a problem," he said, "especially when they don't really know how to emotionally deal with things. Last spring my grandfather fell deathly ill and I was really torn up about it. Our supervisor could see I was really breaking down about returning to Australia to see him or not. Well, maybe due to our communication difficulties in such circumstances, I found an envelope full of cash from him in my mailbox the next day."

"Hmm, interesting." I replied, mulling the information over in my head.

"Hell, even look at our jobs. Basically the Japanese government saw that they were way behind in English comprehension scores globally and threw money at the problem by employing all us foreigners. Ha!" He laughed, and then continued. "Also, if you get invited to a wedding, never give an even-number of cash. It's considered bad luck because it can be divided. Interesting, huh?" Then he concluded, "Why do you ask? You invited to a wedding or something? Traditional Japanese weddings are exquisite!"

"Um, no reason, just trying to get to know Japanese culture as best I can, you know." I hurriedly answered with a nervous smile. "Thanks for the talk, but I got to get going." I hoped I didn't sound too suspicious.

I went home to ponder what Sam had told me. The idea that someone might be throwing money at a problem because they didn't know how to deal with something stuck with me. But what could the issue be? Then my mind raced to an array of horrid images. Could it be someone is feeling guilty about a terrible story? The news! They're had been a heavily publicized news story on all the Japanese newspapers and TV programs. A twenty something man who turned cross-dresser to escape capture, had snuck into a foreign English teacher's apartment a few months ago and slaughtered her in the bathtub armed with nothing but a kitchen cleaver. The story had been gaining great notoriety due to the fact that the English woman's family had flown to Japan to hold press conferences begging authorities to bring their young daughter's murderer to justice. In addition, the Japanese police in charge of the case were found to be very inept in their detective work due to the mishandling of much of the evidence. This had caused an international stir between the British family and the Japanese authorities. The case was on the whole country's hearts and minds. This was an interesting reversal of the common outcry over crimes caused by American soldiers stationed in Okinawa and outside Hiroshima. I could always feel the stares and disappointments every time an American soldier would be accused of rape or murder, which seemed to happen more times than I would like to remember during my stay in Japan. Could this mystery be tied to something awful like this? I never heard of any foreign teacher being killed here in our rural community, and news here travels faster than the Japanese bullet trains, so no way could a story like that stay hidden from me. Could it?

Thinking about such dark thoughts made me anxious and frustrated. Enough was enough; I had to find out who was leaving this money in my mailbox.

82

Looking back on it, I contemplated many different ways to catch my mysterious benefactor. I thought about installing a security camera somewhere near my door or inside my mailbox, or even bribing the mailman to watch my house on his daily routes. But none of these ideas came to fruition; they seemed too complicated or strange-- I mean I didn't want to make any more of spectacle of myself here in this rural town than I already was.

Believe it or not, the tool that ended up catching my culprit was nothing other than mountain mushrooms that my co-worker and Phy. Ed. teacher picked for me. Mr. Saito was a generous old man who often brought me fresh vegetables from his garden or wasabi root from the fields beyond our school. However, this time was different. He brought me giant mushrooms from the mountain side he had picked while hiking Mt. Sanbe over a brisk fall weekend. I thanked him kindly and was excited to experiment with the hamburger bun-sized monstrosities he gave to me.

Over the week I ate the mushrooms in my eggs in the morning and in my dishes at night. They were delicious and a true experience! However, it would turn out to be one I would greatly regret. By the end of the week I was covered in a rash that no inch of my body could escape! The pain and itch was unbearable! By Monday of the next week the rash had gotten so severe I needed to go to the hospital. I called my English Department supervisor to meet me at the skin clinic downtown as I told him of my ailment. I rushed to the hospital and met my supervisor there. The doctor was kind and smiled as I told him of the delicious but dangerous mushrooms I devoured. I was given strong meds and was told not to drive. This small detail would turn out to be the conclusion to my mystery. My supervisor informed me that my car would be fine at the clinic and he would drive me home to rest for a few days.

And rest I did. I had slept almost 2 days straight when I heard a rattle at my mail box. It was at a strange time, well before I knew the normal mail would arrive. I rushed in my drugged state to the door. I stumbled and tripped on my wrapped blanket in nothing but my boxer shorts but I didn't care. I swung the door open red-chested and medicated to see an old man hurrying away from my house.

He turned and saw me. His eyes had a look of horror and disbelief. How could he have known I was home? Nothing had moved in my house for two days and my car was gone. He mustn't have gotten the news of my ailment. Then he laughed a glorious innocent laugh. I burst out in laughter also and began laughing with him. I must have looked like an oni, a strange red skinned Japanese demon. This thought was too hilarious not to laugh at, even in my state of agony. Then our shared laughter soon turned to sadness, he put his hands to his face and began to gently sob.

I grabbed my blanket that I had tripped on and wrapped it around myself, I walked to him and patted him on his back, and tried to console this small old man whom I know I had seen before many times during my time in Japan. His name was Miharu Kenta and his picture even shared the same newspaper as mine did the first month I came to Japan. He was a WWII veteran, and I would soon learn his difficult story. His wife was also the vice-principal at the town's elementary school I would visit once a month. They lived in a nice house with a beautiful Japanese garden only a few blocks from me.

He gathered himself and gestured for me to go inside with him. The he began to recount his story. He could only handle little portions of his time in the war at a time. So we made future arrangements to meet once a week. We told his wife that we had worked out our own culture exchange program. I would teach him English and he would instruct me in the art of Bonsai, so I too could replicate the beautiful trees that stood so proudly in his garden. She smiled at this agreement and always sent him over with fresh sweets and tea. So it was be under this ruse that he informed me of his story and the meaning behind his envelopes.

CHAPTER 5:
Things Not Forgotten in Dead Man's Shoes

He started with his life in the service, the long years missing his home, and of course the caves. He remembered the caves more than anything, the fear, the darkness, the discipline, and ultimately the isolation of entrapment.

He had told me how one day while serving on the island of Corregidor he went to relieve his bladder, as he had many times before in the underground caves where they had made their camp, and found an American soldier fallen and incapacitated. In his shock, he went on to say, he shot the man in a moment of pure adrenaline that he had never felt come over his body before. He went on to tell me that he had never seen an American up close before that time, and that he thought he looked like a child in man's clothes. He would never forget this body, or man, because as he finished firing his sidearm into the American soldier, an artillery shell rocked their cave. It collapsed part of the cave, trapping them both underneath with only a slight opening above them so that the sun would tease him for a few hours each day. He told me the first thing he did was remove the soldier's boots because they were so much nicer than his. He said he found a strange note hidden inside them that he held onto for all this time. He stayed in that cave until the end of the war with nothing but that dead soldier's death stare gleaming at him at all times.

He continued with his story and as it progressed his time in the cave turned much darker, and the desperation of his composure did nothing to hide this fact. At first he told me of eating the soldier's strange K rations he had stored in his gear. He laughed at the awful smell of a tin of peanut butter, and remembered the enjoyment of the cigarettes he savored from the man's pack. In his boredom he studied the dead man. He tried to teach himself English from the man's gear and dog tag. He memorized the soldiers name and religion, Alex Jones, Catholic, and

85

eight digit service number, though he did not understand the second part until he translated it when he arrived back to Japan. The simple yet powerfulness of the one word, Catholic, stayed with him forever, knowing the religion of this man opened so many different questions and characteristics of this dead body that he never wanted to think of. He told me he still had many of the items he found on the soldier in a locked trunk hidden away in his house.

I asked him why he held onto these items as well as the note from the boot for all these years. This question made him nervous as if he had been waiting all these years for someone to ask him. He hesitated. Then all of a sudden the words began trickling from his mouth.

He said those days had become long and he tried desperately in his solitude to climb up from his personal catacomb, but was unable to do so due to the steepness of the cave wall. He tried fastening rope out of the clothes he and the dead soldier were wearing, but he failed to no avail. "I felt as if I was being tested in that cave alone, scared, and hungry," he stated in deep thought. He kept thinking someone would come for him or a bomb would fall from the sky and end his torturous sentence. He told me of how the sun would tease him in its movements across the black crack in the cave. He would bath himself in the light the few hours it pitied him with. His tone turned dark as he continued to recall the days that felt like lifetimes.

But it wasn't until he went on talking of the hunger and desperation he faced in that cave, that he broke down into tears. He went with no food for days and when he became desperate, dying of starvation, he turned to cannibalism. He cut from the soldier only a little at a time just enough to curb the hunger pains. And when he knew that this was not the way he wanted himself to die, he began his attempt to scale the cave once again. But he knew he needed more rope as the clothes he knotted together were not long enough. He looked to the carved carcass of the ghost of Alex Jones and he began to remove the intestines of a long dead soldier. He threw up multiple times from the horrid stench of the carcass. But then no more food came from his stomach, only the taste of yellow bile flew from his mouth. His hands worked on, he knew he was desperate and dying. He tied the ends of the intestines off with the laces from his boots and the small thread that was left from the soldiers pack. He tied a rock to each of the ends and after what seemed like a lifetime of tries he hooked his rock through the small crevasse above him. He began to pull himself up and climb the cave wall. Using the makeshift rope he climbed to his escape. As he arose from his grave he found a plethora of air-dropped fliers scattered across the scorched battlefield. One flew into his left foot. He reached down to grab it, and before he completely opened it he could make out the simple Japanese characters, "War Over."

He began sobbing uncontrollably and Alex continued to comfort him as they sat in Alex's kitchen. The old man slowly rose and told Alex he had something to show him. He said the day he saw his picture in the paper, it was like seeing a ghost. He claimed I looked exactly like the soldier that gave his life so that he could survive. I shook my head in disbelief. He motioned for me to walk to my hallway where he had hung up his jacket and briefcase that he told his wife was for his English homework. He brought the briefcase back to the kitchen table and carefully opened it. There was a small old Japanese box inside. He took out an odd shaped key and gently opened it. Inside it was Alex's dog tags, a strange message written on a telegraph, and what appeared to be the used up wrapper of a K-Ration. He handed me the telegraph with the strange message written on it,

"PJW-Remember 3/31? Need help desperately, not much time left. Please, you're the only one! 2713311869101001 You know what to do. - Alex"

He asked me what it meant. I laughed and said I had no idea. It was just some secret message lost in time.

He laughed in disbelief, as if this might have been some important military message that I was just as lost to understand it as he was. He said he held onto it all this time because he thought it was some important military code that his superiors would have been very happy to uncover. But nonetheless we both were as perplexed by this odd, nonsensical message. He went on to ask if I was related to any Alex Jones' back home. I couldn't think of any and told him that Alex Jones is a quite common name. We shook our heads in disbelief once again. It was just another strange coincidence that tied us together.

We both paused and caught our breath. Then I began to talk about the money. "You can have it all back you know; I didn't spend a single yen." I stated. "I keep it hidden in a tea tins above my refrigerator."

This made him laugh again, and he insisted that I keep it, and that every time he has placed some money in my mailbox has been a symbol of each day that has been gifted to him from the dead American. He said he was honoring his life by doing so. I asked if he had any children that could use the money or anything like that and shook his head as if he had thought about this for many years. I didn't know what to say, but I concluded that we should donate the money to some charity instead. I looked to the dog tags, and saw they read Catholic and an idea jumped into my head. There was an Old Catholic church in Tsuwano, a small charming town about two and a half hours south of where we lived. Today, it is one of the oldest churches left on Japanese soil due to the banishment of Christianity during the Tokugawa regime. Giving the money to the church seemed like an appropriate way to honor the dead soldier. He thought so too, but he said I would have to give the money since he did not want to draw any attention to himself. I humbly agreed. I thought I should honor him for his kindness. I paused for a while and said, "in time when we look back at things, maybe we shouldn't always look at things as wholly right or wholly wrong. Just moments in time that have come to pass, things that are, and things that are to come."

We continued our relationship as my time progressed and finished in Japan. We became friends out of that strange experience that I would never forget. I even continued to send him New Year's cards after I returned to America, and he would always write back. We would talk about the menial moments of life that fill our time in this odd place we call earth. I've never shared his story with anyone else until now, as I promised myself I wouldn't until he passed. Last year I was given the sad news that he had passed at the age of 86. His wife informed me that he died in his sleep and I prayed that he had found peace in his final years. It was a strange feeling knowing that with his death his most intimate memories-that had burdened him for so long-were now carried on in me. I can only hope to honor him with never forgetting his story.

Robert Jacques *is an Educator who began writing at the University of Iowa and continued to write during his time living in Japan. He now lives in Green Bay Wisconsin where he can watch the Packers play every Sunday.*

The Message

Matthew J. Kolell

John's mind raced as he ran towards the communication center. The runner said it was a "weird" message that they thought might be for him. He told himself it probably wasn't even for him, and had nothing to worry about; but in the back of his mind he knew it had to be. His hand checked his left shirt pocket to be sure he had it with him, but then where else would it be.

As he hurried through the door, he tripped and nearly fell into the Sergeant's lap. "Easy private, slow down," the sergeant said. "Take a look at this. It came in five minutes ago. We don't know where it came from, who sent it, or even who its for. You're the only person we could think of." The sergeant held out the note to John's shaking hand, damp with sweaty dust.

John read, "PJW-Remember 3/31? Need help desperately, not much time left. Please, you're the only one! 2713311869101001 You know what to do. - Alex."

"Sergeant, where's the commander?"

"Playing poker in the usual spot. So John, is that for you or... hey, what's..." John was already out the door. He mentally did a quick checklist. First get the commander's permission to leave. He wasn't sure what was wrong yet but he could decipher that on the way. Then make any preparations necessary before he...BOOM!

***

"Ali, check to be sure she's alright and get her any medical help she needs. Fernan, get somebody to help you with Berto. I'll check outside to be sure every thing's clear." Balt took a moment to collect himself to be sure he was okay both physically and mentally, while he waited for the clouds of dust to settle. Sure Berto could be a real prick, but he was a laugh and they had been through a lot together.

Balt placed his sleeve over his mouth and breathed deeply. As Balt walked outside, he spotted the body lying there and silently swore to himself.

As he crouched down next to him, he scanned the buildings and countryside for any sign of danger. The rebels usually struck once and then left swiftly to evade discovery, but you can never be too safe. Noticing nothing, his eyes fell down to the dead man. Balt glimpsed the slip of paper in the soldiers clenched fist. Carefully he pried it from his hand. Again he swore to himself and thought, "What is this all about?" Checking the soldiers pockets, he came across a small book in the breast pocket of the shirt. Balt fingered through the book in amazement; numbers with letters underneath covered every page.

John was relatively new to the unit and Balt, although he took time to get know his men, did not know much about him. Balt recalled that he kept to himself but he was smart and would volunteer for any mission that came up. But this discovery showed how little he really knew him, or the rest of his men in fact. Getting to his feet, he slowly walked to the communication center, mulling things over in his mind. With a deep sigh, he resigned himself to try to find out what the message meant and help this "Alex" if at all possible. Picking up his pace, he started his own mental list of things to do. Find out when the message came in and if there was anything said or any clues in regards to it. Quickly go through John's property to find anything else out. Let his superiors know he'd be leaving and make sure order would be maintained during his absence. Get transportation and arm up. If no clues presented themselves; go to his hometown, inform his parents and dig up any information there.

***

Balt had parked in the garage two blocks away; he knew it was wasting time but his paranoia kept him from parking out front because he had no idea what he was getting into. The city was miles from the border and hadn't seen any of the carnage. It was a quiet neighborhood near the city center where he walked down the street in the glow of the street lamps. His mind raced over the best way to inform John's parents but then to quickly get any answers in regards to the message, because if the message was right, Alex didn't have much time. He scanned the windows and rooftops as he got to the stoop. Climbing the stairs he took a deep breath as he knocked on the door. The door opened a ways, Balt could see a woman looking around the edge. "May I help you?" she questioned.

"Is this the Walter residence? The home of Private John Walter? Balt replied. The door opened some more, the lady's hand went over her mouth as she started crying.

"Please don't tell me..." She took a deep breath and closed her eyes for a few seconds to compose herself. "I'm Vivian Walter, his mother. Please tell me everything is alright."

"Might his father be home as well?" asked Balt.

"He is running some errands. Did you need to talk to him?" she gasped trying to catch her breath through the tears. Balt knew she was pleading with him to have a reason to talk to Mr. Walter and not to be there about her son. He knew there was no easy way to do this.

"Ma'am, I'm Private Walter's commanding officer, Major Kolgrowlski. I'm sorry to inform you that your son died earlier today. He was an excellent--" but before he could finish Mrs. Walter threw herself into him, sobbing and holding him tight. Balt placed his arms around her, trying to give what comfort he could. As she pressed into him, Balt could feel her soft, supple body. She may be around fifteen years older but she had seductive curves that were enhanced by the blue house dress, stockings and heels. And older woman were experienced and could teach you a few... *What the hell are you doing?* Balt thought to himself. *Get your mind out of the gutter and focus. One person already died today, but you may be able to prevent another.*

"I am very sorry for your loss," Balt continued, "but I was hoping you might be able to help me by answering a question or two?" Balt cradled the back of her head into his chest to lend her some support.

There was no response. "Your son was trying to help a friend out just before... Do you know any Alex that was friends with him or would have contacted him?" She was still shaking as she pushed a little out of his hold to look up at him.

"Alex? There was Alexandria, but we always called her Lexi. I wouldn't know anyone else by the name of Alex, especially any soldiers he may have befriended."

"Do you have an address or number where I could try to contact her? And are you sure you can't think of anyone else?" Balt continued.

"I'm sorry I really can't think right now, but let me get you her address," Mrs. Walter replied.

As she walked back into the room she had a small note in one hand and a kerchief in the other. "Here's her address, its about a mile away. She still lives with her parents, Fred and Janet Weis."

"Thank you ma'am. If there is anything I can do for you, please feel free to contact me. I need to..." Balt trailed off as a shout came from outside.

"Viv, is there something wrong?"

Balt managed to extract himself fairly quickly from the grieving couple as he hurried back to his jeep. He had a lead on Alex, now he just hoped it wasn't a wild goose chase.

***

Balt stopped in front of the address he was given; a red brick two story with steps and black metal railing leading up to the front door. He looked up and down the street, and checked the address to be sure this was the right place, as the rest of the residences looked identical. *How the hell can you tell these apart from each other,* he thought to himself as he shook his head. He knocked on the wooden door as he reached the top of the steps. It door opened a crack, still attached to the frame with a chain lock.

"Hello," came a female voice from behind the door.

"Hello ma'am, sorry to disturb you so late," replied Balt. "I'm Major Balthasar Kolgrowlski. Is this the Fred and Janet Weis residence?"

"Yes, I'm Janet Weis. Is there something I can help you with Major?"

"Please call me Balt. I'm the commanding officer for John Walter, you may know him, I believe he's a friend of your daughter Lexi. I received a message from John earlier today that I was hoping your daughter might help to decipher. Could I talk to her please?"

The door closed and then opened wider, so that Balt could now see who he was talking to. Janet was in her upper thirties, with curled shoulder length black hair, brown eyes and nice full red lips. She was wearing a red silk blouse and black skirt with red pinstripes and stockings. Instead of the usual heels, she broke from decorum in her own house and was wearing fuzzy white slippers. "Lexi isn't home at the moment. Do you have any idea where she is?"

Balt stood there, confused for a second, "I was going to ask you if you knew where I could find her."

"I'm sorry. I'm just so worried. Fred is at work. Lexi left last night to go out for a drink with some friends and hasn't come home yet. She's been gone a couple days at a time before but she's always called or let me know where she was. It's never been this long before."

Once again, Balt was in the embrace of a married, crying woman. He could feel her warmth against his body and smell the exotic aromas from her hair. Janet's breasts weren't as large as Vivian's but her face was prettier and she smelled better... *Balt snap out of it. Lexi may need your help,* he thought.

Balt gave her some time to release her anxiety then asked, "Do you have any idea where she might be or might it be possible to go through some of her things to find out anything?"

"I called her friends but none of them knew anything and didn't even see her last night. I don't know if I could go through her things; I was waiting until Fred came home to see if we should contact the authorities."

"I don't want to alarm you but John received a message from an Alex asking for help but some of the note was just a bunch of numbers. Would you know if Lexi would ever use a code like that?"

She began crying again, "That's something she would do. She and John would get into so much trouble in school writing those crazy notes back and forth to each other."

"Do you know how to decipher it all?" Balt asked excitedly.

"No, but there is..." she started to say. "Why isn't John here if the note was for him?"

Balt took her hand, and placed it between his own massive hands. "I'm going to be honest with you. Private Walter was running to see me when he was killed in a random terrorist strike before he got to me. I found the note he was holding and thought it was the least I could do to try to find and help Alex. His parents were generous enough to point me to you in their grief. I have no idea if Alexandria is in any trouble. I want to help find her so that you know she is safe and as a last show of respect to one of my soldiers."

"Oh, I don't know what to do." Her face was a mixture of anxiety and indecision. "When we moved here a couple years ago we found a tiny hidden room in the cellar which we assume was used for hiding refugees at some point in time. We let Lexi use the room and promised never to enter. It seemed right up her alley with all the secret codes she'd come up with. She also made us promise to never let anyone enter unless John came asking for permission.

Squeezing her hand slightly, "Please show me the room. It may help us to find where Lexi is or give us a clue where to start looking. I'm sure Lexi will understand that only your love and concern for her led you to show me the room." Balt couldn't explain why these words were coming from his mouth but he knew he needed to continue with the search because it was the right thing to do. Seeing Janet's grief and worry made him want to help in whatever way he could even if he was too late; not knowing would be worse than finding out what did happen.

"I wish Fred was home to help, but I'll show you." She led him through the tidy house downstairs to the corner of the basement. There she grasped a seem in the wall opening a panel to another room. Balt was amazed at how well concealed the entry was when he saw it. "NOOO!" he yelled, as he pushed Janet from the doorway. He saw the cable, that needed to be disabled, trigger the flamethrowers. Instead of shooting out, the flamethrowers engulfed the interior in flames, igniting the little wooden table and chair and stack of papers. As Balt looked in he thought he glimpsed a picture of a man's face on the desk along with stationary from the army.

Janet thrust a blanket into his hands and Balt quickly set out trying to douse the fire. With the earthen floor and brick walls, Balt was able to put out the fire without it spreading to the rest of the house. Balt had to admit that it was a pretty clever setup to make sure items were destroyed without getting anyone hurt if it was her parents who happened to open the door.

"Did you happen to spy the picture before it burned?" Balt asked.

"No, you pushed me and the first thing I did was grab a blanket and hand it to you. What was the picture of?" Janet replied.

"I'm not certain about the picture but that was quick thinking with the blanket. I need to make a few calls to check on some things. Why don't you check her room and see if you can find anything in there. If you find something, you can get in contact with me through the local branch, I'll be sure to check in with them. If I find anything out, I'll let you know." Balt gave her a reassuring hug, "Things will be alright."

As Balt walked out the door, he was almost positive that the insignia on the letter was the covert operations mark used by the army. Why they would even have their own mark was beyond him, they were supposed to be discrete, weren't they? The picture also kept flashing through his head as well; he'd also bet that he saw that face before, and that it was John's father. He would first try to call his contact in the army and then go visit the Walters again. He checked his watch, it wasn't quite 10 pm. He thought they should still be awake.

***

Balt asked to speak with General Brady. "Yes, I know its late and that he's probably drinking with some company but its urgent that I speak to him right away. I would not be calling if it wasn't urgent and someone's life may depend upon it."

"Yes sir, I'll see what I can do," came the reply.

Balt was getting impatient when after several minutes he finally heard, "Balt, how are you? What can I do for you?" Balt sighed internally; he was well known in the upper circles of command but it always seemed too friendly, that they never took him seriously.

"I'm doing fine, General, I hope the same can be said of you. Sorry to be so abrupt but I don't have much time. I need to follow up on a lead before it gets too late. I was hoping you might be able to give me some information. There is an Alexandria Weis who might go by Alex or Lexi. I got some info that she may be in trouble and that she may work with your department or possibly be trying to gain info about the department. Do you have any idea where I might be able to look for her? And if she might be friendly or not? I have a lead that I'm going to follow up on but I thought I might try you first and let you know that she may be in some trouble, if she is working with you."

Balt could almost hear the general's gears grinding, trying to break free of the alcohol and analyze how much he could say. After a long moment, "I'm not sure who this woman is and I'm sure she is not part of my division but if you think her life may be in danger, you should follow up on that lead. Now I need to get back to my company before they get bored."

"Thank you for your time, General. Should I let anyone know where I will be or if I find out anything?"

"Good night, Balt. If you do find something out, then you can let me know. I would like to know how she might be connected to us at all." Click.

Balt swore to himself. He wished they would give you a straight answer. *This is the situation, do this, don't tell anyone. Nope, not that easy.* He knew he needed to follow up on the lead. With the denial that she was involved in any way with them, he got the feeling that she was affiliated with them in some way, otherwise he would have been more emphatic about trying to get a hold of anyone spying on or gathering information on them. Also, he hadn't actually told the General that Lexi's life may be in danger – the General brought that up on his own... although that may have come from the urgency to get him to the phone.

***

Balt again parked in the ramp and retraced his steps to the Walter residence. Lights were still on. Good he thought, at least someone should still be up. His hand went to his hip to be sure he was still armed, not knowing what he could be getting into.

Balt knocked loudly on the door and listened for any sound on the inside. He was able to pick up a few footsteps by the window and then to the door. The door opened and he could see Mrs. Walter in a pink robe and slippers. "Major, I wasn't expecting you. Is there anything you need?" she said answering the door.

"Sorry to disturb you at this hour, and please call me Balt. Thank you for taking the time to talk to me in your moment of grief. I was hoping I could ask you and your husband a few questions. I know its late but I'm not sure if it could wait till morning."

"Please come in and have a seat. Joseph needed to get a drink and then tell his parents about John," she said as she motioned for him to come in. Balt followed her into the parlor and had a seat. "Is there anything I can get you, some milk or something to eat?"

"No thank you, Mrs. Walter. Please have a seat as well. You must be exhausted."

"Please call me Vivian, Maj... I mean Balt." She sat across from him wiping her eyes, "Now how can I help you?"

"Its about Lexi Weis. Do you remember the last time you saw her or spoke with her?"

She sat silent for a moment thinking. "I believe I saw her about two weeks ago in the market. I mentioned to her that the cantaloupe was very good and that she should pick some up for her parents. And that Janet should give me a call, as I hadn't seen her since John left. Were you able to get in touch with her parents at all?"

"Yes, thank you for your help." Balt wasn't sure where to go from here; he decided to ask about the one thing in the note that might possibly give him another clue. "Do you know if the date or numbers three, thirty-one had any significance for John and Lexi?"

She placed her hand to her mouth thinking. "Not that I can recall, but oh wait, that's Joseph's birthday. They were going to surprise him a few years ago. Joseph loves dirigibles. They made a cake and had balloons shaped like them. They got a captain to give him a ride and tour of the bridge. We all had such fun. But when he first found out, he was so angry at them for disturbing him." She managed to smile a little recalling some fond memories of their family.

"What happened that he was so upset at first?"

"Well Joseph doesn't like surprises in the first place. And then they snuck downstairs and surprised him in his study. I could hear him yelling all the way up here. Which is funny because he has that place so well insulated you can never hear a peep when he's down there but I guess the door was open." Just then the front door opened and Joseph walked in.

"Oh Joseph, I'm so glad you're back. The Major here, sorry, Balt, was asking some questions about Lexi and I just told him about the time they surprised you on your birthday. It's so nice to share happy memories of John, it makes the pain a little less." As she was finishing her last sentence, Joseph reached behind his back, drawing a gun.

Balt, realizing what he was doing, sprung from the chair. He took a giant step; then dove towards him. Joseph managed to get the gun up and fire without aiming. The bullet struck Balt in the shoulder but his momentum carried him into Joseph, tackling him to the floor. The gun flew from Joseph's hand, and even with the bleeding wound, Balt was able to easily pin Joseph to the floor with his arm over Joseph's neck.

Over Vivian's screams, Balt shouted at Joseph, "I have no idea what you are involved with but you better tell me anything you know about Lexi before I beat it out of you!"

Joseph managed to say, "Viv get the g," before Balt pressed his arm harder into his throat, while Joseph started gasping for air.

"Vivian, call the police so that we can get this sorted out. I don't want to hurt you," roared Balt. Vivian was already heading towards the phone. As she talked on the phone, Balt shifted his attention back to Joseph. "You have one last chance to tell me where Lexi is before I hurt you," Balt said quietly into Joseph's ear. As he let up the pressure on his neck, Joseph breathed deeply then spit in Balt's face. "Freedom to the.." Joseph got out before Balt's massive fist slammed into his head knocking him out.

Balt quickly got up and grabbed the gun, then searched Joseph for any other weapons. Vivian stood in the corner crying out, "Please don't hurt me!"

Balt tucked the gun in his pant leg's cargo pocket. He then put up his hands in a placating gesture asking Vivian to calm down. Reassuring her that he meant no harm to her. After several minutes she managed to calm down enough for Balt to talk to her. "I need you to show me Joseph's study. I don't know why he shot me but Lexi's life may depend on it. Please help me, I know you don't want any harm to come to her."

Vivian reluctantly led Balt downstairs. Balt knew he was taking a chance leaving Joseph alone upstairs but he was pretty sure he'd be out for awhile. Vivian tried the door but it was locked. Balt told her to stand back as he kicked his large foot into the door. The door burst open onto the floor. Vivian screamed, "Oh my Lord!" as she peered inside at the figure of a young woman tied to a chair. She sat slumped over, with eyes closed, as a pool of her blood soaked into the carpet.

Just then Balt could hear someone yelling upstairs, "This is the police. Come out with your hands up."

***

Balt stood at the corner, looking at the brothel across the street that the General highly recommended. His mind raced over everything that had happened, and he needed an escape. He remembered the embraces of Vivian and Janet. How good they felt against him and how perfectly their bodies fit against his. Even as Vivian clung to him as her world fell apart around her, he was able to feel the love she had for the two men in her life. Janet hugged him so hard when he told her that Lexi was still alive that he thought he might even bruise. There was so much love for Lexi and thankfulness packed into that hug that his whole body tingled with warmth. Balt took a deep breath, he wanted to feel that love in his life and going across the street would only bring a pale imitation at best. Balt turned around and walked slowly back to his jeep as the red lights faded away.

T	U	I	C	K	L	E	Q	S	H	X	S	F	W	Y	T	E	H	B	N
5	63	43	76	42	78	41	89	40	*10*	11	44	56	90	*2*	99	*100*	17	83	22

P	I	O	K	B	C	W	A	U	M	T	A	A	L	G	N	V	M	W	D
30	31	29	39	3	93	26	34	*33*	69	67	55	*6*	85	80	94	12	36	37	82

Q	T	X	C	K	P	J	D	S	N	B	A	E	O	B	S	T	D	F	G
73	*9*	35	32	47	74	77	38	50	28	60	51	13	*77*	91	98	8	16	20	59

M	N	R	K	T	D	L	E	S	A	K	C	W	M	P	U	I	N	S	L
88	86	*1*	15	46	62	53	58	19	48	84	4	14	64	66	70	96	61	21	87

T	P	A	E	K	L	Q	V	T	R	S	F	R	A	E	S	R	I	U	C
23	81	92	97	57	7	52	27	68	79	24	*18*	25	49	75	45	95	72	54	65

Matthew Kolell *is not a best-selling author nor an award winning novelist. He does own a small business and enjoys gaming, bicycling, drinking Mountain Dew, and spending time with his family. He lives in the Fox River Valley with his wife Sara, three sons, a beautiful daughter, a tall dining room table, and their dog Ajax, a Great Dane mix.*

Spirit Shuffle

Marcus Maichle

"What happens to your kind is of little concern to us," the undine's voice vibrated through the cold water. It had a whale song quality about it. "The fewer of you there are, the better for us, in fact." Angel anticipated the emissary's argument, but still the statement made him shiver even more than the already chill temperature of Lake Michigan.

"The man I am seeking your aid for is a scientist. The research he is doing can be used to stop the dumping of chemicals. That's why he was out here. He's on your side." Angel paused to let the water spirits consider his argument. A few swirls in the water told him that they were giving it thought, and probably discussing amongst themselves. This was the only indication he had of their even being here, since they had no visible form.

Angel himself wasn't actually there, but he had created a visible projection for the sake of communicating with the spirits. He still appeared as himself mostly, but in a mer-folk form. His physical body drifted unconsciously above him at the surface, with a flotation spell keeping his head above water. The swim out here was cold and tiring, not to mention risky, but it was the best way to open this dialog. Meet them where they are. His magic aided him staying safe, but he often accepted certain discomfort and effort as a balancing cost for the power he wielded.

Angel was a mage, a keeper of arcane knowledge, and the magical abilities that come with it, practiced and learned over multiple lifetimes. Like the other members of his order, he had learned secrets of the spirit world; that unseen aspect of everything that makes the world work the way it does. And if they can be convinced to cooperate, they can make things work in his favor. These abilities require long study and practice, and so early members of the order learned how a spirit may return to a new life maintaining the memory and skill gained in the previous one.

"We do not need his research. We know the damage that is being done, and we have told you."

"The research isn't to determine whether they're dumping. We know it too. But we need to be able to prove who's doing it. I can't very well go public with the fact that the Genius Loci of Lake Michigan told me what's happening. The ones that don't try locking me up would come out here looking for you."

"We can deal with them." The turbulence in the water shook with meaning, and there was no doubt that the spirits would follow through on this threat.

"I understand. But what effort would that take? All I am asking is your assistance in locating a small sailboat with a scientist on it. A sailboat for crying out loud. He wouldn't even use a motorized boat out here, which is probably why he's missing. And the longer he's missing, the more motor boats will be on your waters searching. Please, just help me find him. I'll find a way to get him ashore. Without using motorized boats if you wish. It might mean revealing myself to him, which I'd like to avoid. I mean I trust him not to exploit it, as others have, but I'd rather not shake his devotion to science."

"His devotion to science is no concern. But if you are willing to trust him that far, we will help him." The voice stopped for a few moments and the waters seemed to churn and circle around Angel. "Your friend has been located, he appears unharmed but is unconscious and his vessel adrift. Return to the shore. We will bring the vessel to land."

Angel let the projection fade, and woke up in his body, then swimming back to the shore where he'd left his bicycle, kept an eye out on the water. Eventually, he saw Daniel's sailboat floating eerily toward him, even with no wind or current on the lake. When the boat reached shore, he jumped aboard to find his friend laying on the deck.

"Daniel, wake up!" Angel closed his eyes briefly, and reopened them with a shifted awareness. Daniel's aura was still strong. After a moment, Daniel's eyes opened.

"Where am I?" Daniel asked.

"You were adrift," Angel answered. "There are search boats out looking for you. I've been biking up and down the shore hoping to find you, and here you are."

"Shore?" Daniel shook his head. "That's strange. I was out pretty far. How did I end up at shore?"

"I'm not sure," Angel hoped that Daniel wouldn't push for answers. But something Daniel said made him need answers. "I thought you were testing by the shoreline. Why were you so far out on the lake?" At this, Daniel's expression changed, a combination of recollection and puzzlement.

"I don't know how to describe it. There was... something... in the water. I thought I saw a spout of water, then some sort of churning. I'm not sure what I thought it was, maybe some sort of canister that someone was using to dump chemicals. I thought if I could locate it and mark the location before it drifted too far, we'd have something. Whatever it was kept moving though. When I looked in the water, I could see some sort of shifting colors, but no containers of any sort. I was worried that whatever was in that thing was already seeping out, and was about to radio in, but I suddenly felt dizzy, and... well the next thing I remember was you waking me up here."

"All right, the first thing we're going to do is get you to a doctor. My phone's in the bike pack, and I'll call off the search boats."

"I took water samples from the area. Could you take them and make sure they don't get tampered with? I want to find out what's out there." Daniel's dedication to his work always impressed Angel. And this time, may have paid off better than Angel could have hoped.

"Of course," he said. "I'll look after the samples. Do you have someone who can take care of the boat?"

"Yeah, some friends from the University." Daniel answered.

"Good," Angel said. "Let's get you looked at, then."

***

With Daniel resting safely at the University clinic, Angel avoided questions about what happened as best he could, and deliberately failed to mention the samples to Daniel's colleagues. Daniel's theory about a canister was plausible, but Angel did not want to rule out any sort of supernatural activity. He did rule out the Undines, however. They could have created the type of disturbances Daniel described, but if they had somehow been responsible for what happened, then he would never have been able to convince them to turn around and help. The Undines would probably know what was out there, but Angel did not want to offend them by asking for information so soon after enlisting their aid for the rescue, especially when he had an alternative means of getting the information.

Back in his apartment, Angel pulled out the sample bottles and checked the labels. He wasn't experienced enough in sailing to understand the coordinates on the bottles. Fortunately, Daniel was meticulous in recording the time the samples were taken. Angel pulled the sample with the latest time stamp, the last sample Daniel took before whatever happened, happened. Even with currents moving the actual water around, this sample would energetically still be connected with the area closest to whatever Daniel saw. Angel poured the water sample into a shallow, dark enameled bowl, which he set on a table, and took a seat facing the bowl. He closed his eyes and took several deep breaths, concentrating on opening a link between the scrying bowl and the area of Lake Michigan where the sample was taken. He took one more deep breath, and exhaled over the bowl, opening his eyes. The water rippled from the exhaled breath, and as it settled, the reflection of the room around Angel shifted into an image of the lake's surface.

"Okay, let's see what's out here," Angel murmured to no one in particular. "Come out, come out, wherever you are." He scanned for a time, not seeing anything unusual. He shifted his focus further out, to take in a larger view. Nothing happened. He focused on deeper waters and a wider perimeter. All he could see were the usual fish, plants, and occasional litter that filled Lake Michigan. Perhaps whatever was there wasn't around anymore. Angel maintained the connection, but stopped looking so that he could think things through. That's when he saw the letters.

They appeared out of his peripheral vision. Old block style letters, appearing one at a time from the left side of his vision to the right, as if being tapped out on an old-fashioned typewriter. When he tried moving his focus to center the first letters, they shifted along with his gaze. The letters weren't in the water. They were being sent directly into his mind.

It's not something in the lake, he realized. *There's something using the lake as a conduit.* Water is an excellent conductor, both in the physical reality and for magical purposes. In many mythologies, the way to the afterlife was through a lake or river. Angel watched as the ghostly characters continued to fill his field of vision.

"ELN- Remember 3/31? Need help desperately, not much time left. Please, you're the only one. 2 7 13 3 11 8 6 9 10 1 0 01 You know what to do. - Alex"

Alex. Angel had met many Alexes in his life, but there was no mistaking who sent this message. It was literally a lifetime ago. As a mage, one of the first things Angel had learned was how to interact with the spirit world and how to negotiate with the ruling powers there. It was how he was able to begin this lifetime with the full use of arcane knowledge and practice which he'd spent previous lifetimes learning. If he focused, he could also recall the events and people from his past lives. It was clear that Alex wanted Angel to remember a particular time, 3/31. As if he could forget.

***

March, 1931

"Eddie!" a voice called. Angel turned to see the young man catching up to him on the busy Chicago street. Angel smiled. He had smiled back then, and even recalling the memory made him smile in the present. Alex had that effect on people. It wasn't just his handsome looks, but also his vibrant energy and enthusiasm. Of course, that's where the trouble started.

"Alex!" Angel suddenly tried not to sound so excited. "Um, I was just heading out for the day," he said, motioning back toward the Tribune building.

"Oh," Alex said. "Is the file room still unlocked? I was going to ask for some help in looking up some photos to compare to some recent ones I took. I really think something is showing up in them."

"Well, I still think you're wasting your time. Stick with your training and you'll be able to contact the spirit world directly. This trying to use modern invention as a shortcut worries me, and I doubt the spirits who work through it will be ones you want to meet."

"I'm not looking for shortcuts, Eddie. I'm looking for proof. What good will it be to contact the Spirit World if everyone thinks I'm crazy."

Angel, or rather, Eddie as he was called in this lifetime, worked for the Tribune as a file clerk. He archived pieces of research and stories that never made it to print. He also had access to various anonymous tips that people called in, sightings and stories of things that the editors deemed too incredible to do a story on. He sometimes looked into these stories himself, if they had a ring of something magical about them. Alex was a photographer for the paper, and a natural at getting exciting shots. He seemed to have a sense of when something was about to happen and have his camera aimed at just the right spot. Eddie realized that this sixth sense was a form of psychic gift, and befriended the young photographer. Alex seemed to know that his gift was something unusual as well. He asked a lot of questions, and soon, Eddie confided in him about being a mage, and how he worked behind the scenes to help keep things smooth between the spirit realm and mankind.

"Alex, I told you. You can't go public with what you're learning. It'll end badly. With your gift, I'm surprised you don't see that."

"Maybe my gift isn't showing me that because it won't happen that way."

"I may not have your specific gift, but I have lots of experience, and going public always goes badly." Eddie felt a twinge of pain at the memories.

"Whatever. Is the file room open or not? I want some of the pictures from the things we looked into."

"Yes, someone was still reviewing an old article to do a follow up. File room should still be open for a while, just promise me that if you find something like proof, talk to me before you do anything with it. Any pictures from an investigation we did would be filed as an article on Xylophone recitals."

"Xylophones? That doesn't seem newsworthy at all."

"That's exactly why no one ever bothers to look in the folder. Not to mention, there's plenty of room in that drawer."

"Thanks, pal." Alex tipped his hat to Eddie and turned to go back to the Tribune building.

"He's going to be trouble," Eddie muttered to himself. "The handsome ones always are." Eddie continued on his walk, deciding whether to continue about the city or head home.

"Hey Eddie," a new voice called. This time, Eddie didn't smile. He'd just passed a building and the voice called him just as he cleared the corner. The speaker had been waiting for him. The suddenness of this approach, and Eddie's recognition of the speaker raised his suspicions, causing his magical reflexes to kick in. The air around Eddie crackled slightly as a protective shield formed around him.

"Hey, now, old friend. No need for the show of power here."

"I'm not your friend, Bruno." Eddie calmed slightly, realizing that if this had been an ambush, it would have happened already.

Bruno was another magician, but not a mage like Eddie. He took a more brute approach to his connection with the spirit world. Where Angel had learned about the spirit world and maintained friendly relationships with the spirits themselves, Bruno took up the unsavory practice of binding spirits and forcing them to do his will. It was a quicker way to achieving the kind of memory reincarnation the mages lived. A mage typically spends his first lifetime of study learning how to communicate with the spirit world, how to travel there, but most importantly, he learns the culture of the spirit world, and spends his time there cultivating trust with the spirits, those of the 4 elements and the ether. Some rather powerful spirits could be called gods. This leaves little time the first time around, for learning the kind of spells wizards of old are known for, like flying, turning invisible, and throwing fire and lightning. But because of their good relations in the spirit world, when a mage dies, the spirits in the afterlife (or more correctly, the between-life) assist him in bringing his knowledge with him into the next life.

Bruno, and those like him, would not have become mages because they were not willing to put off gaining power for another lifetime. When they begin to learn power, they spend their time learning how to manipulate and force spirits to do their will, a shortcut that allows them to go right to learning the flashy spells. These magicians disregarded the agreements with spirits. They were oath breakers, or, as mages called them, 'warlocks.'

While the warlock was not as advanced in magic as Eddie, he was more than dangerous enough if he chose to be. If he'd wanted to harm Eddie, he would have taken advantage of surprising him coming around the corner. Now that he was aware of Bruno's presence, Eddie was skilled enough to avoid any spell.

"Come now, Eddie," Bruno affected a patronizing tone. "When will you see that we have this power for a reason'?"

"Of course we do. But that reason is not to dominate. It is to preserve a balance in the natural order." Eddie answered.

"I couldn't agree more. Some have power, some don't. Isn't that balance enough? You speak of the natural order. It is in Nature for the strong to dominate the weak. It has always been so."

"And yet you take orders from criminals." Eddie challenged.

"Power takes many forms. The organization is powerful because of the many who follow strong leadership. But that devotion is delicate. If I took the position by force, it would drive many away, and fracture what makes the organization strong." Bruno's demeanor now took on a salesman approach. "But something is about to change. I've foreseen a vacuum in the power structure. A position at the top is soon to be... vacated. The men will welcome a strong leader to fill it."

"And you intend to be that leader? Ascend the ranks and be in control? That's not what we are here to do."

"Think of it, though, Eddie. These men take what they want because they are strong enough to do it. They use force against those who try to stop them, the ones who protect what 'belongs' to the rich, enforcing man's laws, not nature's, and it comes down to a shootout. What if they could simply make the enforcers look the other way, or pass through unseen? There would be no need for killing. It would put an end to violence."

"It would still be an abuse of power. Just because you might end killing doesn't justify such abuse." Eddie realized something in what Bruno had said. "'If *they* could?' You don't intend to teach magic to mobsters, do you?"

"Actually, I was thinking you would be my captain and handle the instruction."

"Not a chance! Even if I only taught harmless spells, what's to stop them from making a copper look the other way so they can shoot him in the back? I'll never do it." Eddie's voice rose with conviction.

"A pity. From what I hear, you're a good teacher." Bruno gave a brief shrug and then... disappeared.

Eddie stood for a moment, trying to get over the nagging feeling that overtook him. "What is that guy up to?" he thought to himself. Organized crime was pretty firmly entrenched. Eddie himself had intervened quietly in a few cases to try to help the law stop certain mob activities. But he didn't dare try to take them on directly. Such action would create a great conflict and too many people would be caught up in the middle. Bruno wasn't considering the possible consequences of his actions. Eddie would never give anyone access to magical knowledge without first assessing the student's sense of responsibility. That's why he rarely even took students. That's what was nagging him. Bruno's last comment, "From what I hear, you're a good teacher." The only person who had even approached Eddie about learning magic was... "Alex!" Eddie shouted out loud, and turned back the way he came. He'd been walking a bit before encountering Bruno. It looked like Bruno had used a teleportation spell. Eddie didn't want to be quite so flashy in public. He ran into a nearby office building. Finding an office door that wasn't locked, he paused and focused his magic. He opened the door and stepped through it and emerged back in the file room at the Tribune. No one was there.

One of the file drawers was still partly open. Alex had been here to retrieve the pictures he'd been looking for. He wouldn't have left it open like that. He had left in a hurry.

Eddie closed the drawer to avoid drawing attention to the otherwise obscure and uninteresting files, and ran out into the Chicago streets. He tried getting a sense of where Alex had gone. He tried thinking of places where Bruno might take him. Eddie spent the majority of the night searching, including venturing into some of the gangster dens he'd looked into previously. There was no sign of either Bruno or Alex. When he returned to his apartment, there was an envelope under his door. Inside, was a single tarot card. Eddie looked it over, the card was "The Moon." He also recognized the artwork, it was from a deck that he had given Alex. The two had often used the cards, or references to them to send messages to each other. It helped them develop an intuitive sense of how the other interpreted the cards in certain circumstances. The "Moon" was a card of mystery and concealment. Yes the moon gave off light, but it was a reflection of sunlight, and not the same thing. "Like a negative," Eddie thought. Although he really wanted to go to sleep, he returned to Tribune Tower, let himself in and headed to the photography darkroom.

Alex was dozing in a chair, but woke when Eddie entered. He had a red work light on, and looked over at clock.

"Took you long enough," he said.

"I was looking all over the better part of Chicago, and some of the worse parts, too," Eddie answered.

"For me? Why?" Alex asked.

"Because I was worried that Bruno had taken you."

"Bruno, right. The other mage. He just wanted to talk."

"He is not a mage, Alex!" Eddie exclaimed. "He doesn't care about life, or freedom, or anything good. He's only interested in power for his own sake. He's one of the bad guys."

"Really? He didn't seem that bad. I think he wants to help me with my ideas about photography and proving that ghosts exist." Alex sounded hopeful.

"Alex, I told you, there's a reason that spirits can't be seen by everyone; mainly, because they don't want to be." Eddie tried to stay patient, but he'd been up on a desperate, and apparently unnecessary search for hours.

"So this Bruno is a villain because he agrees with me, is that it?"

"No, Alex. He wants to use you, so he's telling you what you want to hear. Did he tell you that he's working with the mob?"

"So have you," Alex countered.

"I was trying to uncover information to stop them from hurting people. That's different."

"He wants to stop them from hurting people, too. I mean, if there's no way to actually stop the wars, why not help them become nonlethal?"

"By teaching magic to thugs? Don't be a fool, Alex!" Eddie was clearly not winning the battle to keep his patience but he was determined to win this argument. "They won't stop with harmless parlor tricks, or sleep spells or illusions. They will use magic to kill and control people. Power is all they care about, and they don't care who gets hurt in the process."

"I wish you could understand. Just because someone doesn't do things your way, it doesn't make them evil."

"No, of course it doesn't. But his way of doing things does make him evil. Please, Alex. Just stay away from him." Eddie stifled a yawn. "Alex, I'm exhausted. Can we talk about this tomorrow?"

Alex looked at him. "Yeah, I suppose. You go on home. I won't be able to get back to sleep anytime soon, so I'm going to do some work here. Good night."

Eddie walked out of the room, pushing the door closed so that Alex could work. Alex thought about Eddie spending hours looking for him. He appreciated the concern, and thought he should at least have said 'thank you.' But he was confused and angry at this point. He also knew he wasn't going to get any work done. He just sat and stared at the wall.

Eddie reached the front door and stepped back out to the street. He started walking home, his thoughts replaying the discussions with Bruno and with Alex. He needed to sleep so he could think clearly in the morning. He had to convince Alex to be patient and do things right.

"Damn!" he thought to himself. "If only I'd been more careful." He wasn't sure how Bruno found out about Alex, but he did know that he now had his work cut out for him.

Eddie's thoughts filled his mind, and he kept rehearsing arguments in his head. He was so occupied that he didn't notice the car pulling up next to him until the Tommy gun extended out the window and fired.

***

Shaking off the effects of remembering, Angel looked back to the note where he'd written down the message. A series of numbers. These would refer to specific Tarot cards. Although he knew them well enough, Angel retrieved his cards from a desk drawer and laid out the ones referred to in Alex's message.

2. The High Priestess. 7. The Chariot. 13. Death. 3. The Empress. 11. Strength. 8. Justice 6. The Lovers. 9. The Hermit. 10. The Wheel of Fortune. 1. The Magician. 0. The Fool. These all referred to major arcana cards. The final two digits, a number preceding another, was their reference to the suit cards. A single 0 being Staves. 01 was the Ace of Staves, then.

"What are you trying to tell me, Alex?" Angel laid the cards in a line. Unlike a reading spread, he figured Alex was trying to tell him something narratively. Except for the last card, he used all Major Arcana. It was archetypal, but somehow, Angel knew it was very personal. Whatever was happening, it involved both him and Alex directly. The High Priestess and Empress caught his attention. They represented spirituality and authority, respectively. Why them and not the Heirophant or Emperor? The female characters were symbolically associated with the more communicative approach that Eddie had espoused, over the 'masculine' and forceful aspects. The Chariot and Death were in between them.

Angel reflected on the meaning of this set. Alex was dead. The Death card simply felt literal in this case. The Chariot seemed to imply Alex as driver, directing his own path. Somehow, he'd managed to enter into the afterlife in the manner of the mages. But Eddie had been killed before teaching Alex very much. And if he'd been doing things Bruno's way, he'd have a hard time in the Spirit world. But the Chariot leading to Death implied that Alex was somewhat successful in having some control over his crossing, and being in the Spirit world.

These were followed by Strength and Justice. Angel's intuition told him this was about Alex's accounting for himself with the powers of the spirit world. He had a psychic gift, and assuming he'd continued to study, he'd have a strong presence. He probably had been influenced by Bruno, and the Justice would be the powers of Spirit holding him accountable. Would that prevent him from being able to recall knowledge in his next life? Eddie had seen Alex to be a good person. He didn't know how things turned out with Bruno. He'd done some research of records, and found no mention of anyone like either Bruno or Alex being involved in Chicago's criminal underworld. Either something happened to prevent Bruno's ascent, or he'd been successful and also avoided discovery. Maybe Alex managed to prevent it.

Of course! The next two cards. The Lovers first, then the Hermit. Alex probably did team up with Bruno for a time, and then... what? Probably Bruno turned on Alex, used him and abandoned him. It would be in his style. He would have helped Alex get enough knowledge to be useful, but not enough to challenge him. That would have left Alex to learn on his own, a Hermit. But he would have been good at that, and the Hermit has the benefit of solitude to reflect.

The Wheel of Fortune card represented the cycles in life. Times of misfortune are followed by times of prosperity. Along with the Wheel was the Magician followed by the Fool. Angel was instantly reminded of Eddies last argument with Alex. "Don't be a fool!" he'd said. So it seemed that Alex had to go through some ups and downs, and realized that Eddie had been right, and he'd been a fool for following Bruno. But his read on the Justice card was that Alex might somehow be prevented from reincarnating... unless he got some form of assistance from the physical side. The wheel wasn't turning. "You know what to do", the message had said. And there it was, the final card. The Ace of Staves showed a hand holding out a single wooden staff. That was it! Alex needed someone to hold out a branch for him. He needed a link between Spirit and Material realms. Angel had seen the message while scrying out over Lake Michigan, and the disturbance that Daniel had noticed was out there too. Water was a strong conduit to the Spirit World, and if Alex needed help crossing, he'd be using just that conduit.

"You need me to create a link to you, so you can reincarnate." Angel spoke to the cards laid before him. "Sure, Alex. I know what to do. Can you give me any clue about how I'm going to do it?" After scanning the cards a few moments, it was clear that Alex's cryptic message would not give him that much. "Right. Well, if it were easy, everyone would be a mage."

Alex could have told him how, but Angel still would have had to figure most out on his own anyway. Magic was very personal, and Angel was in a different life already. Besides, Angel had been Alex's teacher, it was up to him. It was rare for him to even teach someone about reincarnation to begin with, and even then, he'd only prepared students ahead of time so that they could make the journey. He'd never attempted to help anyone through the process from the destination side before. This would be tricky and he needed to come up with something that Alex would recognize. He also needed to clear his head and decided to sleep on it. It was still a little early, so he made one more quick call to check on Daniel, who was apparently doing well, but was told to rest, since no one really knew what had happened to him. Angel suspected that Alex's attempt to reach Angel through Daniel included an attempt to communicate telepathically to Daniel, but ended up causing distress instead. He'd have to check on that too, as well as getting Daniel the samples back. There was still work to do there. None of it was going to get done if Angel exhausted himself. He had a lot of information to process, and he often could think better if he slept on it. He lit some incense, did a brief meditation, and went to bed.

Waves carried Angel aimlessly. Dark skies rumbled overhead. It was somewhat like the experience of the spirit world between lives. Yet he was still part of the real world. He knew he wasn't dead. Something about the waves sounded familiar. He'd been here recently. It was Lake Michigan. He was aware of the shore, and the familiar Chicago skyline. He realized that he also wasn't drifting aimlessly, but rather specifically floating to the North. The waves started to pick up, and flashes began to streak across the sky. Angel felt himself tossed about on the waves, and yet he still moved constantly northward. The winds grew in speed and whipped in every direction. The water became choppy and rough. Lightening interrupted the ever darkening sky and finally a downpour began to fall. Angel was no longer being moved, but felt compelled to keep going north, and so he swam. He pushed and struggled, somehow managing not to drown. When he finally felt like the storm was going to win and pull him under, he remembered being a mage, and reached out with his magic. He'd still been aware of the northward direction he was being drawn to, so he stretched his senses to where the shore would be. He sensed a beacon. Of course, there would be a lighthouse. At this thought, he could sense one, and drew himself toward it. Indeed there was one, but this wasn't the source of the beacon he'd sensed. This wasn't a standard light, it was a magical, spiritual signal coming from even more inland.

Then he saw it. It was like a branch reaching out over the water, carried on the back of a great, cloaked bird of some sort. A branch, like a staff... the ace of staves. The beacon light shining from it was more than just a locator. It was a beam of magical energy that he could grab onto. Of course! That's what Alex needed. He needed a line thrown to him, something he could use to pull himself across from the tempest, a chaotic realm between the spirit and physical realities. Angel stretched his arms into the beam of light and grabbed onto it as if it were a solid thing. As he tightened his grip, he felt the beam go taut in response, pulling him suddenly out of the water and directly toward land in a collision course with the great bird.

Angel woke up but didn't open his eyes. Instead, he sat up, took a few deep breaths, and focused on recalling details from the dream. It was one of the skills he'd developed long ago, directly related to how he could recall knowledge from past lives. He recalled the waves, the storm and the lighthouse. Then he focused on the beacon that had drawn him in. It had seemed like a staff carried on the back of a great bird, but it wasn't that. It was something permanent, something anchored. A structure. Before opening his eyes, he recalled one last detail, something he'd been aware of when the dream had him drifting – north.

When Angel did open his eyes, he realized it was still night-time.

He grabbed a notepad and pen he kept next to his bed and wrote down the dream in detail so he wouldn't have to remember later. He was never sure what tiny detail he might need later, but he was pretty sure he understood this one pretty much. His subconscious had continued to work on the problem of helping Alex, and drew a solution from bits of memory. To confirm what he thought, Angel booted up his computer. Magic and intuition could do many things, but Angel knew enough to take advantage modern resources as well. He just preferred keeping the two separate.

The bird like structure reminded him of a landmark he'd seen on a recent trip he'd taken with a friend to Wisconsin. The Milwaukee Art Museum building was designed to resemble a sailing ship, with spires that opened and closed like a sail, but they also resembled wings. A central angled mast or spar reached up, festooned with cables attached to the building itself on one side, and supporting the pedestrian bridge on the other. A great staff carried on the back of giant bird.

Looking at the structure, Angel was amazed by how magical it seemed, literally. It was more than just an emotional response to the elegance of it. The sails of the building faced the Great Lake, but instead of collecting wind to propel a boat, Angel could picture them gathering natural energies to be used for magical workings. He wondered if the architect, Santiago Calatrava according to the website, had consciously built a magical focus. It was more likely that he had been a mage in previous lifetimes, but at some point decided to forget the knowledge and reincarnate in a more normal existence. Mages sometimes did this to preserve a balance, or simply as a form of retirement after lifetimes of arcane practice. It was still possible for some aspects of the magical lives to linger. If this were the case with Calatrava, he could easily have been inspired by an artifact he'd known in a past life, and re-created it as a building.

Angel started having doubts, though. If the building did collect energy, it would have been a huge center of magical disturbances. With the weather off of Lake Michigan, there would be enough natural energy to at least make the building a beacon for mages throughout the Midwest. Again, the website addressed his concerns. The building had sensors on it that signaled the wings to close anytime the wind exceeded 23 miles per hour.

While this information allayed his doubts about the building, it presented him with a new challenge. He needed the wings open to harness the energy of a storm, but as soon as one started, the structure would close down. Angel checked for more details on the structure. The wings were raised by hydraulics, so he could manipulate the fluids and force the arms to extend despite the controls, but that would take a lot of concentration at a time when he needed to focus on helping Alex. Not to mention, forcing the mechanical parts would put strain on the structure, and Angel didn't like using force to begin with. Angel thought about his options. If he could prevent the sensors from closing the wings, at least for a while, he'd have time to tap into the energy gathered from the storm and hold the wings in place more firmly. He also considered that there would be a manual control, but he was already forming a plan for that probability. He browsed for more information on the museum and the surrounding area, printed a few pages of information he'd want to review, and then with a few more clicks, he purchased a ticket for a morning train to Milwaukee.

"If Merlin had had a computer," he mused to himself, "Camelot might still stand today."

The train ride gave Angel time to prepare. Around Chicago, he always took his bike. It didn't pollute, could get anywhere, and was surprisingly fast, especially when he used magic. But he felt he needed the time to focus and work on a few things he'd need. He was beginning to understand the urgency of Alex's message. There were no storms in the forecast, but one was on its way. He could feel it. That meant that it was probably supernatural in origin. If Alex knew about it too, that's when he'd be counting on Angel to be there for him. Being on the train let Angel do some additional work while still getting him there quickly. For the first time since receiving the message, Angel felt he understood what to do and how to do it. It was time to prepare a message of his own.

He pulled out a notebook, piece of parchment, a quill and a small jar of ink. The ride was smooth enough to allow for writing, but he also used a simple spell to keep everything steady. In swift, but deliberate strokes, he spelled out a message in an archaic alphabet and language. For a moment, he wondered how long it would take him to have the old language converted to a digital font, and whether the intended recipients would respond to a text message. Then again, recalling Eddie's conversation with Alex about shortcuts, he decided to let that idea rest. After completing his message, he drew his personal sigil, sending a trickle of his personal energy through the quill to seal it. He let the ink dry, rolled the parchment into a scroll, then tied it with a ribbon from his pack, and put everything back in. Then he sat back, mentally rehearsing everything he needed to do later.

The train arrived in Milwaukee shortly before noon, and Angel set out immediately for the art museum. He needed to start the first part of his plan soon. It was a short enough walk and, as Angel approached the building, his senses began to confirm what he'd suspected from the images. Even in calm weather, he could feel a certain radiance from the structure. A small crowd had already gathered in the courtyard and around the fountains, waiting for noon, when the daily display of the closing and opening would take place. People took pictures, some had video cameras, and children either played in the fountain or stood staring with everyone else. Occasionally, Angel heard someone say "Is that it? Is it moving?"

Angel stared too, and he could sense the change almost before he visually saw the movement. Still, he was more aware of subtle changes than most people. Working with entities that are barely perceptible tended to develop keen senses, so it was easy enough for him to see when the mechanism started lowering the wings of the structure. Angel raised his arms out to his sides and over his head, matching the angle of the top pair of struts on the museum. Slowly, yet faster than the wings on the building, he lowered his arms in a graceful arc, then slightly faster, he raised them again.

Angel began to dance, mimicking the motion of the building, and adding his whole body. The dance was an improvised interpretation of the Art Museum as a living thing. At first no one seemed to take notice of him. By the time the struts on the building reached a fully closed position, he'd begun to attract a little attention. There were some murmurs through the gathered crowd, and even a few insults thrown his way. It didn't bother him, he'd been called names most of his life, and his focus right now was on the flow of magical energy and how it was affected by the closing of the structure. There had definitely been a focusing of energy in the wings of the building, and he could feel it slipping through as the struts lowered. It began to gather again as the mechanism activated again, this time raising the struts back into place.

Others started to take notice of him as well. A few children, for whom the slow motion display of the building was not interesting enough, began to follow Angel's movements. A few grownups turned their attention to him as well, probably thinking he was an art student or street performer. A dark haired woman who had been photographing the museum, the fountains, and the children in the park had taken a snapshot of him when he started dancing, and as his pace quickened, so did the clicking of her camera.

Angel had accepted the fact that his 'performance' would attract an audience, and was prepared to simply focus the best he could, not letting the attention distract him. When the children started joining in, however, he realized that the attention could actually help him. Keeping a small portion of his attention on the magical calling he'd been sending out, he turned and smiled to the children, and then started to exaggerate his movements, demonstrating the dance he was doing, and then performing it again. The children took the cue, and by the time the arms of the museum started back up, they were performing Angel's dance in time with him. Then, Angel sent out a psychic suggestion, nothing that would force anyone to act against their will, but a strong enough inspiration that aided people past their inhibitions. Gradually, more and more people joined Angel in his dance. The clicking sound stopped as the photographer let her camera hang from its strap while she joined in the dance. Her first time through, she followed a moment behind, and by her second time through, was perfectly synchronized.

More than a dozen people joined in the peculiar wing-dance that

Angel was leading. It was like something that would show up on the internet, if anyone had still been taking pictures. As the mechanical arms continued rising, Angel brought his full attention back to the calling he had started. He knew that it was being heard, and that the crowd was also drawing the attention of the spirits he was reaching out to.

The wings of the architectural marvel returned to their full extension, and Angel could feel the focusing effect return. He had been right about the structure, and he was sure it was strong enough for what he needed later. At that moment, it also served as an aid for calling the air spirits he wanted to reach. Gathering up the energetic vibration from the participating crowd, Angel channeled his will into one final call for the air spirits to manifest, and sent it through the "staff" that stretched out over the art museum. This final act ended with Angel standing tall, arms stretched out overhead, and all of his backup dancers doing the same in a 'great finale' pose.

Scattered applause could be heard from the rest of the crowd who had been watching, briefly reminding Angel that he and his spontaneous volunteers had just finished what appeared to be a public recital. Turning, he saw the glowing expressions, mostly of joy and surprise, of the people who had joined in his dance. Smiling broadly, he bowed his head quickly, then grandly gestured to the rest of the dancers, as a conductor would acknowledge his orchestra. His impromptu curtain call was cut short, as he heard waves crashing on the shore around the other side of the building, and crisp breeze whipped past him.

"Thank you everyone," he called out. "Thank you," he repeated nodding to the other dancers. "You have no idea what this means. I, uh, really need to be going now." With one last bow, he jogged away, headed around the building.

"Oh damn!" said the voice of the woman with the camera. "Wait! Don't… oh, hold on!" Angel didn't stop, but he could hear her still addressing the crowd. "OK, everyone do this one again, on 'three'. One… two…"

Angel continued around the corner. As he rounded to the side facing the lake, he felt the breeze grow into a strong wind. He slowed to a steady walk, and steered himself into the wind. The wind stung his eyes, but he fought to keep them open, knowing that he'd need to notice the slightest detail to catch sight of the Sylphs.

When he saw the first sylph, he thought he had made a mistake in his conjuring. What materialized in front of him was the face of an old man. Sylphs were ageless, immaterial beings, and their appearance was determined by their own perceptions. When Angel saw the others, he understood. They had all gathered behind this one "elder." This was a spirit that even among other ancient beings was respected as one of the very wise. The lines and wrinkles that among humans are considered a sign of frailty, were in this case, a reflection of the reverence offered to this being by the others.

"Your dance was a very pleasant offering, Mage," the sylph said with a voice the sound of the wind itself. "It has been some time since we have seen a congregation of any size participate in such a calling."

"Thank you, wise one," Angel replied. "Though I must admit, the others joining in were not part of my original plan. That rather happened on its own."

"And yet, inspiring such spontaneity is a sign of the quality of your act. We are honored that you called to us in such a way."

Angel bowed slightly. "It was natural for me," he answered, "and it seemed appropriate." He had always had a stronger connection with the spirits of air than he had with Undines of water. The sylphs manifested the essence of the element of air, and wind. They were attracted to and appreciated movement, grace and flight. Dance was a perfect offering to these spirits, and Angel had always loved to dance.

"As you can see," the elder sylph continued, "we have heard and answered your call. What is it that you would ask of us?"

"A storm is coming. I'm sure you are aware of it." Angel began. The sylph nodded, both confirming that the storm was known to them, and indicating that Angel should go on. "I'm trying to aid a friend. He's another mage, but not as experienced. He's in the spirit realm and I need to create a crossing for him to transincarnate. I can use this structure as a focus for this working, but I need it to stay open during the storm, and its mechanism will automatically close it when it detects the wind."

The assembled sylphs looked around, some examining the art museum, some looking out over the waves of Lake Michigan, and a few, including their leader, regarding Angel. The wind increased and swirled around the assembly as the air spirits conversed. Angel did not interrupt. He knew what he wanted to ask of them, but they already seemed willing to help, and they might even come up with a better idea than his.

"We can, of course, prevent the winds from reaching the building," this time, the mage heard additional voices in the wind. They were speaking as a group. "But would it not be easier to disable the devices that detect the wind, or that mechanism that moves the arms?"

"Easier, yes," Angel replied. "But it would also disrupt the operation of this building, at least for the near future. It is quite important to this community, and I'd prefer not to do it injury."

"You are wise to consider the consequences of your actions," the sylphs spoke jointly. Then the elder sylph stepped forward.

"Have you considered the entire course of helping your friend? If he is inexperienced, will he be as conscientious about his mark on this world as you?"

"He has made mistakes," Angel admitted. "But I trust that he has learned from them, and will continue to do so. His promise to serve the greater good will be his end of the bargain."

"And you ask nothing else of him? Nothing for yourself?"

"I don't need rewards, but I need allies in my line of work. The terms of his return will give him opportunities to choose his path. If his choices are wrong, the spirit world will alert me, and I'll handle him myself."

"You would eliminate him if he proves a threat?"

"I'd prefer to just render his magic useless, but yes. If it comes that, I will."

The elder sylph paused to consider Angel's offer, and the wind whistled around him as the others shared their thoughts. Finally, the sylph said, "We will aid you. When the storm comes, we shall form a barrier around this building. The power generated by the storm will reach its sails, but the wind will not. In return, we require your promise that you will not allow him to become a warlock. Do we have a deal."

"Yes," Angel answered, bowing. Before he could find an appropriate expression of gratitude, there was a whirl of air, and the spirits were gone. "Now I know where the term 'flighty' comes from," he thought. But this still seemed unusual to him. Sylphs were the most communicative of the elemental spirits he'd worked with, downright chatty at times. He supposed that it wasn't really that unusual for them to simply whisk away since they would be back as soon as the storm began, a mere few hours away now. To them, a few hours would be like stepping away to powder their noses. Angel smiled briefly at the image of wind spirits trying to apply powder.

The next few hours didn't go by as quickly for Angel as they probably would for the sylphs. He kept replaying the events over in his mind, from Alex's first attempt to contact Angel through Daniel, to the cryptic message spelled out in the scrying water.

Thunder rumbled. Angel watched as the scattered clouds in the evening sky thickened before his eyes. The sky flashed and the waves grew higher as a gust of wind swept in over Lake Michigan toward the rocks where he stood. The gust washed over him, nearly taking his breath away. He turned, which put the wind to his back, but now he needed to face the building. The wind rushed past him, shaking leaves on the trees and hissing over the rocks. As it reached the spines of the art museum, he very faintly saw the outlines of thin, strong forms floating in the air. The sylphs had gathered in a sphere shape around the building. They appeared to be wearing long cloaks, although as spirits, their garments were actually extensions of their own essence. The beings reached out toward each other, their cloaks linking as if sewn together to form a huge sail.

Then the full force of the wind reached them, and they inhaled as one. Unlike Angel who struggled to breathe when he faced the wind, the sylphs seemed able to inhale endlessly. They were the very essence of wind, and they absorbed all of it. The sylphs were stopping the physical manifestation of the gust, but the energy of it passed through them into the spread wings of the structure behind them.

Angel felt the energy resonate through the spines, and he focused his concentration on that gathering energy. He suddenly felt as though he were experiencing the same kind of empowerment that the sylphs were absorbing from the wind. As he watched, he noticed something happening through the windows of the building. One of the museum workers was looking out at the weather conditions, then up at the unmoving beams spread out over the building. The employee reached for a two-way radio and spoke into it.

"Damn," Angel thought. The employee was obviously calling someone on the crew to report the weather conditions and the fact that the wings weren't closing. There was sure to be a manual control and the wings would close. He didn't need much time, but probably more than it would take for someone to pull a switch. Desperately, he drew in the power that was gathering around him, and stretched his arms out toward the structure. Concentrating on the wings remaining open, he created invisible brackets of pure magical force to hold the struts in place. Angel hoped that any control operator would notice the arms not folding in and stop trying to close the structure. But just in case, he decided it was time to hurry.

Angel concentrated for a moment longer on the spell holding the wings in place, making sure the spell would remain in place for the time he needed. Then he turned his attention to the large mast that rose up from the opposite end of the building, the one he'd designated as the "staff." Sending his thoughts out, he directed the energy gathering in the wings to move up to the staff. Wisps of pure magical energy flowed up from the spines to the larger mast, like lightening in slow motion. To Angel's perception, the image reminded him of cotton candy being spun onto a paper roll, except that instead of bunching up, the layers overlapping and increasing the brightness, although to everyone except Angel and the Sylphs, there was no visible change.

Next, Angel turned to face the roiling waters of Lake Michigan. Drops of rain were just beginning to fall, and with the wind, they struck Angel with a determined force. Angel found the sensation oddly exhilarating. The mage called to mind the images of the spirit world he had visited between many lifetimes. He recalled the Names of spirits he had spoken to. In his mind's eye, he drew the ancient sigils into the air in front of him, forging a connection between worlds. When he felt everything in its proper place, he clapped his hands once over his head, and with his palms remaining together overhead he drew the essence of magic from the tip of the staff to his hands. The power surged as a beam of light into his hands. Angel remained facing the lake, but knew that the single beam had gone dark after sending the energy to him. However, like a siphon, when the energy left the staff, a natural flow of energy gathering back in the wings of the building began to replenish it.

Angel brought his arms forward, took a deep breath in and blew sharply against the wind. His breath lanced forward, ignoring the laws of physics, and along with it, the power gathered in his hands extended in a beam to the space where the spirit sigils hung in the air. Angel drew the beam downward, stretching the beam into a vertical line. Then he aimed his hands back toward the middle of the line and drew them apart. The line began to stretch open and a new scene formed in the space he was drawing, as if he were peeling back a fabric. The new space was dark, with swirls of color and flashes of light. Angel realized that there was a parallel storm happening in the spirit world.

"So that's how the unexplained storm hit here," Angel thought. This must have been Alex's doing. He had created a disturbance that got Daniel's attention. He must have been able to affect environments across the barrier between the two realms. If one of his abilities included weather magic, then Bruno had indeed taught the young man some dangerous things.

The beam of light from his hands faded out as he used up the energy he'd drawn on, and he lowered his arms. The portal remained open. Angel paused and watched it intently, concentrating on the edges and making sure the magical creation was stable. When he was satisfied, he allowed himself to look away so that he could un-sling his pack and retrieve the scroll he'd prepared on the train ride over. Without opening the scroll, he mentally reviewed its contents. Satisfied that he had prepared all that he could, he drew his arm back and threw the scroll into the open portal. Seeing the scroll fly against the wind reassured Angel. When the parchment reached the portal, it stopped and hung in empty space for a moment. Then, a glowing bubble of energy formed around the scroll, and the whole thing suddenly launched deeper into the swirling realm, out of Angel's sight. It reminded him of the pneumatic tubes used in bank drive-through lanes.

"Okay, so maybe the spirits don't mind technological advances so much after all," he thought.

Right now, though, there was a life in the balance, and Angel focused his awareness behind him again. This time, instead of drawing energy to himself, he stretched his right arm forward, gesturing as though he were holding an actual staff, and mimicking the angle of the mast from the museum. Energy shot from the tip again, going directly into the portal. Angel envisioned it as a beam from a lighthouse, except that it remained pointing in one direction rather than pivoting. It didn't need to. The beacon was more than a light, it sent ripples throughout the surrounding portions of the spirit world. For Alex to have sent the message, he would certainly be within the range of this sending. Angel waited. The sylphs remained in their positions, even though Angel's spell was now holding the wings in place. They had made a commitment to help him, and would not leave. Angel hadn't noticed the attempt to manually lower the arms, but he was sure it had happened. If repeated attempts had been made, he was sure it would have made considerable noise. The fact that he didn't hear such noise reassured him that after the wings didn't fold the first time, the crew in the museum must have decided to take a chance on the building weathering the storm, rather than risk damage by forcing the arms down.

"Eddie!" a voice called out. Angel squinted into the swirling beyond the portal, and saw a figure approaching.

"I'm here, Alex," he called back. The figure was a hazy silhouette, walking toward him underneath the beam of the beacon, as if following a line painted on the ceiling. "It worked," Angel said, smiling. Alex smiled back, and Angel found himself remembering every time Eddie had seen that smile. It had always filled him with hope for the young man. Even on that last day...the day of the shooting. Perhaps it was the memory of the shooting, but Angel was suddenly aware of a change happening on the other side of the portal. Something was wrong.

Without warning, dark, whiplike strands struck Alex from somewhere below, entangling his legs. Alex reacted quickly enough to grab the beacon light, and he was able to hold onto it as though it were solid. But Angel could see that he was struggling against the pull of the strange tentacles. The portal was wide, but he still could not see where the strands were coming from. He needed to be up higher. His thoughts started to race, and he almost lost his concentration. The beacon flickered ominously, and Angel forced himself to stay focused.

"We are here to aid you, Mage. What can we do?" asked the voice of the elder sylph, which had swiftly flown from the others to Angel's side. Very few summoned spirits would change their actions once an arrangement was in place, but here was a sylph offering to change the plan. He had agreed to aid Angel, and although keeping the wind from reaching the sensors was the specific action, the spirit seemed willing to give further aid.

"I need to see what's below Alex. I was going to levitate, but then realized that the people in the museum would see me. I can't risk that."

"And doing that in addition to your existing spells will leave you little focus to act on what you find," the spirit added. There was a reason mages consulted spirits. Often, they had knowledge long forgotten, but they were also much better at thinking things through. After a brief moment, the spirit continued. "The windows have been fogged over. No one will see you. Allow us…"

Angel felt a pressure from below his arms, and wind whipped around him. The sylph was controlling the winds and directing them in precisely focused points. Angel steadied himself in preparation, and allowed the winds to lift him into the air.

As he rose, he was able to see the area below Alex. Following the tentacles to their source, he saw another silhouette. This one was hardly recognizable as a human form, and unlike Alex's hazy appearance, this one was purely dark. Its arms were extended, and instead of normal hands, its fingers had elongated into the terrible strands that were trying to pull Alex down. Angel knew at once that he was seeing the spirit form of a warlock.

"Bruno," he shouted. "Let him go!" The dark figure drew slightly closer, and Bruno's features became visible.

"Eddie!" Bruno greeted, with casual familiarity. "So good to see you, old friend."

"I told you before, *warlock*," Angel shouted, emphasizing the title. "I am not your friend."

"So you keep saying, and yet here you are helping me complete my plan."

"*Your* plan?" shouted Alex, in disbelief. Angel did not react.

"Of course, silly boy," Bruno laughed. "I taught you exactly enough so that you would figure out how to call your dear mentor and get him to throw you a lifeline. I also helped with the storm. You're good with creating disturbances to get attention, but this thing needed to have some meat on it. Now that our friend here has opened the door…" Angel's eyes narrowed as Bruno continued, "I am going to be the one who goes through. But first, I'm going to steal your essence to increase my own power in the next life."

"Shut down the spell," Angel heard the elder sylph beside him. "Your friend is lost, and you must not allow the warlock to come through."

"No," said Angel in response. "Trust me, I can handle this." There was no response, and the winds holding him up started to lessen. "Please, I promise the warlock will not make it through the door. I take full responsibility." Spirits take responsibility seriously, and the sylph understood the deep meaning in Angel's statement. If he failed, and Bruno were able to return to life as a warlock, Angel would stop at nothing to oppose him.

"Your way, then," said the sylph. "Be sure you succeed." As the winds strengthened around him, he turned back to Bruno.

"This is your last chance, *oath breaker*," again, he put emphasis on the words used describe his enemy. "Let...him...go."

"Oh, Eddie," Bruno taunted. "How could I break an oath when I wasn't the one who made it." There was a change in the swirling mists behind Alex and Bruno. Angel made a note of several shapes taking form, but did not turn away from Bruno who continued talking. "It was your friend here who came to you for help. I just used him to get you to do what I needed. You mages have always been too trusting."

"And you warlocks have always been predictable." Angel answered. Before anyone -except possibly the sylphs- realized what he was doing, Angel reached his hand up into the beam of light, cutting it off. Alex began to drift, with Bruno's dark tentacles still tangled around him. Angel pointed at Bruno, and the beam lanced in that direction. It struck Bruno in the chest, and the dark figure sprawled backward a short distance. The impact caused Bruno to lose his grip on Alex. The hazy outline started drifting farther, but Angel kept his full attention on Bruno.

"If you had taken the time to learn your magic the proper way, you would know that words have power, especially in the spirit realm, *warlock*!" This time, there was a pulse in the beam when Angel spoke the last word.

"Aaagh!" Bruno screamed as though struck again. "Okay, you've proven your point. But what will you do now? Your friend is drifting away, and you will lose him forever."

"He will be fine," Angel said. Bruno's expression became one of confusion. "Oh, I followed your plan, 'old friend,' but not to the letter. Before lighting the beacon, I offered a contract to the powers of the spirit world."

"Still wasting time with contracts when you could simply take what you wanted," Bruno continued to taunt, despite his situation.

"It pays to have allies," Angel said. Bruno looked startled for a moment, and Angel realized that the sylph had chosen that opportunity to make himself visible to the warlock. Nice touch, Angel thought. "If I had simply pulled Alex through, I would have made him a warlock like you. Instead, I made an arrangement that will allow him to come through as a mage."

"Impossible!" Bruno screamed. "Given the chance, he'd be as bad as me."

"Then I guess he's lucky you didn't give him the chance." Angel smiled a moment before becoming serious again. "The contract allows the powers to determine a number of factors that will influence his upbringing and the formation of his personality before the recollection takes place. I think he'll have a more solid moral compass when he remembers how to do magic. If not, well then I've made a promise to make sure he does no harm."

"This is craziness. You can't always be there making sure he's a good boy. You may have stopped me here, but I can still come back, and I'll find him."

"Predictable and clichéd," Angel sighed. "I don't think you'll be coming back. You see, even with the assurance regarding Alex's future, the aid of the spirits still came at price. I offered them a favor in exchange for their help. Balance must be maintained." Angel watched the expression on Bruno's face. He could tell that the warlock was still trying to understand what was happening and find a way out of it.

"What did you offer them?"

"Spirits don't like being pushed around by magicians. They take it very personally, and they never forget. Alex was misguided, but hadn't actually gone against the ancient oaths between mages and the spirits. I guessed that they wouldn't care what happens to him as much as they would be concerned about an oath breaker coming back. In exchange for granting Alex a recollection in his next life, I offered to deliver a warlock to them for justice."

Bruno's eyes widened. "You wouldn't!" Desperation registered in his voice. "You said you sent the contract through just before lighting the beacon? How do you know they'll accept your offer?"

"Several spirits arrived while you were busy gloating. One was behind Alex and caught him before he could drift farther away. The rest have been waiting to take you away."

"No! Eddie, don't let them take me. We could be such a powerful team. Please, Eddie!"

"It's Angel, now," he said, using conviction when he said his name. "I am a mage of the Order of Mithras. I proclaim you, Bruno, a *warlock*, and I deliver you to the authorities of the spirit world." As he finished stating his intent, four spirits leapt from their positions behind Bruno and grabbed him. Bruno may have been a spirit, but he was the spirit of a mortal. That fact had placed certain limitations on the powers that ruled the spirit world, according to the ancient pacts. They could only claim him if one of his own, especially one who had kept the oaths, delivered him into their authority. Angel took no pleasure in condemning Bruno, but he felt great relief knowing that the warlock would not be getting another chance at life. Still, he turned his head as the spirits dragged Bruno, screaming, deeper into the storm. The beam of light had completely faded, but as he turned back to the portal, the hazy figure of Alex was again walking toward him. As the form neared, the features became clearer.

"Eddie?" Alex asked. "Or, I hear you're called Angel now?" He stared out at the new incarnation of his old friend, floating in the air with what appeared to be a giant pair of wings stretched out behind him. "It seems appropriate," he said.

"Alex," Angel addressed his old friend. "It is good to see you again. Understand this. When you pass through this portal, you will be born into your new life. You will grow up without remembering your past life, but when you come of age, the recollection will come to you, and you will have access to all the knowledge, ability and skill you have now. Your gift will be active again, too. I have sworn to aid you, and I will keep tabs. When you remember, you would do well to seek me, and continue learning as a mage learns. If you choose another path, I will have no choice but to oppose you."

"I understand," Alex answered. "I know it will be a while before we can talk again, so… thank you. Thank you for believing enough to come after me."

"You're welcome. Now, I need to start setting things back to normal here," Angel prompted. With Bruno being carried away, he could feel the storm dispersing. While most of the energy was required for opening the portal, he didn't want to keep it open after the storm passed. It risked too many people coming outside and seeing.

"I'm ready," said Alex. He stepped forward through the portal and his form scattered for a moment into particles like glowing dust. Then it re-formed into a floating sphere that flew past Angel, over the art museum and out into the sky somewhere over Milwaukee. The winds shifted, and Angel could feel the sylph lowering him back to the ground. Angel stretched his arms out in a wide gesture toward the portal, and then brought his palms together. The portal, in response to Angel's gesture narrowed back to a straight line, then faded, along with the sigils. He turned back, and reached his left hand out with his palm toward the building, the invisible brackets dissolved and the essence that had made them up floated back to Angel.

"Cleverly played," said the elder sylph, still standing next to him. Angel was aware that the other air spirits had dispersed from their formation and were gathered around as well. "Even for a mage, you are an extraordinary man."

"Thank you," Angel said, bowing to the spirit. He place his hand over his heart, and then extended it to the sylph. A small orb of softly glowing light rested in his palm. "My gratitude for your assistance," he said. To spirits, all spirits, emotion had a powerful essence, and Angel's offering of gratitude was no mere symbolic gesture. The elder sylph accepted the gift, smiled at Angel, and vanished.

The walk back to the train station was long and sluggish. It had only been several hours, but the act of working so much magic that afternoon was taxing. Angel got a ticket to return to Chicago. The following morning, he would get in contact with Daniel again, and get back to work preventing big companies from dumping chemicals in Lake Michigan. As he sat down, he pulled out his notebook, and jotted down the details of what had happened, making note of the date, which would be the birth date of Alex's new incarnation. Then he put the notebook back into his pack and promptly fell asleep.

Marcus Maichle has been making up stories since grade school. He currently lives in the Milwaukee area, and looks forward to being able to tell stories to his niece, Amanda.

Down by the Drool

Catalino Tolejano, II

Down by the Drool

Just over six months ago I ate someone's brain. Normally I would think that to be the peak of the story, not the beginning. If my life were a movie, I guess it would be. But in the real world, I had to go on living.

And unfortunately that has landed me here, holding onto the roof rack of a racing SUV with one hand, while strangling the driver with the other. He floors the accelerator in a mad attempt at leverage against my grip, boosting our ridiculous speed even more as we rocket down the dim city streets like the Coyote on an inevitable course of destruction. Luckily, it's after 3am and the city is asleep, granting us a partial reprieve from the swarms of traffic which would have swallowed us by now. But the red lights zip by in a kaleidoscope of blurring lights and buildings, causing my mind to wonder how long we can push our luck like this. I'm drawn from my blur of lights to the pieces of the shattered side-window, embedded in my knuckles and gouged into my forearm, where I can feel the tears in the flesh. I take a moment to enjoy the simple fact that I can feel it at all. The wonderful sensation of my pain dissipates, fleeting as it is, overcome by the sensation of my hand as it fights the tension in his throat and the frantic, clawing fingers struggling to release him from the crushing vise around his neck. Unfortunately for this thug, the last of his backstabbing crew, he won't live long enough to understand why at a muscular three-hundred-plus pounds he still can't break my grip.

For six months I've struggled against a subtle yet constant craving for human brains, partly because I've been experiencing some alarming side effects of brain consumption, but mostly because I just have this desire to frustrate myself every damn day! And Jolly here, like his former thug partners, is going to pay dearly due to all that pent-up frustration. Don't get me wrong, he more than has it coming, but every once in a while you have a very short fuse. I guess tonight was not the night to try to kill me.

147

I realize, as Jolly begins to lose consciousness, that he must have been keeping us amazingly steady on the road while struggling against my crushing grip. The red lights shift thankfully to green, but things go from bad to worse as we start to sway back and forth, the accelerator still floored. I wait, for what feels like an eternity when you're stuck on top of an out of control vehicle, just long enough to feel certain Jolly isn't faking unconsciousness. As we gracefully bounce off one of the parked cars, lining the streets like bowling bumpers from when I was a kid, I start calculating the timing and risk of how I'm going to get down and gain control of this death trap. I really do feel like the Coyote!

I steady myself, waiting for the next bounce so that I can hop down, when a sedan races up from behind us and pulls alongside. *I wonder who else is out at this time of night? I don't recognize that car.* The big sedan drifts a little left and right like it's going to ram us, but then shoots forward in front of us instead. I can't see the driver beyond an outline really through the tinted rear window, but I am fairly certain he's alone. I'm blinded by the sedan's sudden brake lights and the scream of the tires on the pavement in front of us. *Is that me screaming?*

I hear a whisper in my head and like some surreal dream I'm standing on the sidewalk. *What was I just doing? Wasn't I... well this is weird!* I'm drawn from my joy over the last sucker whose money weighs down my purse. I look down at my new treasure, but can't see my feet past my cleavage. Not because of inhuman size, but because **I have cleavage.** *W. T. F!* I lean out just a little and take another adoring look at my new Alexander McQueen red Booties, which complete tonight's party ensemble! *What kind of messed up experience is this? How in the hell? Am I dreaming - that I'm some woman wearing red 'booties' of all things? Did I die in the car crash and just miss it somehow?*

I look up, just as an SUV is barreling down the street past me with some idiot riding on top, as a black sedan slams on its brakes right in front of them. The idiot on top, I notice very clearly (*Hey that's me!*) is just staring blankly ahead as the SUV rams into the rear of the sedan, mashing the two vehicles together. *Ahhh hell!*

"I can hear you, idiot, get out of my head," screeches a sultry woman's voice, obviously not my own. I sound like a girl? I feel like a girl, but I know I'm not! *What the Hell? I must be having some sort of memory or messed up thing going on, but it feels like nothing I've ever experienced!* I bring my arm up to wipe my forehead and notice how lovely my red nails, with the little 2pt diamond bit in each, look as they sparkle in the darkness. *Did I just notice how pretty my nails are? Come on!*

I, or we, as I start to notice I'm not alone in this experience, see the sedan trunk crushed inward as the SUV grinds to its left, lifting up the rear of the sedan and smashing it into a parked car and then a concrete telephone pole base to the right side, nearly cleaving the car in two.

"I said 'get out' you stupid amateur. NOW! You're going to get us both killed!" I sound like a crazed girl now. *This is the most bizarre thing I've ever felt.*

It all only takes half a second, but it plays like slow motion as I watch the vehicles and debris getting closer. The SUV ricochets off a parked car between us, maybe ten feet from my surreal location, then tilts onto two wheels and smashes nearly square into another parked black sedan.

The black-on-black collision mashes the cars into one twisted hulk, catapulting the rooftop rider *(I can't look!)* up a good ten plus feet and forward to careen off the side of a building and into the street at the intersection. I lose track of the body between the cars and look back at the first sedan, wedged up against a sparking light-post with its door hung open with the driver dragging himself out. I hustle toward the SUV and its sole inhabitant, and stop dead. The soft breeze has brought the smell of blood wafting from the vehicle. A yearning descends across my whole body, making me close my eyes and I think and hear that same female voice, now quivering with anticipation. "I'm so hungry, my boobs ache!" *What. The. Hell. Did I just think and say?!* I open my eyes and the colors of the night suddenly jump out at me, like I'm looking through my own undead night-vision again, with everything vibrant and exciting. There's an almost palpable feeling of excitement in the air. I'm looking at the accident from the same perspective. I lick my lips, contemplating my options, then decide I should get out of here before I lose control. At least, I think I'm the one who thinks this! *But it's not really me, is it?* I cross the street quickly, heels clicking on the pavement as I scuttle rapidly, cursing my poor toes as I pass a body out in the street. Knowing it would be too much to avoid, I keep away from any blood.

A soft, more seductive female voice, strong with an inexplicable power now, and which I very creepily recognize as my own, says "Bye!" and things go dark and tasteless.

I'm lying face-down now, only half in the street actually, with my legs up on the curb like a discarded rag doll. *I'm back in my body again!* I go through a quick run-through to make sure all my limbs at least respond! Deep in my belly I feel a familiar yet more visceral need to feed. The pain, if you can call it that, is both exquisite and terrible as I reset my broken fingers and wrench my distorted limbs back into place so they will work properly. I can feel a few broken ribs and some very soft spots all over, every sensation directing me to feed in order to help my body regenerate. I hear the voice of brain addiction sing its siren's song, lovingly and just for me. *Hey, I never said I was entirely sane!*

I get up, slowly, surprised when both legs function, albeit poorly for the moment. I shuffle toward the curb and the SUV, perhaps too confident in my legs' power, as negotiating the treacherous height of the curb lands me almost on my face again. At least I fell forward. *Jolly isn't going anywhere, anyway.* As I fumble about between the cars, beneath the vehicles to my left I note that pair of red Booties disappear into a doorway down the street. *I can't believe I still A, know what those are, and B, that it wasn't some delusion. I'm done with this undead stuff.* I'll have to table that, though, as there are more pressing concerns. Like Jolly and the mystery man.

I can tell I'm healing already, as I'm more stable rising this time. I wipe some of my blood from my eyes, distraught that I'd be thoroughly caked with blood from my dying body, if, that is, my heart still beat like a normal human. But it doesn't. The blood flows maybe a little I think, but by some means I cannot divine. And 'divine' is the only word I can think of that makes any sense. With the parked cars for support and my claws dug into the cheap sheet metal to keep from slipping on my blood, I make my way up the curb and over toward Jolly and his new friend.

A blood-soaked and slightly overweight man, middle-aged and stark white in contrast to the night, is methodically, maybe even softly, pistol-whipping Jolly. Jolly is just mumbling and gurgling as far as I can tell, as he and the mysterious assailant share an intimate ear to ear conversation between pistol blows. The assailant is obviously the sedan driver who'd crashed our little party, literally. I deduce this with my exceptional powers of observation, or maybe from the blood trail which traces from the man's feet back to the open sedan door. Jolly starts to plead or maybe cry, and it seems their pleasant conversation is done. The man steps back from Jolly, slipping in his own bloody trail a little but regaining his stability. He's obviously fatigued, possibly due to blood loss from his several wounds, and strains to lift his pistol to target Jolly's head. I can see shreds of his shirt and muscle as he lifts, noting that it's amazing his arm even functions. Then, with a scream from somewhere in the back of my subconscious mind, my body surges into motion on its own, as my conscious mind catches up and realizes the deadly intent.

"Not the brain!" I'm not sure if that was internal or came out of my mouth. Right now, I'm just glad I'm not wearing red Booties.

I close distance so quickly I don't think the man notices while focused on his deed. The blood-filled eye blotting out his peripheral vision probably didn't hurt either. I slap the gun and arm upward, then pull it from the weak grasp before he can line up on Jolly. As he turns in violent reaction to me, I shove him harder than I would have liked, launching him into the side of a car caught in the tangle of vehicles. The man spits air and blood from the impact, dropping his pistol which bounces off the car and ricochets over to my feet. *Perhaps my luck is improving!*

Jolly looks at me, offering a faint smile and nod of thanks. I don't know if I'll ever forget the way his face quickly distends into terror as my world goes black.

It's hard to explain the cartoon-like, surreal shadow world my consciousness inhabits when my Berserker - that's what I call the state - takes over. I thought about calling it "Hyde" or "The Hulk" since those are relatively universally understood, but I think "Berserker" is a better term for me. Maybe someday I'll come up with a term more appropriate to a bloodthirsty fugue-ish state when I lose active control and give in to my appetite for brains. This is only the second true state I've experienced, so I'm still working on it. Shadows dance around as lights warp and twist into something like a bad claymation horror flick. A dark shadow form builds next to me, filled with holes and missing pieces, clearly twisted and evil, as its malevolence washes over me. The car becomes a pinata with pink and yellow paper sprinkled about it. Inside the hole in the pinata, I see a coconut head on a voodoo doll bobbing around inside. The shadow rips the hole open wider in the pinata and grabs the coconut head. It drools a shadowy acid as it cracks the coconut repeatedly around the interior structure of the pinata. It drools on its elongated claws then jabs them into the top and bottom parts of the coconut. With a screech of delight, it pulls the top off the coconut, allowing coconut milk to splash across the interior of the pinata. Then the evil shadow is some sort of shadowy cartoon monkey. It starts digging out the coconut meat in crazy delight, pulling out whipped cream just for the topping. *I don't actually carry whipped cream for eating brains. It's just an illusion in my mind - I think!* The shadow form's holes and missing pieces fill up, completing its shape back to whole. When the monkey finishes, it points to another coconut-headed voodoo doll on the ground behind me. When I look back, the shadowy monster has returned and slowly engulfs me with its form, straining to continue on its mission to get to the other coconut. As its eyes wash into mine a flood of memories crash into my head and I drop to the ground beneath its menacing shroud. The shadow surges forward and looms over the second voodoo doll, but the unbearable pain paralyzes my brain as names and places burn into my mind – as if such things know my mind is not their home. I stand and utter a silent but horrible scream, which shatters the shadow form.... and I'm suddenly standing in the wreckage of cars, screaming up into the night sky as I tower over the sedan driver who tried to murder my dinner.

I look down and he moves slowly, reaching into his pocket as he sits slumped against the car, coughing blood to clear his airway. Internally I hear a joyous cackling, inviting the thought of him trying to draw a weapon. *Not before I rip off his arm.*

He pulls out an envelope, instead, leaving bloody fingerprints all over it before dropping it to the ground between his knees. "Peesss. Heepp uurh..." he utters incoherently trying to recover the envelope from the pavement in front of him. It's pathetic. I don't have the patience for it, but allowing him to try may help him realize how seriously damaged his body is right now. He's strong, though, and is able to at least get his hand on the envelope.

"I don't want your money nor your bribes, asshole. Who the hell ARE you, anyway? You're not one of these cronies! And you wanted Jolly dead, so I'll give you props for that, with the enemy of my enemy is my friend thing. So keep your money." I look back to see Jolly missing the top half of his skull and all of his brain. Then memories, vivid and in disturbingly clear 3D, flash wildly through my head and I'm watching the man beneath me as he pummels me with a pistol through the shattered SUV window. The disorientation forces me to a hand and knee, allowing the man a chance to lean forward close to my ear. I can feel his cold breath and the drip of his bloodied drool on my hand.

"Please. Help her..." He manages to inch the envelope closer to my knee. He gets a pincer grip on it and clutches it to his chest, then struggles with all he's got to hand it to me. It's tragic and heartwarming, I'd guess, so I take the envelope. He collapses back against the car in satisfaction and just stares at me.

"Do the right thing. Help me. Help. Her. Find key..." He whispers the last as he closes his eyes and slumps somewhat, like he died in an old movie, ironically at the exact moment he would divine the secrets of the Universe. His chest is still moving, though, and he coughs again indicating he's not quite dead. Yet. He's definitely unconscious, though. *Just great! Luckily there isn't a lot more blood, so he's got a chance at surviving.*

"Do the right thing? You've got the wrong guy, friend." I sound sure, but a scary voice resounds in my head. *This may be your Destiny. You will be the champion and use my dark power to not only destroy your enemies, but save the girl! Turn your dark power toward Good! It is your Destiny.* I think most people would hear Yoda as this voice. These days, my conscience sounds like Darth Vader. Not sure which one scares me more. I set the envelope down on his lap.

"It's a sure way to get caught, found, or killed. All of which involve Feds and a bunch of problems. No thanks, man." My words fall on deaf ears, of course, so I dig out his ID quickly as sirens creep closer. "Marvin R Wyatt? What the hell kind of name is that? And you live on Shadow Drive? Seriously, that is too creepy. " I realize that I'm standing over a dying man, holding his ID and talking to him. "Okay, I guess maybe that isn't so creepy."

I look around, finding new lights lit in some of the surrounding windows, illuminating residents with phones at their ears. *Damn!* I head over and pick up the gun Wyatt won't be needing, then take Jolly's gun and magazines, conveniently on the seat next to him. Just to be sure, I do what we in the gamer world call 'looting the body.' Jolly's body stench is almost nauseating, but I manage to get his phone along with cash and a few other trinkets before jumping over the vehicle to make a hasty exit! Figuring the condo building in front of me will be the best route out, I start to climb the wall Spider-man style. *Well, it looks like that but I can personally attest that it is not, in fact, as easy as it looks. Still, a quick shimmy up the wall and onto the roof should get me some escape routes outta here!*

I stop about ten feet up the wall. The sirens are close now. I look back at that damned form, slumped amidst the walls of shattered sheet metal and bleeding vehicles. I jump back down. The nagging guilt or whatever would pass for a conscience compels me to go back and grab the envelope. He doesn't look like he's breathing at all. As I start to lean down, hoping to check his vitals, I hear the high-revving engine of a police cruiser accelerating from just around the corner. The lights are close enough and reflecting off the buildings as they near. *No checking now. We'll have to look him up to see if he lives.* "If you die, Wyatt, you'll never know." That's all I say to him as I shoot back across the vehicles and up the wall. At least I have something to do now! Who knows, maybe this mission of his will be some sort of Humanity Quest for me. *His mission, my Quest. Who knows, maybe I'll find some lingering Humanity through all this.*

As I look down from the roof momentarily I wonder. "Would I want Sancho Panza or Rocinante for this? Maybe I'll end up dead. Dead-er? It's like a woodchuck rhyme. How dead would an undead get if the undead were killed dead again?" *Truly I have a dizzying intellect!* I leave as the gathering of more and more lights in the street drive away the beautiful darkness.

**

[Phone intercept transcript excerpt 011408_223 pulled for BPI DIV analysis]

[Call began 1:14:08am EST 2011_06_11]

{0:01s}

<No pertinent data>

{1:29s}

[Subject:] What the hell is wrong with you? Where are you now?

[Male Caller 17:] I'm in Nome, Alaska.

[Subject:] I'm SERIOUS! You were flagged in LA a week ago and you need to get out of town. You're going to get yourself killed. Or worse, caught. I need more time in order to convince people around here that you're different. Or at least to get the opportunity to have that discourse. Until now, we've only seen Ghoul activity that's horrifyingly violent and horrific. Inhuman and irrecoverable. BUT, you've managed to remain both civil and follow a moral compass with only the occasional transgression. That needs to be explored and

studied if your kind will ever be more than demonic beasts needing to be put down at the earliest possible opportunity.

[Male Caller 17:] Is that all there is? A lab rat to usher in a new scientific breakthrough and messiah 'my people' from violent dog breed to a tolerated form of monster? That's why I have to stay in LA. That's why I can't run every time there's danger. Dammit, I'm a man and I occasionally need to act like one. Or at least feel like one.

[Subject:] So this is about some sort of male ego testosterone thing? Don't be ridiculous. Bullets and medical examiners won't care if you died in a glorious fight or if you crawled in a hole. Either way, you'll be dead and I'll be pissed at you. Forever.

<Argument continues - no pertinent data>

{8:02s}

[Subject:] Right. Here's the jist of my Ghoul Progression theory, based on your own statements. Tell me what you think. You've stated you have been having daydreams or memory flashes, and I'm confident now that they're Carla's memories. I think you absorbed some of them when you killed her and ate her brain.

[Male Caller 17:] Look. I wasn't...

[Subject:] Stow it. I don't want to talk about her death. We're focusing on the theory. So, you have flashes and memories that are probably triggered by your actions, just like they might be triggered in her if she were doing that activity. Now, adding to that, you say you had some sort of telepathic or out of body experience, the latter being more appropriate I guess, and you not only were aware but it seemed like that person was aware of you. And either she or you got hit with a thirst or appetite for blood when you went by the crime scene. Let's presume that she was or is a Ghoul or Vampire or some other SUP-class being and"

[Male Caller 17:] You know I like it when you call me a SUP! If 'Sentient Undead Predator' didn't mean I was evil, it would be quite dashing!

156

[Subject:] Can you please let me finish. You're bloody intolerable. Based on your data, the evidence we've seen, and the fact that Ghoul physiology like most SUPs is still mostly incomprehensible to us; my theory is that as Ghouls devour brains they absorb memories and 'information' from those brains which lingers in their psyches indefinitely, adding subconscious or conscious knowledge or skills to the subject, but ultimately driving them to insanity or schizophrenia due to the constant struggle in their own mind.

[Male Caller 17:] So we eat ourselves crazy? That's the theory?

[Subject:] Well, I guess if you want to oversimplify it. While your physical system is ready for your addiction to brains, your mind - that of a human with rules and societal order - is not. I don't know yet what makes you so different, but I think if we could truly study you we could make some real progress toward understanding what Ghou... what you have that you're able to resist that temptation and deal with the mental issues.

[Male Caller 17:] What about my ghost-ride in the shoes-woman's mind?

[Subject:] I'm not sure about the out of body thing, yet. Have you had any further incidents? What about your visit to Wyatt's place? I know you went, even though I told you not to risk it for them. You don't owe him or this Alex anything.

[Male Caller 17:] I didn't go for him and I didn't go for Alex, either. I went for me. Because I need to do the right thing and see this through. Maybe I'll be a person [subject stressed "person"] who makes a difference, not just this killing machine with an inconvenient conscience. Or maybe it's a convenient conscience, keeping me from being that machine? Sorry, soapbox got under me. I think I figured it out, though. Problem is, if I'm right, I have to go to Seattle for the next step.

[Subject:] I like that, 'convenient conscience.' Seattle, huh? I might be able to meet you for coffee or something if you let me know what day you're going to be there - I do get to take a day off here and there! Where better to have a cup of coffee...<intermittent static or

interference>

[Subject:] You're where? Where are you that I'm losing you?

[Male Caller 17:] I5. Just outside of Yreka. About to enter Oregon.

<Incoherent yelling and feedback - no further pertinent data>

{19:32s}

[Call Ends. 1:33:40am EST 2011_06_11]

[Delivered to BPI DIV 7:22:00pm EST 2011_06_11 via batch 349765_20110611]

***

There are times we all make mistakes. I think my most recent is that I chose to come straight to what I believe to be Alex's house, but that's what they'd do on TV - rush to the location without rest or any semblance of thought beforehand. And it all works out! At least, that's what I tell myself. It's a cute little ranch house, small for my tastes, with little land based on what I can tell from the front yard and surrounding properties. I've stopped a few houses down to take a look.

I don't sleep, for the most part, and not for lack of trying since I... changed. I feel like a living, or dead, biological hypocrisy. I'm nocturnal, but practically cold-blooded now as I don't generate body heat. I'm sensitive to light, especially bright sunlight, yet I'm lethargic during the day even if I do warm up! Let's not forget the don't have to breathe and non-beating heart thing. Again, biological hypocrisy.

Relax. I'm getting all worked up and I'm just sitting in the car! *So, let's be smart. What had I learned from Wyatt's place? Do I even want to go any closer to Alex's place?* I hate trying to pull up memories. Janey says it could be a critical ability, if I can 'tap the memories of my victims, then perhaps I can not only learn their knowledge but gain empathy toward what drove them to their wicked ways.' A little too hippie for me, and I think she reads too many comic books. *Yes, as in present tense.* But she's got a good soul, *not to mention looks and brains as the Fed version of Lisbeth Salander,* so I'm trying to bear

158

with her and try out her ideas. *Relax.* I breathe in deep, and exhale smoothly. I'm sure this does nothing for me physically, but mentally I still think of it as a calming effect. Bringing up memories of mine own are easy, so I'm going to start with the note. *The damn note outside Wyatt's. Zero in... concentrate...*

"Just great!" I looked at the note again. It still hadn't changed since the last section of wall I sat on:

> *'MRW-Remember 3/31? Need help desperately, not much time left. Please, you're the only one! 2713311869101001 You know what to do. - Alex'*

That's it? I have to wonder why I am even bothering with this. Wyatt was a pretentious prick and I don't even know this Alex person! My mission hinged on a cryptic and practically useless note! Plus, even when I was really alive I wouldn't care nor get involved with this. What the hell am I thinking now?

I had the message written down on a post-it note and hoped it would at least provide some wisdom for getting into Wyatt's condo. See, for a guy like me, crawling up walls and other feats of physical prowess seem to be no problem since dying - it defies science. But that doesn't make it any easier to get into a condo that has all the windows and doors locked, paired with an active security system.

Fortunately Wyatt the P.I. loved the camera and the spotlight, so it was pretty easy to track down the media-hound's residence, even for a techno-idiot like myself. I had weighed my options and the landscaping brick seemed to be my best one for entering the 4th floor corner condo. Wasn't until later I really thought about how anyone else would have broken in this way, but I was in a hurry.

Okay, I need to fast-forward this memory. Shattered the window, swung in. Turned on the video camera so I could look over things later if needed. Luckily, Wyatt's "Open Concept" condo seemed to also reflect his lack of affection for personal items. It had been a veritable wasteland other than a few pieces of art and a wall full of Wyatt-centric photos. And the memories keep rolling...

The bedroom had made even me feel bored. The hardwood floors looked, upon a quick inspection, to be real wood and too nice to conceal any secret compartments. Then there had been the office, or what had been probably the master bedroom originally. The heavy door had been locked, and the code on the note had definitely NOT had anything to do with opening the keypad lock. Kicked in the door. The line "I think I hear one of them silent alarms" from some movie was taking my mind off the ticking clock until cops arrived.

My grin stopped as soon as I turned on the lights and looked into the room. There were not one but two bloodied men tied to ornate wooden chairs, in the middle of what looked like an epic war zone, facing a clean desk with a computer nicely perched atop. It must have been one helluva fight, however it went down. File cabinets were knocked over with files strewn across broken or toppled bookshelves. There were small blood splatters all over the room, with hand and body prints in blood everywhere. I think even Dexter would have trouble figuring out what went on in that room!

I had walked over to the man on my left first, not expecting much as I noticed the yellow pool beneath his chair and the smell which indicated he had been there far too long. As expected, no pulse. Not even warm. Kinda like me. When I swung around the front I came to the fairly certain medical conclusion that the large knife buried in his heart's location was the cause of death.

The other man, slumped in his similar chair, had not been easy to figure out. I had approached from the front, noticing that he had maybe been dumped in the chair and not really bound, as opposed to the first who was still tied down. I have to admit, he was probably a pretty smart guy. As I got close, still surveying the room, he had buried a knife in my gut which must have been on the other side of the chair waiting for me to get close. His face, hard with desperation and a grim satisfaction at his killing thrust, was starkly contrasted by the look of absolute terror frozen in death after I regained conscious control from the ensuing Berserker episode. While the cartoon-like episode, for the third time in my undeath, had been quite clear that I feasted on his brain; I couldn't help but be disturbed by his empty skull and that dreadful face of terror staring at me as if he understood and pitied me. I guess sometimes we see what our subconscious wants us to see?

I remember looking at the desk which triggered a wave of twisted memories from this man washing over me. This is bad. *Memories within memories always wreak havoc on my mind and just generally screw up my chi, for lack of a better term. No one is worth this.*

{{A very disheveled Wyatt had been sitting on the front of the desk. His lips move but I can't hear him. He was paging through what was presumably a black calendar or address book, and shoving the opened page toward me and then my colleague. While I couldn't read the page nor hear the words, I knew that he was taunting us with the information we wanted. Had we killed him first, it would have been ours! I could feel the rage boiling inside me. }} *I can feel the pain swelling in my true self, like my own brain is about to burst. I can't do this for long.*

{{Then Wyatt was burying his knife in the other man's chest, a silent scream gurgling out of Smith's mouth. As he looked at me, fear like I'd never known arose in me, and I swear his eyes turned red, vicious fangs I hadn't seen protruded from his maw, and he, while still looking at me, licked a long drink of blood from my colleague's navel to his chest as if to make it clear to me that I should be afraid. I then knew absolutely that this man was going to happily kill me, unless I gave him whatever answers he sought. So when he asked, I told him everything he wanted. Not quite freely, so not to seem too pathetic and weak, but the beating was worth it if it meant I could live, maybe see my boy... I told him about the girl. Why we had gone there, to find out what he knew from her and to silence him and anyone he may have told. He had been so fast, so strong, we had barely held our own in the fight and obviously lost still. I told him about our crew. Everyone. I told him about Jolly and the freaky contract thief he and the boys were probably cutting up right now over by the docks. How everyone who'd ever touched anything to do with that woman's new work, whether they knew it or not, had been on the list. I told him that Jolly knew where she was, said he'd been there to make sure she was secure before coming down here. How it was dark and stank wherever she was - some town underground. I told him that even after I told everyone to leave him alone, assuming he let me live, that Jolly would probably still come for him. And he nodded those crimson, dead eyes at me and stuck his nose to my cheek. He licked my face and I never saw the punch coming; and all went black.}}

I had found the book, afterward. Alexis Reidman had coffee with Wyatt April 19th, in Seattle. They walked over to "Queen Anne Baseball Park" and his only note was "C trip" which meant nothing to me. Well, nothing so far. It was more than enough to help me find her address and information. I looked in his filing cabinet but of course there was no file between Reichert and Reilly.

A small, blinding ray of sunshine hits me right in the face through the windshield and while literally blinded, my mind catapults out of the thugs' and my memories, back into the car. These memory trips, especially a memory within a memory, hurt like nothing I can explain. Last thing I need is this, during the sunny day when my whole being yearns for the night. I feel like I haven't eaten for days and my stomach is slowly driving my other systems into withdrawal. And even I, dead or alive or undead, get stiff after this much time in a car.

****

Cranky, recently blinded, lethargic from daytime, and sore from being behind the wheel, I'm feeling terribly hospitable now. My head feels like a gremlin is inside with two stone hammers banging on the inside of my skull, just to see where the soft spots are. I know better than to try this new 'memory surfing' as Janey calls it, but sometimes male stubbornness wins. I decide to at least get out of the car. Probably should go in. A myriad of lame stories go through my mind about why I might be here if someone asks. *PI maybe? Jehovah's Witness? Ooh TV repair man?* I obviously watch too much TV! Maybe I should change my nifty call-sign from Olmec to Macgyver?! *Then it hits me. Why am I even doing this? This isn't TV. It's not a comic book nor fiction.* I just stop and stare dumbfounded at the house, having made it to the curb from my car. *I could leave right now and be done with this. The game was fun but I'm spinning my wheels for what?* Something I know nothing about and that may, at best, only cause me more pain or even get me killed. *Again. Well, more permanently.* Or at best get me more enemies for sticking my nose where it doesn't belong. I could leave now and let it go. No fights, no more murder! *A break from thugs and all the societal refuse would be a welcome change.* My life, or un-life, has been about survival. Just mine. This does nothing to that end. I don't know that I'm even doing the right thing. *Nor if I actually care that it's right. Wyatt, I've discovered, was or is not a nice person. Even if my 'memory' was just the embellishment of a drugged thug. So why do I presume he had good intentions? Because he said so?* Feelings aren't fact.

It's a cute little house. Even in this awful sunshine, it reminds me of my home as a kid playing out front with my brother or drawing on the walkway to the door. The blinds move ever-so-slightly and I tell myself it's just a memory of when my mother would check on us but try to not disturb. *Would Alex do all this to help me? Would she even care?* I already know that answer. And my Mother would want me to live, even like this. Wyatt's a killer. Alex is obviously involved with him, and is important to him.

I do something I should have done at the beginning. I get in the car and leave. I tell myself the form peering out from behind split blinds is just my Mother's ghost, still watching out for me.

*****

I've been on the road an hour and I still don't feel like I'm far enough away. I kept driving North, heading out of the US entirely. It's the smart choice. *Don't lie to yourself, you're afraid.* Clear and simple I don't like what happens to me. *I AM afraid, of me.* Maybe it's better for me to be Janey's lab rat and document my life now that I'm not alive? Maybe my destiny is to show the haters like the Feds that a Ghoul isn't just a mindless killer. Maybe it's important to have a story to tell? *Dammit!* I guess I'm learning to deceive myself, too. Even if that's the case, then helping this person is exactly what I should be doing. By leaving her to suffer or die, I'm just living up to their expectations. *I hate Fate.*

I feel like a fool and a hero all at once as I turn back into the storm I've been trying to outrun. Someone was at the house, and I know it. And I can't deny that I saw the kids' play set and sandbox behind the house on my way out. And that makes me angry. More at myself than anyone, because I know I saw that and still left. Talk about feeling low.

Of course, someone at the house implies an organization or at least organized individuals, unless it's actually someone who belongs there. I'll never be that fortunate. And the last thing I need is to rush to the top of another Most Wanted list! There I go, making excuses to not get involved. I guess this is the time that tries my soul - so far I'm not fond of how poorly this trial has gone. At least it'll be dark by the time I get back.

******

Jake and Danny weren't bright by thug standards. That says a lot considering most hired muscle is already expected to have limited brain capacity in favor of said muscle and a dog's eagerness to impress how well they followed commands. The smartest thing they did was to sleep in shifts with one 'on duty' and the other off. The dumbest things, yes I have to equally list three, were toss-ups:

- They took sleep turns at night - when even other thug predators come out.
- They left all the doors unlocked, including the back patio - apparently so they could smoke.
- And they brought a video game system to play bad-ass gun-toting car-jacking thugs on the TV.

Lets just say they were ill-prepared for a Supernatural Undead Predator (*or SUP as Janey says for the Fed classification*) very-well equipped for the darkness. I don't know if Alex's house is always a messy disaster, but presuming not I can only hope that Jake and Danny thought the mess would alert them to other intruders.

Apparently Jake and Danny also weren't the most loyal individuals to have in your organization. Since I'd hate to rob the thug gene pool of these fine specimens, I chose not to kill them. Fortunately for me, they have some sort of twisted honor code and felt honor-bound to tell me what they knew. Apparently I had "bested them in a battle" and they had their Code to follow. While I'm fairly certain there wasn't actually anything from the Geneva Convention which applied, I wasn't about to argue with them about cooperating! I wish every criminal I met were one of these guys. Imagine the fun!

Jake and Danny indicated that they had overheard the information I sought regarding Alex and her whereabouts, but regrettably couldn't share it with me. Apparently the code only allowed them to reveal so much. "You're going to have to torture us to get it!" Danny was so very proud of himself.

I reluctantly agreed, wandering into the kitchen but never really out of site and they sat quietly in their wooden chairs, discreetly testing the bonds and duct tape which secured them to their respective chair. Sitting tall and proud of themselves, chests out and jaws set, I gathered we'd seen the same films. So I grabbed a few miscellaneous yet common items from the kitchen and returned to my stalwart prey. Their eyes passed over the items, both of them swallowing when they got to the corkscrew. As they looked back to me I pulled out one of the same sturdy chairs, opened a clawed hand, and raked it down the back of the chair splitting it into two pieces at the end and throwing half at each of their feet. They jumped at the shotgun sound as the chair was destroyed, and both fell over backward as they tried to dodge the pieces thrown in their directions. Perhaps too dramatic, but it proved effective.

"Dude - we never said you had to maim us or nuthin!" Jake was a little less enthusiastic about the torture, I guessed. "Couldn't you just punch us in the face or something so we don't look like total losers? I don't know if this extreme measure is necessary." I half expected a surf board to fall into the room.

"Wow. Dudes." I said it as deadpan as could. "I hadn't thought of that. I figured two tough dudes like you'd want me to cut on you for a

165

bit, make it a deeply painful experience? How will I know you're not lying to me if I don't torture you proper? I would never insult you by being too soft! Perhaps you should suggest a measure of pain which would be amenable to your egos in order to procure my information? What do you suggest?"

Danny and Jake agreed to two facial punches, for visual effect of course, and to remaining secured to the chairs. They were very clear that my willingness and intent was paramount enough to their Code to arrange a deal. At my insistence on appearance, they agreed to being knocked over and some minor damage being done to the interior of the home to make it at least look like they struggled. After setting the scene and giving each of them a good shiner and some bruises 'on the house,' they explained that they'd overheard Alex's location was on a ship on the south side of Salmon Bay. Since I had treated them fairly and in good faith, they didn't feel bad about giving me the name and the berth.

I threw in some claw scars, allowing them to, *honestly, in their words,* 'tell the girls how they'd fought with a real supernatural Ghoul dude and lived to tell about it.' For this I got the bonus that Johnson, the Employer who hired them, had apparently been looking for something here. But Johnson didn't find what he was looking for! He was after a key to some sort of code. He found something else, which they said made him less of a 'buzz-kill,' but he was really after some key. Johnson had told them he represented "a non-terrorist organization, which operated contrary to the interests of the authorities, and had a critical agenda for changing the World." While they were old enough to compare this job to the X-Files, I sincerely doubted they were old enough to have watched that show in its day. Of course, I felt like this was the Twilight Zone, so I guess I shouldn't judge. I DID wonder if the organization was Cobra. From GI Joe. Never mind.

I spent some time trying to learn about Alex. Alexis, I corrected myself, was apparently a Math Teacher. There were pictures of Alexis and two children, presumably hers, all over the house. No signs of a Dad or significant other for Alexis except in the girls' rooms where there were pictures of a man, presumably their father by the notes and frames. I pulled out the crumpled sticky for some kind of clue.

MRW-Remember 3/31? Need help desperately, not much time left. Please, you're the only one! 2713311869101001 You know what to do. - Alex

I pulled out my Tablet, a web-surfing dynamo, and Google Mapped the numbers again. Nothing. I imagine that Johnson had already done the same, hence he's looking for some sort of code or encryption key. I partially read a Geo-caching for Dummies book once, and decided to try my math skills (*pathetic by kindergarten standards*) at finding ways to make the number into coordinates, math teacher style. Square root of 2713311869101001 is 52 089 460.2. *Ha ha! Comes up Garden Gate Elementary School in Cupertino CA! That makes sense. She has kids, maybe hid whatever it is at their school?*

And this went on for a little bit as I tried elementary methods of making new numbers and converting them to coordinates. Then maybe combinations to something at the house but found nothing. I'd already expended time trying to figure out the number. Like Johnson, only the key would provide the real answer. Only I know that her being a Math teacher is going to be an important clue.

I felt myself drifting away from my objective. Jake and Danny were getting too annoying. And while Alex was probably suffering, I was looking for answers I didn't need. So I re-tasked myself to verify that a vessel named *Genesis,* per Jake and Danny, was actually still docked in Seattle's Salmon Bay. Easy enough. I'd even found pictures of the cargo vessel, taken by someone calling himself or herself "Watchdog of the Wharf" who posted a variety of conspiracy theories about most ships entering and exiting the bay. Some people!

****

"You sonuva bitch!" The slap landing across Jim's right cheek seemed to take him by surprise. "You bugged my phone. My apartment. My everything, because you suspected a Ghoul would

167

contact me?"

"Janey, you're overreacting. I bug everyone when I think they're in danger." The look on Jim's face clearly showed that he knew that was the wrong thing to say. He didn't even try to dodge her slap to the same reddened cheek. "Please, no more hitting. It's protocol. People fall under Influence and other forms of persuasion all the time. You're not this naive!"

"Spare me the I did it for the team tripe! I'm not ON your team. I'm on loan to this Division from DoD in order to conduct my own research, attached but extraneous to your operational privileges. I'm here to come up with a less shoot-everything-different-on-site approach. And you KNOW it!" She was actually huffing now, muttering a low growl.

"Janey, you of all people know, then, that this is not about emotion or sentimentality. I need the facts, from wherever I can get them. And YOU know that none of us are exempt from this. You were already in Seattle when I got the script. Not that it mattered, there was only one way for us to play it."

"Bull. Fast and hard with guns blazing is not the only option. It's just YOUR only option. What if you had actually caught him? Then what? Summary execution and the World is a safe place again, except for the 348 known other offenders out there?"

Jim was obviously immune to tears. "Look. I know you like this guy, research or not. But he's a killer. He knows it. At least he's accepted it, whether I believe your theories or not. And you know it too. Maybe he isn't all bad, but a *Riddick* meets *Dexter* in a sort of bad-ass killer with mixed emotions is a tremendous threat. At least your and our psych profiles agree on the risk with this guy. I can see how you're drawn to him, but think of your life. Your career. Again, you're not this naive." This time her fist was closed and Jim chose to stop it. She pushed and he just held it. "Janey. We. Hunt. Killers. It's what we do here and what they are. We are successful and protect people using the research and the data that you and your predecessors gather. You tell me: How many Ghouls, in the last decade let's say, were not at some point very successful at blending in and killing discreetly? Then how many were civil when apprehended?"

"None. But this one is different. I know it, not just theory. Maybe you're right about where it'll end, but we could learn so much before the eventual insanity sets in!" She could see he didn't understand the point.

"How many team members were killed by Ghouls in the past decade?" Jim tightened his grip on her fist at the thought of it, then let go in surprise.

"A lot. I don't know. " She looked down, wringing her fingers on her lab coat then placing a sweaty palm on the glass window of the lab wall. Then quickly started to clear the smudges off the glass.

"Janey." His voice was calm, like he was speaking to his children. "How many people has THIS Ghoul killed? He CHOSE to run last year, and killed Carla. You say he's smart, strong-willed and able to keep the insanity at bay. And I agree he's clever and skilled. That makes him a nightmare -- not a lab rat – for me. I can't let something that powerful, unpredictable, and prepared for us just roam freely. Hell, the insanity is an advantage to us! Look. You know the numbers and the odds better than anyone. What do they tell you if you're wrong about his good intentions?"

"You've read my reports, Jim." The possibility of being so utterly wrong finally brought tears to her eyes. "If he's half as bad as you seem to think, combined with what I know, then we're better off leaving him alone. Maybe wait for the insanity. It'll save lives in the long run. You spoke once about him being the Scorpion from the *Frog and the Scorpion* story. If he's the anomaly I think he is, AND your killer?"... She shuddered ever so slightly, but he felt it. "Then he's neither the Frog nor the Scorpion. He's the River. And we're all gonna drown."

Jim didn't know what to say to that. So he just watched her cry while he tried to figure things out.

****

The steel door creaks and moans as I peel it away from its casing, a patchwork of plating installed recently and somewhat haphazardly. The frame is strong though, the welds are hard enough to break, and blood all over your hands makes them very slippery! Even after wiping them on your clothing. I take a little longer than I need in dismantling the door, giving myself some time to think about how this is going to go. The hallway I'm standing in, along with the rest of the ship as far as I know, is blanketed in darkness from me having destroyed the electrical system earlier. But this room is still lit, indicating they have separate power. Something to think about as I take my time with the door.

The four men in head-to-toe tactical gear with mask and ear bud radios are in a half-circle facing the door, just watching as I slowly dismantle it. I'm both scared and impressed that they appear to be calmly waiting for me to finish fumbling with this door. *This demands more evaluation!* Deeper into the narrow yet lengthy room is a hooded woman tied to a chair which faces my door. It seems intentional that she is facing me as opposed to the door behind her. It's like they want to make sure I can see her. I can smell the sweat and blood in this room, not all if it fresh either. It doesn't take Ghoul senses to tell this isn't a room for the squeamish. Shrouded in the now-partial darkness of the hallway, I can feel whatever passes for Ghoul adrenaline building in my system as I start assessing them individually.

Each man is armed with only a pistol and a variety of melee weapons, from knives to fighting sticks it seems, which varies per man. *Odd considering the opposition before this room had machine guns. I'm suddenly aware that I'm guilty of the same thing I yell at movie heroes about. I should have grabbed one of those machine guns!* As I near total removal of the door, three of them pull their pistols and the figure center-right pulls a small hand-held crossbow. *A freaking mini crossbow? Wasn't there a GI Joe character with that?* They each hold the weapon in front of them, pointed at the floor, like they'll wait until I finish what I've started with the door before we begin something new. *I guess they want my undivided attention!*

Down by the Drool

Tearing the door into three pieces of bent metal and away from the hinges now, I stack the pieces nicely next to the doorway, outside the room. Looking to the men and back, I decide to grab the section with the door handle as a shield. *Yes, I brought a shield to a gun-fight. Maybe I can go all Captain America on them?* I set the shield down, straighten my clothes a little noticing more bullet holes than I'd thought, roll my shoulders and neck, then pick the 'shield' back up and step into the room. I can hear the woman's soft whimpering, along with the smell and taste of fear in the air. I expected to find more men hidden in the corners by the door, but only a small table sits in the corner to my left, a closed briefcase on top. *What, only four of you?! I'm kind of insulted by this!*

The man with the crossbow, "Chavez" labeled on his left breast, speaks with a young but hardened voice. Reminds me of the bad guy in the first Highlander movie. "I'm glad you came. Surprised, but still glad."

All I hear is "Nice to see you again, Macleod!" like in the movie!

"You're supposed to be this cautious, intellectual, ancient friend turned traitor. I asked Johnson once why they don't have pictures of you in any of the facilities and all he could say was that your 'banishment' - his words - demanded that your visage be removed from all sight. Never to be seen. It was quite gloomy. Imagine what must be going around in the minds of The Circle, now that I've reported your name from little miss Alex here! I'm sure you don't understand, with all the changes in the last century, what's really at stake. When she assured me you'd come for her, I was quite surprised. You've been so adamant about caution. And the records say you've never interfered, before. Why now? What can she possibly mean to you? Even she doesn't quite know. Tell me."

"Nice to see you too!" I couldn't help with the Highlander line. I don't know who he thinks I am or if this is some sort of delusional game? Maybe he thinks I'm Wyatt? "Believe me kid, I didn't want to come after her. Hell, I already quit once." My voice betrays me to Alex, obviously confused, but they're all focused on me and don't notice. "But I don't think YOU understand much of anything. Here's

171

my offer: You let me leave with Alex and I let you all live. I'll continue to stay away and you can go about your merry way playing Cobra or whatever it is you're doing here. I think that's a pretty fair bargain." There's about as much bravado as I can muster in my voice. The steel door handle starts to bend and crumble from my white-knuckled grip, drawing my attention as it buckles and moans.

As I look up from the shield, Chavez has leveled his crossbow at my chest, speaking with a much more deadly edge in his voice. "I've got a counter offer. This shouldn't be too much for someone who's already dead. It's not like you have a life waiting in whatever cave you crawled out from. I know you want to save her." *Why do they always think they know me? That assumption really irritates me. Is it just arrogance?* "We'll let her go, quietly and peacefully without harm. Well, further harm. But we keep you instead. Not that it would end differently but I'd be happy to avoid making a mess."

I'm so sick of people after me. "I just tore a steel door apart. Why do you think your crossbow --" The wooden bolt from the crossbow hits me square in the chest before I even realize he pulled the trigger. *Wow that's fast!* I stagger back a step and just stand there, dumbstruck in more ways than one, looking from the bolt to the man to the bolt again. *What happened to talking? Smart! Real freaking smart! New Rule: No stupid banter with the bad guys.* I look at each of the other men expectantly, but none of them have moved. The room starts to shrink, though, as the edges darken like a shadow is slowly being drawn from outside my vision into the room. I know this all too well. Only this time, I welcome the Berserker.

They guy furthest to my left speaks for the first time. "Is that it? I thought this guy was super-fast and all bad-ass predator?" He sounds like he's early twenties and still waiting for puberty to hit him.

"Shaddup, Wilson. He's nuthin special. One wooden shot to the heart and they're all incapacitated." The man to my right is definitely an older man, "Carson" written on his name tag. *Heh, Johnny Carson maybe?* I laugh a little, and the room starts to darken even more from the shadow now dancing across over half my vision. It seems almost alive, slowly creeping out toward my enemies like dark tendrils. My laugh comes out as a gurgling and pathetic cough. *The bolt is stuck in my left lung probably. Good thing I don't really have to breathe for oxygen, just for things like speech!*

Chavez walks over to the table and sets the crossbow down next to the briefcase, apparently confident in my immobility. "Carson is right, Wilson. There are a few truths about these undead suckers, no matter how old or powerful they are or claim to be. A stake in the heart will always incapacitate them, for one. But they don't usually slow down enough and just let you shoot them in the chest! There's always a motive to kill with them." He takes off his mask, dark features and hair spilling out, and opens the briefcase. "And this, I'm guessing, is why our big bad wolf here would come out of hiding and into the hornet's nest!"

Inside the briefcase is a large vial secured in a nice foam cutout, with several other chips and data equipment embedded around it, complete with a Bond-worthy giant temperature gauge and clock! Flashing lights indicate climate control with temperature tolerances for the cargo, even! Chavez turns and smiles a toothy grin at me. "You never mentioned the serum in your offer. I'm guessing you didn't think we'd find it at her place? Or do you not really care about the world? I wonder myself, sometimes. If you'd acknowledged it at all in your offer, I would have a baseline on its value. But since you didn't, and her 'statement' says it's done or close to done, I think this may be just as or more valuable to us than even you. Maybe if you had at least mentioned it, I would have felt your offer was more than a stall. But you insulted me by not even acknowledging it!" He turns back and closes the case hard, locking it again taking it over to drop at Alex's feet. She jumps away as best as she can when it bangs at her feet. "Let's not forget how you seem to honor your deals from the past. With this I have no need for you, actually. But I think The Circle will want you alive. You know what I mean. So let's talk about things. Gemini, says you'll know his name, spoke to me for the first time since I've been in Ops. Apparently your name was enough to get people to speak to us lowly grunts. He sends that he wants you to be friends again. Personally, I think you're all old news." Chavez sighs as if bored then visibly shudders as if thinking of something nasty. "Let's box him up boys!"

The black masks come off all but Vestyn, who hasn't moved since drawing his pistol. Carson slides toward Alex, who starts whimpering in her chair. He hovers over her, body language screaming nasty intent, and asks "What are we supposed to do with the woman?" I swear drool drops onto her thigh as he purrs the most creepy sound I think I've ever heard. She goes impossibly pale and stiff. *I guess she can tell even with the mask on.*

Wilson steps right up to me from the left, whispering quietly with disgust. "You don't scare me, boogeyman. You were supposed to be tough yet Chavez nailed you like nothing." *I think he might actually be thirty and still waiting for Puberty!* "Seems to me you give Vampires a bad name, not even putting up a fight. You're about as scary as a jack-in-the-box. And what's with your eyes getting all dark or bloody? You gonna cry, tough guy?" *Vampire? Who do they think I am?* Quite loudly this time, Wilson continues. "Christ I thought we were going to see some real action this time?! Every time we get assigned to someone bad-ass I had to sit in the truck or guard the back or some crap. Now, I'm in the front finally, and what? This guy?!" He whirls away and continues his rant.

Chavez pats Wilson on the shoulder as he saunters toward me while Wilson rants his way over to open the heavy steel door behind Alex. *They think I'm a Vampire.* Having taken Chavez word earlier, I realize I haven't even tried to move, believing I was incapacitated. *So sue me for not knowing better!* Chavez leans in close, his breath pouring a noxious stink with every word. "Here's the deal, old man. We're going to take the serum, and you. After Carson is done with Alex, and assuming no one else wants some quality time with her, I'm going to put her in a room with something hungry and leave her. Maybe you if I can find a way to arrange it." The shadow has taken over my vision now, and I see the room in a glorious myriad of darkness and the kaleidoscope of colors, as if it were night and all the things in the darkness were made of bright colors just for me. "You should know, the last thing you'll ever know is that all your pain and suffering is my doing. I wish I could really know what's going on behind those black eyes of yours." He searches my face for a moment as if trying to remember something, then seems to give up. I feel the Ghoul adrenaline again, as if it were building this whole time and I hadn't noticed until now. "And just to be clear. Wherever you've hidden the kids. I'll find them, too. And I'll take them apart slowly just in case you've hidden any other secrets with them." He smiles. I'm not sure if he's insane or just that sadistic. Probably just trying to get a rise out of us.

Alex lets out an angry scream and fights against her chair until Carson kicks her shoulder, knocking both Alex and the chair backward and onto the floor. "Quiet!" In case his message wasn't clear. He pulls her mask off and gives her the evil eye as her red hair mattes to the damp floor. As Chavez looks at them, I tighten my grip on the shield and tip my head to the side, cracking my neck. *Just like someone in a movie would right before they kick ass!*

Chavez turns back toward me, his smile from ear to ear fading as I bring my eyes back parallel to his. "One problem..." I tell him as my shield hand shoots up under his chin and clamps down on his throat, hard enough to cause his eyes to bulge a little. The door segment shield hits the floor with a resounding thud on the metal grating. *At least he shuts up!* "I'm not a Vampire, moron." The blackness and the shadow are there, but there is no comic special effect this time. I may not be quite the Berserker this time, but I know I'm smiling as I close my grip on Chavez' throat to about the size of a quarter and my left hand shatters the wrist of his right arm before it clears the pistol from its holster.

The crunching sounds of Chavez' throat and arm are almost inaudible as a mix of "Shit, Ghoul!" and gunshots from Vestyn reverberate in the small compartment. The noise is maddening, as I still don't know how to shut off my hyper-sensitive hearing and lost my earplugs in a fight up on deck. I use Chavez' twitching body as a shield from most of Vestyn's bullets then launch the body at Vestyn. I follow right behind it, instinct driving me but not controlling me this time, arriving at Vestyn at almost the same time as the body.

Vestyn tries to dodge right and bring his barrel up to my head; but

I'm already inside his reach, bringing his gun and forearm over my left shoulder. Since his arm is right there, I tear into it with my fangs while the gun drops to the floor with the loss of muscle control. He's moving so slowly. They all are. It's exactly like all the martial arts masters say combat should be to the prepared mind - like everyone else is moving in slow motion compared to you. As his eyes meet mine from behind his mask, both the gun and Chavez' body hit the floor. A split-second later my claws have swung upward, digging into his right elbow and his chest at the right shoulder. The arm separates from his torso with a popping sound like a water balloon, and he wails the only sound I'll ever hear him make. *Right into my right freaking ear!* I punch-shove him back away from me so hard he makes a dent in the wall and almost seems stuck there before slumping to the floor.

Carson is bringing his pistol to bear on me as Wilson is rushing me with a Randall Model 1 knife, of all things. *How do I know what knife that is?* I've been shot before, and already this second, so I figure Carson is more of a threat right now. I improvise and throw Vestyn's arm at him, hitting him right in the face with the wet end forcing his shots to go wild. Wilson tries for a good straight stab and glances a few ribs as I twist away from the lunging blade to Wilson's right. As I spin I howl something primal and pull the wooden bolt from my chest. Which I immediately and unceremoniously bury in Wilson's throat from behind as he is still moving past me with the knife. I can feel the thrust shatter his spine at the neck and he collapses forward about six feet into the wall near the destroyed door. *Three down!*

Carson is wiping the blood from his eyes and firing somewhat erratic as he retreats for the back door. I move toward him in a slightly curved approach, taking a few rounds in the torso and leg but most missing me. His fear, now pungent even with stench of blood and nastier smells that come with dying bodies, is like a lure to my dark appetite. I grab and break his gun arm at the wrist. He pulls an old Marine Ka-Bar *(Again how do I know what the hell kind of knife that is?)* with his left and buries it in my right shoulder. I barely feel it as the Berserker shadow and Ghoul adrenaline are in full effect now. *And yet I'm still in the forefront this time, with still no cartoon. It's blood lust, maybe?* His eyes widen as he looks from the hilt to my face and back, twisting the blade with no noticeable effect. I crush his left wrist with my right hand, then pull his hand and the knife from my shoulder. The sound of the knife hitting the floor echoes in the room as he steps back, fury and terror in his eyes, and kicks at me with some sort of heel side kick. *He's so slow compared to me right now.* I just step to the side and grab the knee with my clawed hands, then swing him like a rag doll in a full circle before releasing him into the wall opposite the others. I'm on him before his broken body hits the ground. I'm there but it's almost like I'm observing for the moment. I tear open his skull like a coconut in what has to be a disturbing display of blood and violence. I don't even notice the giggling sound I make as I feast on his brain, but the sensation is overwhelming and I'm not in control at all any longer. Only this time it's not like the cartoon dream and my whole body shudders with ecstasy as I feed. *Maybe it's because deep down I don't feel remorse about their deaths? Or maybe because I'm not really fighting the Berserker now?* The brains are gone all too quickly and my hunger screams for more. *Were I at all rational, I might recognize this moment as that critical point where the addiction morphs into madness. Were I rational, I might decide to stop with this one brain. I know that even one feeding, while magical and healing to my undead body, costs me a terrible price in humanity.*

A pistol unloads on me from across the room. Three rounds tear into my arm, leg, and torso from my right side facing the shooter. A fourth clips the top of my forehead knocking my spin out of control to slip in the bloody mess and fall to the floor. As the 1911 runs out, I'm on all fours shuffling inhumanly toward Vestyn, like a Komodo Dragon shuffling across the ground. My feral side is in overdrive now and I pounce on his gun arm and shred it from elbow to shoulder. *He may already be dead, as his face was in the floor before I got there.* I crack his head into the floor a few times with my left arm, noticing that my right side is relatively useless at the moment. I watch as I repeat my coconut trick and gorge myself again.

I dig out the bullets even as the amazing brain meal repairs my body. It's like a symphony of sensations as the burning and pain and healing and ecstasy of the food all seek for dominance in my head.

As I sit, a few seconds feeling like an hour, I tell myself I need to learn about the organization that employs these thugs. The brain addict in me decides I need to consume Chavez' brain, of course, to gain the knowledge he had. *Logical, right?* No, I must feed on all their brains. Maybe I am and maybe I'm not in control at this time, but my sense of self-preservation for the first time agrees with the Berserker addict. There is no coping cartoon measure this time as I lose myself in the feast of the other brains. The rush is so amazing that I don't even realize what I'm doing or where I am. I find myself crouched over Alex, licking my fingers and smelling the sweet scent of her flesh. Her eyes are wide and just staring at me, as if she's frozen in time. *Oh no!*

She takes a deep breath and I blurt out an exasperated laugh of relief, which makes her scream then quickly quiet herself and go still again. I tilt my head to look at her. She's very pretty. Perhaps a little older than me. And still scared so much that she's trying not to breathe as I am still crouched over her. I can't imagine the horror of watching me feast on her captors' brains then sitting here eying her up as dessert. Correction. Looming over her with fangs and drool and claws, covered in fresh blood, eying her up as dessert. I'm suddenly aware AND in control and quickly step up and back from her. I'm suddenly embarrassed at what she may think and if it were possible I'm sure I'd be a deep shade of red right now. I'm sure she's humiliated and scared but all I can do is stand back and look at her, not sure of what to do.

Thankfully, boots clomping on the metal flooring of the hall, coupled with the "clear!" and other sounds of tactical teams approaching bring me out of my trance. I kill the lights in here and can see quite clearly down the darkened hallway teams of Fed creeps sweeping along toward us. They just love to wear big flags that say 'ATF' or 'Federal Agent' on them. It's enough to stop me from doing or better yet saying, anything stupid. Still woozily drunk from gorging myself on brains, I stumble toward the door behind her. I look back to her in the darkness, wondering if I should untie her or even apologize for almost eating her? Or maybe grab the briefcase? Flashlights floundering around in the hall and at the shredded door give me the answer. *Run, you moron!* I stumble out the rear hatch, hoping I've left her in better hands than mine.

178

"Thank you" whispers softly from the room behind me. True or not, I take it as meant for me.

I hope Janey forgives me for not making our coffee date. Again. I'm just not that presentable.

Epilogue

"This was a mistake, 'Olmec.'" The low statement, ground out over the 2-way radio caught me off guard and I almost jumped out of my chair, still managing to bang my knee on the rental car's steering wheel.

"Olmec? Why would you call me Olmec? I was thinking 'Roy' would be better?" I had figured out where Alex had hid her key to the note. It actually did provide coordinates.

"Someone's been watching a little too much *Die Hard* it seems. 'Olmec' is your code name in your BPI case file, Braniac. I can see that the file is right that you're lucky, not smart. You should probably find a way to get hold of it. Might help to know what your pursuers think of you."

"Yes, I often find myself caring what the psychotic band of Feds think of me as they chase me all over the Country. What are you going to do when they come calling for you? I doubt the mess you left at your office will give you any sympathy when Jim and his cronies find you." I flip on the camera feed for the tree camera I set out to watch the rock that had been covering Alexis' briefcase. Wyatt's eyes glow with a hazy light in the night vision of the camera. The half-ton rock has already been moved and the briefcase sits atop it, right next to Wyatt who is madly pacing around the rock in a circle. He stops and then determinedly moves off camera.

"Oh, don't worry about me, my friend. Worry about you. I've read your file. I hope it's true what they say about you. If so, I can't wait to see what happens to you in the next few months. Tell me, how many times have you fed ...few...days?" There's some distortion or interference in the signal.

"What? Screw you. Lets talk about the case and its contents?" I check the camera and Wyatt is still somewhere off camera.

"Did you familiarize yourself with the contents?" *Phew, he's still on. I need to figure things out with this guy.* "Do you understand both the power and the undoing you hold?" There are some scratching and breaking branches sounds, as if Wyatt is walking in the woods. I hadn't seen a car approach before he came on the radio. *Maybe he didn't drive here at all?* "Assuming you're not insane enough to use it, yet, and aren't dumb enough to have kept hold of it - what do you want? Money? Power? Answers? Training?" The breaking and crunching over the radio stops.

"You think that... what, training? What do you mean, training?" There are long seconds filled with silence and the trudging sound of feet in the snow.

"Look Olmec, I know what's in the case. Hell, I gave it to Alex so that other 'associates' of mine would never have that power. I don't actually mind that you have it nor know it. You're not even a threat WITH it. But I DO mind that you're too young and stupid to be able to protect it. And THAT, my friend, is alarming to me. I may be a little nuts but I've been around a long time. I see the Pros and the Punks in the undead world and most often neither last. I think you're gonna be a Pro. But you need guidance if you're going to live."

"Guidance? I found the case, buddy! I discovered the 3/31 reference to the E7 Lattice! I leave out *Thanks to Google.* I got here long before you and made sure to place the contents somewhere safe. Somewhere safe elsewhere, I guess. You know what I mean!" I had found the piece of Alex's garden lattice outside, which held the key. How funny that it was a literal clue to an easy break, once you had the key. It pointed to this spot, West of Balmy Beach near Ninette in Manitoba Province, Canada. East of Highway 18 on the side of some dirt road, with not a residence in sight. I was very proud of my success! "So who needs the training? What are you going to teach me about? How to show up second?"

A tapping sound startles me and I look out my window into the very large barrel of a shotgun, rapping gently at my driver door. At the end of an outstretched arm, finger on the trigger, is Wyatt. He's smiling and holding the radio to his head as if I won't hear him over the whirring noise as I lower the window.

"How about we start with the scent you left on the radio and how easy it is to track, eh Olmec?"

Floundering in obscurity and the call of several comic-induced dreams of avarice, **Catalino Tolejano, II** *lives in Southeastern Wisconsin along with his wife and son, deep behind enemy lines of great friends and phenomenal family. Held together by an eclectic plethora of entertainment ranging from his original Atari 2600 to Netflix and Blu-ray on the PS3, the Tolejano family manages to survive by foraging on Organic foods and the frequent infusion of life-sustaining pizza, fast food, or take-out! Catalino frequently raids M&M stockpiles, comic/toy/gamer conventions, and the occasional triathlon event; further contaminating his mind with material for future stories.*

The Favor

Patrick A. Waldoch

The Favor

<u>Now:</u>

Chaos erupts all at once. The damage alarms start blaring, and everyone on the bridge is talking to someone for some needed information, adding to the noisy chaos. My chief of the ship grabs my attention while we're being shaken about "Captain, I'm getting automated damage reports from all over the ship! Hull stress warnings going way beyond original design tolerances! We've got ventral hull breaches! We're not going to hold together for much longer!"

"Captain, Engineering! The lower thrusters are overloading! The heat from the atmo is roasting the engines more than they can take!"

"How much longer will they last, Chief!?"

"I don't know, maybe a minute?! Maybe less?!"

<u>A few weeks ago:</u>

I'm sitting on the bridge in my captain's chair reading my mail and I see a message I never expected to see, from a friend from a long time ago.

Alex needs a favor.

Ex-senator, Alexia Torres. She preferred Alex, trying to separate herself from her past, but I always insisted on Alexia. Long story. She helped keep my butt alive for six months when I was a guest of the Unitary Government Prison system back when I was, shall I say, "leaving" military service. Not only did she help keep me alive, she helped open my eyes to the nature of the Unitary Nations of EarthSpace's government, it's military and heck, maybe life in general. That knowledge kept me alive well after I left the prison and entered mercenary life.

The message capsule from Tortuga with mail and personal packages for the Bootlegger's crew is usually a welcome diversion. If it wasn't for Tortuga's very neutral status in the known galaxy, this wouldn't be possible. Henry Morgan, Tortuga's Planetary Governor, Lord, Owner - take your pick - has set up the place as safe haven for many lawless ruffians, pirates, mercenaries, and separatists, but he's managed to keep enough ties to the rest of the galaxy by acting as a cut out between the various governmental and corporate establishments and the freebooters, like us. One of the middle-man services he runs is a mail drop, electronic and otherwise. Without it, the crew would never have any sort of communication with their families and friends outside of the ship. Okay, so I pay a pretty decent amount for the drop-off service, but its worth it for the crew. I normally don't get much by the way of messages or deliveries, except for things pertaining to the ship so when I saw this one, I was floored.

MAP-Remember 3/31? Need help desperately, not much time left. Please, you're the only one! 2713311869101001 You know what to do. - Alex

I remember 3/31. Unitary Government Prison Facility quadrant 3, sector 31. Aleixa and I were cellmates for a while. She and her gang kept me alive, while various people working indirectly for the Warden tried to kill me, to keep some dirty dealings my former Captain was doing out of the spotlight. (Of course shortly after I left the prison to go to my tribunal back on Earth, I was captured by pirates and sold to Morgan, but that's a different story.)

I owe Alexia but even now with the Bootlegger's full armament and crew, I'd never be able to take on 3/31's defenses and prison guards, and manage to get her, let alone ourselves, out alive. Still... wish I would have tried.

She told me back then how when she was a Unitary Senator she would arrange some of her shadiest deals with people by sending them messages with coded location information. From the specified location, they would broadcast a coded number sequence given in the message, which triggered a remote transmitter that gave further instructions. It was a way for her to get deals done without it being directly traced back to her. Costly and convoluted, but it worked. This message looks like one of those as she described them to me. She somehow arranged a message from somewhere to reach me though Tortuga. She never told anyone she didn't trust about her messaging system, so that leads me to believe this is genuine, but I've got my doubts. Last I knew, her sentence should be up, but I don't know for sure. I can't imagine that she truly felt she needed to be so secretive with me, but then again I am a pirate now, at least according to governmental information sources, and maybe she just felt she really needed to be careful. Or more likely, she couldn't trust the message delivery channel. She seems desperate, at least in the terseness of her message. The problem is she never really told me the details or structure of her code system. What does it mean? There's only one number sequence here. So where do I go to broadcast the code? I'm gonna need some help puzzling this out.

"Miss Yvette, please put me on 12MC intercom circuit. I need to address the senior officers."

"Yes Captain. You're set."

"Captain to all senior staff, report to the wardroom at 1730 hours for a think tank session." I get virtual acknowledgment lights on my display from the senior officers in no time. As 1730 is only twenty minutes from now, I get up and address my helmsman, or woman in this case.

"Miss Haggerty, you have the bridge for the next few hours, into the next watch as necessary. Get someone to relieve you at the helm. Oh, get us prepped for departure as well."

"Do we have a course or location Captain?"

"Not yet, but we will."

****

"XO, may I enter the wardroom?" I ask Johnny Samuels, my executive officer. I keep a military-based structure on the Bootlegger, which is different than regular pirates or some mercenary groups. It helps to keep discipline and order, and promote a feeling of security for the crew. They all know they have to answer to someone and that cutthroat pirate attitudes are not allowed on this ship. Now asking the XO for permission, that's an old wet navy courtesy and tradition still in use by the USN today. The wardroom is generally run as a social location for meals and special events, and the executive officer is considered the nominal head of the wardroom. Normally, tradition dictates that work not be performed in the exec wardroom, but we *are* an independent mercenary vessel, not a fleet navy ship. I don't have to keep everything like a military ship. Besides, I've got a surprise for the senior officers that they'll enjoy.

As I walk into the wardroom, I can see all of my senior ship's officers seated and ready, and passing around some coffee and doughnuts. They see me and they all rise while I take my position at the end of the long wooden conference table. I had this room apportioned with extra luxuries like a long real cherry wood table and matching chairs. A bookcase on both long walls containing a small library of old fashioned paper books, ranging from a few reproductions of earth classics to modern day stories produced on frontier worlds with little electronic means of production but plenty of local varieties of trees. We use this room for entertaining and meals, but I like to meet here for these brainstorming sessions to keep them informal and not let anyone feel restricted by rank.

"Please sit everyone. I took the liberty of having the mess prepare formal dinner for everyone, on me, as I have a feeling were gonna be here a little while. So put those doughnuts away!" and with that announcement a cheer goes around the table as the stewards come in to set the place settings and bring out some various alcoholic drinks. We don't always eat so formally but I thought the extra expense was worth it. Normally, if I'm having a formal meal in the executive wardroom, I'll advertise it and the officer level staff need to get permission with the XO or myself to join at least six hours in advance and it costs them a bit extra on their shipboard credit for the meal compared to the dirty-shirt wardroom, otherwise know as the cafeteria. "Let's get started and maybe we'll even have some ideas to kick around by the time dinner is served."

"On behalf of the crew seated here, thank you Captain." Johnny offers as a toast with some of the wine the stewards brought out.

"Here! Here!" goes around the table a few times.

"Settle down you reprobates, and pass me a glass of that wine. Now, does everyone have in their comm-tac a copy of the message I received?" I get a round of nods and continue. "Good. Some of you may or may not know this story, but Alex or I should say, Alexia Torres, is the ex-senator from the Harris system." I get a few whistles when I mention her real name. She was well known for being the 'dirty senator from Harris' when in reality she was probably the least dirty politician in the Unitary EarthSpace Senate. She was just a convenient scapegoat when the time came to keep the other politicians' hands looking clean. I continue, "We were cell mates for about six months, years ago, when I was being drummed out of the Unitary Spacial Navy for the unspeakably treasonous crime of not following orders to help commit genocide. Most of you know that already. Before I was to go to trial I was shipped to the Unitary Government Prison Facility 3/31, as in quadrant 3, sector 31. Alexia was already an inmate there and had formed a mutual protection gang of what would normally have been easy marks in a prison. Alexia and her gang kept me alive for those six months by watching my back for the attempts on my life, as the Warden was working on behalf of my old Captain and his 2nd officer to spare them any embarrassment as to the exact nature and conditions surrounding my actions in disobeying my orders."

"What were those conditions Captain? Why were you being tried for treason?" That was from my new third officer Lieutenant Mathew Bell. Good man, picked him up on our last stop at Tortuga. Confed officer who got tired of the nearly mindless and wasteful actions against the Unitary military forces that are typical of the Confederated Colonies military.

"That's a story for another day as its not relevant to what's at hand.

Anyway, Alexia described to me how she would set up some of her shady dealings by arranging messages similar to the message you all have now. If you knew the prearranged codes or locations, you would go to the location then broadcast the code contained in the message on a radio broadband frequency, which activated a hidden transmitter. That transmitter would then broadcast a second message back containing the details of the dealings in question."

"So, what's the location code Captain?" Julia Woods, our ship's doctor, pipes up.

"That's the million dollar question."

My second officer, Lieutenant Commander Sunny McBride, a young woman comparatively speaking for her position, but damn capable, pipes up. "Captain, I just took the number sequence and used the ship's main computer try various permutations to run against the ship's navi-computer database. I also programmed it to try using various alternate methods of star chart coordinates. Nothing on any of it so far, but it could take hours to come up with anything."

Like I said damn capable. I tried some permutations just before we started but I was manually querying the navi-computer. I didn't think to let the ship's computer run the various permutations of the number sequence.

"Great thinking. Let's think outside the box to see what else we can come up with. It may not be a star chart position directly."

"If there are coordinates in the numerical sequence, then it may only be part of the numbers there." The ship's Chief engineer, Matthew Finley, speaks up from the far end of the table. Big guy and it's easy for people to think he's just a dumb hulking brute but he's the best ship wrench anyone could ever ask for. He should be designing starships.

"I've accounted for some of that in the program chief, but the computer is only as smart as the input set I gave it."

"So, not that smart you're saying?"

And they're off. The rounds of teasing and good natured jabs start off while they are working on the problem. I let them go on for a while, listening in and making a comment or two as we go and take a few notes along the way. This is by far the best crew one could ask for. I'm sure every Captain says that, but I wholeheartedly believe it's true.

Dinner is served while we continue discussing the message. The only one besides me not speaking up regularly is Chief Nate Green, my ship's boatswain, aka The Chief of the Ship. He's a non-commissioned officer but he's the most senior non-comm on the ship and was with me before there even *was* a ship. We were both guests of 3/31, but we didn't actually meet until after we were off the station and captured by pirates. He kept to himself at 3/31. He isn't a very formal man, a career non-com, more comfortable eating in the enlisted mess, than here, but I made him the Chief of the Ship for a reason, and that makes him senior staff.

He has a look about him like he's got something on his mind but takes a few minutes to order his thoughts. Then with his commanding presence, he stands and addresses the table. That presence quiets the various ongoing discussions with out any word from him. "Ladies and gentlemen, I think we're looking at this all wrong. I remember Alex from my time at 3/31." That gets a few eyebrows up. Nate's never really spoken about his stay there to anyone and I've never mentioned it. "She was as smart as they come and she knew how to make a deal happen. If she wants help from you Captain, she's gotta make sure that you understand enough of the message so you can act on it. She got information in and out of that prison regularly. I'm thinking she's given you the location right at the beginning, she's still at 3/31."

Damn, I really hadn't thought of that. She might have earned a few extra years somehow and is still stuck there. He's right, if she intended for us to go somewhere else, she would have made it at least easy enough for us to figure it out.

"I think I'll make a call to Morgan while we're still in orbit and see if he's got some recent information on 3/31's census." Morgan's an information broker extraordinaire. It's what makes him so useful to everyone on both sides of the law.

"Please excuse me ladies and gentlemen. Please continue to enjoy your meal without me and keep thinking about the message. I'll rejoin everyone by dessert." I run out to my stateroom to go make the call.

*****

It takes three days for Morgan to dig out information on 3/31's most recent population, and as of four weeks ago Alexia was still listed as a prisoner there. It also seems that they've been having repeating comms system glitches for some time now and have requested a new comm array to be installed. That might be Alexia's doing, and it may explain her message's warning about not much time left. As I'm laying on my bed in my stateroom, I'm trying to puzzle out the logistics of getting to and from the station. The station was placed at the L5 point in the orbit of Goree 1, a large gas giant not too unlike Sol system's Jupiter. No human habitable planet in that system and the only other planet is a another gas giant roughly similar in size and orbit as Saturn in Sol system, but without the pretty rings.

Using some rough and dirty math: after emerging from a fold at Goree 1, it's over a two week trip in normal space to travel to the station -- assuming a moderate acceleration pace of two g's for eight hours, coasting in for about fifteen days, and then two g's deceleration closing in on the station. And then the reverse back out again, but probably doing a three and half g burn for maybe ten hours. I assume we'll need to run like hell getting away from the station and getting us back to the gas giant to fold out of the system. That will use up a very large portion of our reaction mass, but the station's placement was designed for that. Makes breakouts and space pickups both time and reaction mass costly for smaller ships. Add in the reaction mass we'll use up as part of the fold and we'll be nearly empty by the time we're done. That's cutting it close but its doable. Now, how about the station itself? I don't have the firepower nor manpower to assault the prison, period. End of story there. I have a few fake Unitary military IFF encryption codes to bluff our way close to the station, but I don't have any codes to make a legitimate looking prisoner transfer to take anyone away. But, I can fake a prisoner drop off. Okay, that gets us in close but only until we dock, then the game's up again. I don't have enough uniforms and legitimate equipment to fake it against real Unitary forces should anyone, like Warden Harper, come aboard.

I look over at the clock and see I've been up most of the shipboard night watches just trying to work out a plan to get in and get Alexia out. There's enough guns and torpedo launchers on the prison to knock us out of the sky without too much trouble if we tried to slug it out. Alexia has got to know this!

I open my stateroom's comm-tac and set it to route an inter-ship direct call, "Chief Green, this is the Captain."

Takes a few seconds but Nate replies back faster than I expected, he may be still awake. "I'm here Capt'n. Is there a problem?"

"No, no. I know its late, well early technically, but whatever. Would ya come to my stateroom immediately. I need you."

"Well Captain, it does an old man like me some good to finally hear you say that. Shall I bring some flowers and chocolate for a proper old fashioned wooing or are we going to skip all that and just get right to business?"

"Will you just hurry and get over here. I need to pick your brain."

"Oh well you should have said so in the beginning before I got my hopes up then suddenly dashed! I'll be there in five." If he wasn't my karate sensei and my oldest friend here, I'd kick his butt just for grins, but he could easily wipe the floor with me and make me beg for more if I tried. I take a few minutes to change into something more presentable than underwear and put up the rat's nest that currently poses as my hair before he gets here. I'm hoping he can help me with insights into Alexia like before. I have to figure out how to get into 3/31 and get her out, and still keep the ship's hide in roughly one piece. I hear a chime at the door.

"Door, open. Come on in Chief."

"I made sure to take the most visible route here, and left orders that I can be found in the Captain's quarters, at her request, with every Able or Leading Spacer I could find along the way."

"Yes, yes and I'll make sure to tell everyone on a 1MC message tomorrow how you passed out after five minutes in my quarters."

"Oooo, now you're getting nasty!" Changing to a more serious tone, "What can I do for you Marlene?"

"It's Alexia. We gotta help. I just can't figure out a decent way to get her out of there without us getting killed. Its roughly seventeen days real-space travel from the gas giant out to the Lagrange point where 3/31 sits and similar back to the planet's gravity well to fold back out to safety again. I can get us in with a fake IFF transponder and military codes, but if we dock it won't take them long to figure out we're not a real Unitary ship, and if we just hang there and broadcast Alexia's code, it won't take them much longer to figure out something isn't kosher either. "

"So we don't dock. We come in and just as we would start to dock we claim some sort of emergency and abort. We can even fake up some sort of explosion on the hull."

"That gets us time outside the station for a while but that doesn't get us docked at any point either."

"I think Alex has already worked out that part."

"Why?"

"If she got a message to you through Tortuga then she knows enough about you and this ship to know you can't go in with guns blazing, even if we faked getting in close first. I was on that prison for longer than you, and the Alex I remember was resourceful, especially for being stuck in a prison. I'm willing to bet she's got a plan to get out of the station and it will be at least within some achievable parameter, even if its difficult."

"Okay, but we still need to figure out her plan."

"No, we just have to be able to react to whatever she already has planned. She's probably burned up every favor and a lot of money setting up what ever she has planned. Remember,we don't know what she actually wants either. We're assuming she wants a ride off but maybe she's not looking for that but needs us to do something else and

196

is planning to tell us via the second message. We need to keep our minds open here while we plan until we get more information. You're emotionally attached to the situation, and you need to be careful that it doesn't adversely affect your thinking."

"Alright, I buy all that, including my emotional attachment here." I knew calling him over was a good idea. A good boatswain isn't afraid to tell his Captain where her faults lie. Neither is a good friend, and I'm glad I've got both.

"Now, I do think the smart money is she wants or needs something off the station, otherwise she would have made her first message a bit easier to decode to point to some other coordinates. We, however, have another problem, Captain. When and how to broadcast the number sequence. The second we broadcast the number sequence, the station is going to ask what that was about and then when we get the answering message we're definitely exposed."

He's got a point but now a real plan starts forming in my mind. "Go get Chief Finley and the both of you go planet side to the bazaar and find me an old MEGS array."

"What are we doing with an old MEGS sensor array?"

"First, go get Matt and tell him that the Bottle o' Rum rides again."

****

It took another few days to get everything ready so by the time we emerged at Goree 1, it was already ten days since I received the message. Add our sixteen days of transit time since we folded in system and we're almost to the prison station almost four weeks later. Our fake military ship ID has held up so far. The prison thinks we're here to get them their new comm system they've been asking for. Hopefully.

I walk over to my signals officer's station, "How long since we transmitted our start code to our satellite back at the gas giant?"

"Eighty five minutes ago, Captain. "

"Excellent. It's almost show time folks." I head back to my chair to wait for everything to start. We directed a tight beam laser comm transmission back to our orbiting satellite to start broadcasting Alexia's number sequence. We're roughly four Astronomical Units, or AU's, away from Goree 1 and one AU to the station, we've got roughly 10 minutes left to wait before we'll hear any sort of answer from whatever Alexia has worked up. Since light travels at roughly eight minutes per AU, it took almost forty five minutes just for our start code signal to reach our fake ship satellite at Goree 1, then the satellite's broadcast transmission of Alexia's number sequence will take another forty five minutes to reach the station, and now we're waiting to get a reply from Alexia. Which will probably be followed shortly by the station questioning us as to what that signal was. Having a fake ship seem to appear near the gas giant and having it transmit Alexia's code, we get to pretend to be a USN Corsair class ship for a while longer, buying us just a little more time before the shooting starts. Well.. at least I hope it does. Just because I'm the Captain and the crew can't see me sweat, doesn't mean I'm not sweating it on the inside.

"Johnny, you ready to play captain again?" I ask my XO who's seated to my left.

"Sure. I kinda like having the ship to myself." He grins at me. "So who will contact us first, the station or Alexia?" Johnny asks. Johnny's dressed as a United EarthSpace Ship Navy Captain and the rest of the bridge, sans me, as their equivalents. Since my face is known, here especially, I have to make myself scarce when we communicate with the station.

"Alexia. She's waiting for our transmission. The station isn't. They'll get it, pass it around a few heads, then buck it up the chain of command until the Warden decides to call us about it."

"Captain, I just received our transmission from Goree 1." Mrs. Yvette at signals pipes up over our conversation.

Johnny replies to her, "Excellent. Who's first to reply? I think the station will be, even after the passing through various levels of command. Alexia's a prisoner, once our message gets in, she'll have to make her way to a hidden transmitter from where ever she's at. She might not be ready to reply. Twenty bucks says the station is first."

"Twenty? I thought I paid you better than that? I'll tell you what, I'll give you three to one that Alexia is first."

"Sixty to my twenty? You're on."

"Incoming message. It's a one way transmission. No military protocols at all. Part of it's encrypted." My signals officer reports as Johnny is fishing a twenty out of his pocket. I guess I should have expected an encrypted message, otherwise the station would be able to read it. Problem is what's the decrypt key?

"The header is in plain text, Capt'n. It just says the key is the last message. Routing to your station now."

Or I could just trust Alexia knows what she's doing and have expected she'd make it easy enough for us to decrypt and no one else at least for the short term. I feed the entire original message into the decryption program as the decryption key and I get a video file.

"Hiya roomie. It's been a long time since you've heard from me, but as I alluded to before, I'm in trouble here. Seems my scapegoat days weren't finished. A few months ago, some of the Senators in the EarthSpace government decided they could pin some other shady dealings on me that went sour and have recently come to light. They backdated a few records, changed a few names and bribed a witness or two and next thing you know I've got murder charges and every goon in the prison gunning for me to help avoid a trial. That M.O. sound familiar?" Yes it does. Intimately familiar. "I need to get myself and what's left of my people out of here. I burned up every favor I had and most of my money arranging twelve vacuum rescue suits and a backdoor way into space, near the prison yard area." That's opposite side of the docking collars. Looks like plan A is definitely a go. "I've got a small comm unit set to listen for a reply from you. Once you're in position to pick us up, broadcast the number sequence I gave you but in reverse and I'll know to head out. We'll be hiding from the guards by the time you get here but I don't know how long we'll be able to hide before we are discovered, so please hurry! I'm gonna owe you big time for this I know, but you know I'm good for it. "She smiles as she ends the recording. Yeah, she's good for it. Between using up a fake ship ID, buying the information from Morgan's Nest at Tortuga, and buying a used MEGS system for another fake ship satellite, this entire operation has cost me plenty. I've already paid the crew out of my own money, since this job won't have a payday.

"Alright, I get it now." Johnny says to me as he's grudgingly handing over his twenty. "My reasoning was good that she knew she may not be able to get to a comm system right away. I just didn't think about the fact she'd have a pre-recorded message."

"Ya got it in one." I guessed she'd probably use a pre-recorded message, but I could have been wrong and out sixty dollars. I look down at my display and see I already have access to the 1MC comm circuit hooked to my station. "Everyone, this is the Captain speaking. We're about to head into the lion's den in a few hours. The plan is to head to the far side of the station and pick up our passengers, who will be in vac suits. When we're in position, we'll let them know to come out. I'm assuming at that point the station is going to start to figure out something is wrong. If they don't, that's wonderful for us. We'll pick them up and high tail it back to the fold point as fast as we can. We may have a few torps to worry about on the way out but nothing we shouldn't be able to shoot down once we're away from the station and her guns. I've already paid everyone in their ship's account what I promised for doing this job. It means a great deal to me that as a ship you all agreed to take this personal job on. I do hope that doing this favor will gain us a valuable new contact for the future. Thank you all."

"Um, 'Captain' Samuels," Lisa the signals officer pipes up. "You have an incoming message from the station."

"Just as you figured Marlene." Johnny says as he leans over towards me. "Put it up on the main viewer please."

The transmission is only about a minute old for transmission lag. Lisa puts up the transmission and I see a woman's face I haven't seen in a long while, Warden Harper. "Captain Samuels, we've just detected a transmission from the planet. With the comms glitches we've been having I don't know if its real or not as it seems like it was just a sequence of random numbers. Shortly thereafter our comm system blanked out completely for a few seconds, similar to the our previous outages. Now our MEGS is detecting what may be a ship back out at the planet, but our detection is so intermittent we can't tell anything for sure. Did you pick up any transmissions and do you see anything near the planet? I'm hoping you can tell us something. It's probably nothing but I'd be so grateful if you could tell us anything." Wow, is she laying it on thick! She might as well hold up a sign that says, "I'm easy!"

The transmission continues, "As a means of returning the favor, I am having my kitchen staff prepare a special meal if you would do me the honor of joining me for dinner and a special evening once you've docked." Oh gag me. From what Alexia told me, she tries to have "dinner and a special evening" with just about every good looking captain that comes to the prison.

"Do I tell her that I don't play for the team she thinks I do?" Johnny laughs at me. He's as gay as the day is long on Venus.

"Ha! I don't think she'll care. She plays both sides of the field herself. I'm sure she'll do whatever she can to seduce you, but let her keep her fantasy for now. Tell her you didn't read any transmissions but that you're getting intermittent readings from near the planet on our MEGS as well. Tell her it seems like the power signature is lower than expected for a ship, and suggest that it's a damaged message drone bound for the station. Offer to pick it up on your way out and retransmit any message back to the station."

"Very good. Now as this is an USN military ship and not an unsavory pirate ship, and I'm it's Captain, get off my bridge before she sees you in my reply."

"Yes sir! You have the bridge. I'll be in my quarters for some rack time before all the fun starts. Make sure you get some as well 'Captain'."

"Aye, aye ma'am. I have the bridge." Johnny mockingly salutes as I leave for my stateroom.

****

"General Quarters. General Quarters. All hands man your battle stations. Captain Pritchard, please come to the bridge. We're arriving at the station," a disembodied voice and accompanying siren screams out in my cabin.

"Acknowledged." I've been up for a few hours already just trying to rehearse possible scenarios of how this can go. Almost useless as there are just too many variables here that I can't account for, but it does calm the nerves before going into battle. I dash out of my cabin as quickly as I can. My quarters are near the bridge, as most Captain's quarters are, so I'm there in no time, and see that my third officer is in command.

"Mr. Bell, what's our status?"

"We're approaching the station and I've sounded general quarters as directed by the XO. They just hailed us with docking instructions, which we acknowledged. I've also called for the XO."

"I'm here, Captain." I proceed to stand in the strategic information section in the rear of the bridge, which keeps me out of the main view-screen visual pickup, while my XO sits in my chair. Mr. Bell moves over to the XO's chair to complete the picture. Communications with the prison is in real time now.

"How's our arrival time matching up with our second broadcast for Alexia?" To hopefully buy us even more time as a fake USN ship, Mrs. Yvette suggested we time a rebroadcast of the reverse number sequence though the satellite to arrive just as we arrive instead of us broadcasting from the Bootlegger. It required just a bit more accurate math to make the timing work than first message but Lisa worked with Mr. Singh, my navigator, the math whiz.

"They are receiving the message now."

"Perfect! Johnny, we're going to pretend to dock and at the last second call the station and claim a malfunction in engineering. Matthew already has a staged 'problem' to show them. Then assume a holding pattern north of the station with a vector ready to dash to the back of the station. Helm, get ready to pour on the speed after that. Ops, please put up our current heading on the main viewer."

The main view-screen comes to life with Prison Facility 3/31 filling the entire view. It's easily four to five times our size, and with a bunch of defensive measures to boot. It looks like a starfish that had all five of its arms on one side of its body. I don my glasses and gloves to access the Combat Information Augmented Reality or CIAR display so I can see more information via the virtual world. Calling up the MEGS feed, I see with those sensors that the nearest weapon emplacements are tracking us, as expected, but the docking-arm gangway for our listed berth hasn't been extended. It should have been out when they sent us docking inormation so we could visually verify our instructions. They haven't called about the second satellite broadcast either. And the weapon emplacements are reading more infrared than they should unless they are ready to fi...

"Susan! Punch it! It's a trap! They weren't fooled! GO! GO! GO! Get us to the back of the station now!" I run right for my chair as Johnny and Matt shuffle themselves back to their regular stations.

The Bootlegger leaps forward to get to the backside of the prison in a hurry. Won't take even a minute but every second counts now. The prison's guns and torpedo launchers that were pointing at us, all converge their ordnance on the spot where we were only bare seconds ago in a brilliant flash of deadly light.

I mash my finger on one of my virtual comm circuits, "Weps! Get that point defense active, those torps will swing around in just a few seconds! Fire rear chaff to confuse them!" Our last second rush caused those torpedoes to radically change direction in order to re-acquire us, so weps should be able to pick them off while they reaccelerate.

"Already on the torps, Captain. Guns and chaff."

"Start targeting their torpedo and missile launcher emplacements Gunny. I'd prefer if we can slow down any other torps coming our way."

"Captain, we're swinging around the backside now and I can see our targets. Someone from the station is shooting at them!" Ah hell. My MEGS officer, Mr. Colmes automatically feeds the data to my CIAR so I can see the ugly details. Damn, there's small arms fire coming from some vac-suited snipers at various points on the stations external surface.

"Helm! Get us between Alexia's group and the station! Rotate us 90 degrees to port so our topside's to the station. Getting in closer will keep a few of the station's guns from being able to get a bead on us. Lisa, get me flight ops comm line."

"Ready." Damn, she's quick on her comms board.

"Timothy, there's some small arms fire coming from the station but I expect the big stuff any second. We're rotating to protect our new guests and your rescue shuttles during the pickup. Get space-borne ASAP! And keep our new guests quarantined when you get back until I can verify their identities." Just in case. I've got a feeling this was a setup.

"Way ahead of you. We launched the second the Bootlegger reached the back of the station, you can scold me later when we're back in the barn." Damn right I'll scold him, after I kiss him. He left without orders, but damn if his timing wasn't good. With the hanger bay effectively sheltered, they'll be shielded from the station's active fire and can pick up Alexia and her people in relative safety. Using the combat shuttles is marginally faster that just picking up Alexia and her gang directly, more like a hot combat zone pilot pick up, which those crews have practiced plenty times before.

We begin trading plasma cannon hits, but we can't maneuver while we're trying to act as a shield for the pickup ops, so all we really do is slug it out with the station. The problem is we'll eventually lose that slugging match if we don't get out of here quick. We're already losing armor and guns on the topside pretty fast. Damage reports are coming in from everywhere topside. Damn, this was the exact scenario I was trying to avoid at all costs.

"Captain, the smaller swarming missiles knocked out most of the dorsal point defense and a torpedo managed to get though coming up on our rear!" Johnny calls out to me.

"Oh hell!" As Chief of the Ship, Nate shouts over the 1MC circuit to the entire ship, "All hands brace for impact!"

The torpedo smashes into our rear and the main thrusters take a beating, as well as everyone inside the ship. It takes us a second to get our bearings back, even strapped in.

"Engineering- conn. How bad was that?!" I call to Chief Finley and his crew. God, I hope we make it out of this.

"We got lucky. We've lost the number four thruster but it's restarting. I'm guessing we'll have seventy five percent thrust capacity when it comes up. I'm also shipping some badly injured up to the infirmary."

Chief Green jumps into the conversation, "Belay that, sir. I'll send medical to you. Keep your people running things sir, we can't afford to have any delays. I'll see they get taken care of. Signals! Please tell medical to get a team to engineering aft thrusters." Smart man Green. Finley's men need to keep working.

"Weps to conn! We've got six more torpedo launches on THIS side of the station!" Oh hell, I check the CIAR plot and see their headed roughly for our topside bow, just were we've lost some of those point defense lasers.

"Helm, nose down fifty degrees. Johnny, relay to the pick-up shuttles our maneuvers." By angling our nose fifty degrees 'down,' which is really fifty degrees away from the station, the pickup shuttles' coverage area is cut more than half but it protects our bow some and it allows some of the further aft point defense guns an angle of attack on the torpedoes. However, the station's point defense lasers are dangerous to the shuttles and with the number of them that can point in the shuttles' direction, they would be mincemeat if they don't stay under the cover of the ship. But as long as they watch their locations, they should still have enough cover to finish the pickups. It's either we maneuver or give the incoming torps a free shot at us.

"Brace for impact!" Green shouts again. A torpedo hits us

amidships topside and I can feel it reverberating straight to the bridge, as we're just a bit forward of the strike point. Unlike our waterborne cousins, space-fairing ships have their main bridge and control centers deep within the ship and a flying bridge near topside towards the front that generally only gets used during tight maneuvers like docking in dry dock or in coordinating a ship within large tight space fleet formations. Everyone is tossed around in their chairs from the impact, but as we're all strapped in no one goes flying around the bridge like some bad old movie depictions of space combat.

Johnny leans over to me, "Marlene, it looks like we're venting water from the number three tank. I'll get a crew to pump that one out into other tanks ASAP. Don't know about the power core, but we still have power. Mr. Bell, go to the power core and help Commander Finley out by assessing its status, since he's at the aft main thrusters."

"I'm on it." Mr. Bell leaves the bridge for the power core, which is on the center-line of the ship but aft of the bridge, roughly in the last third of the ship lengthwise. The power core is the heart of the ship. If it goes, we lose space fold capability, main maneuvering, the main thruster's fusion containment bottles, gravity systems and power for most of the weapons. The fusion backup generators can power maneuvering thrusters but at a much lower output level, the life support, MEGS and some secondary systems, but power has to be severely rationed just to keep all that going. The kicker is the gravity systems. With that out, we have no internal gravity and no compensation at all for impacts or thruster acceleration. It takes a heck of a lot to take out a D-energy power core but it happens all the time in combat. We have got to get out of here now if impacts are reaching it.

"Captain, Lt. Commander Stormbringer reports he has everyone and is docking back now."

"Thank God! Helm, I want us another forty degrees further nose down and full thrust the second those shuttle are back in."

"CAG to the bridge. We're all aboard! The last pickup was right near the hanger." How does he do that?! It's like he times things right out of my head.

"I'm maneuvering now." Susan replies with almost a snicker in her voice. I think she's got a thing for our CAG, but then again so do half the women on ship. Me, I'd like to kick him in the pants like every other hot head pilot, except he's a damned excellent pilot and has a sixth sense for fighter tactics.

"All hands, we are leaving! Conn to weps! Saturate the area behind us with every gun we've got that can bear aft. Helm, keep us going on the normal vector at full acceleration away from the station until we're out of effective weapons range then plot with navigation to get us the hell back to Goree 1 as soon as humanly possible."

"Captain? Captain?" Petty Officer Yvette tries to get my attention.

"Yes Lisa?"

"The station just transmitted a coded radio message." Crap. I expected it, but I was still hoping that we might get lucky.

"Did you get a copy?"

"Yes ma'am. It wasn't very long, so I don't believe there was much encoded into the message."

"Good, see if any of our codes match up to it by any chance.

"Wanna bet it was a call for reinforcements to intercept us before we get to Goree 1?" Johnny says to me.

"I wouldn't take that bet if you gave me a hundred to one odds." The USN probably has a few ships that were waiting at the other planet in the system listening for a radio message from the station. I had hoped we could have knocked out the station's comms system with a sneak attack but they got the drop on us. While the transmission will take maybe three hours or so to reach Goree 2, it's still gonna take us two weeks' time to travel back to Goree 1 via real space, to reach Goree 1's gravity well so we can fold away. It will take the reinforcements at most a few hours to be waiting for us in orbit of Goree 1.

"Brace for impact! Torpedo astern!" Chief Nate hollers again, and again the ship reverberates with the impact and explosion.

"Sorry Captain, we couldn't stop that last one in time. It was smart enough to duck behind another one for cover."

"Save the recriminations, Mr. Sann. Just make sure nothing else is following."

"We're clear astern Captain." Max from the MEGS shouts out. Well that's a small relief.

"Crew to secondary damage stations." Chief Nate is getting damage repair efforts underway. "Let's help engineering get everything fixed as best as we can so the Captain has a functional combat vessel. Let's move people! Captain, permission to help coordinate damage crew on site?"

"Go on, Chief. Find Mr. Bell and get him to help you, he needs the experience."

"Conn to hanger. What's the situation with our guests?"

"Kincade here, Captain." My deck chief, Megan, responds. "Our guests are a bit beat up from begin shot at. A woman who claims to be Alex Torres is asking for you. I told her you'd be down when you can."

"Thanks, Megan. Get whatever medical needs they have taken care of and keep them there. I'll be down shortly."

"Aye, Captain."

"Bell to the conn."

The never-ending chaos of a bridge in combat... "Go head Mr. Bell. Please tell me good news."

"Alright, I will. The D-energy reactor is running fine. Some minor control system damage but everything else checks out alright. I've just hooked up with Chief Nate and will help him coordinate repairs per your orders."

"As you were then, Matt." I disconnect the comm circuit. I think my Third Officer replacement is going to work out alright. At least better than the last one, whom I was forced to execute as a traitor. Even though Chief Nate is technically his subordinate, he knows to defer to him for operational matters, as Nate is the senior non-com on board and has many more years of shipboard experience. A good officer knows when to look to his non-comms.

"Mr. Samuels, you have the bridge. Get the damage assessments and take action as you see fit. Get my ship ready for more combat. Keep a periodic active scan of Goree 1 and watch for any fold emergence."

✶✶✶✶✶✶✶✶

I make my way to the hanger pretty quickly to go greet our new guests. I keep my AR glasses on so I can review the MEGS data starting when we first saw Alexia's group leave the station. Looks like her group took some small arms fire on their way out and some of her people were injured and killed. Guards happening upon their position wouldn't have been able to suit up and offer space capable small weapons fire right as they were leaving. Changing the zoom level and panning around a bit, I can see that there were space suited snipers already in position outside with a line on the hatchway Alexia's people were using.

Well it's a pretty safe bet that Alexia didn't set us up, unless she was making it look good by getting shot up, which is rather ridiculous, as the shooters had no easy way to tell which vac-suit was her. She was probably sold out at some point earlier and that person wasn't with her group in space suits for the same reason. That sort of makes me feel better. I really didn't want the image of Alexia selling us out but it was possible.

I reach the hanger deck and see a triage going on right on the hanger floor. Several of her people are being treated for bullet wounds and some amounts of exposure. I see a stocky looking woman with a Hispanic coloration being treated for a wound to her thigh but she looks fully cognizant. That would be Alexia.

"Hiya, roomie. Please excuse me if I don't get up right now. My leg is just a bit less than one hundred percent, but your doc says I'm lucky my femoral artery wasn't hit."

"Hi, yourself." I say to her as I give her a big hug. "Welcome to the Bootlegger. How many did you lose in this set up?"

"You came to that conclusion too, huh? I lost four and another five of us are injured. Your man Stormbringer went out of his way to go get my dead as well. Thank him for me will you?"

"I will when he gets back. We're not out of this yet. The station got off a message that I'm sure is being listened for over at Goree 2. Don't get too comfortable yet, I'm sure we're gonna have to fight our way out somehow, but let me worry about that. It's good to see you Alexia. Other than the leg, how have you been holding up these last few years?" left unspoken is my guilt for not getting her out sooner.

She stands up and tentatively tests her bandaged leg with a crutch, "I'm doing fine, even for being in prison. People came and went and I did my best to keep them from being victimized by the other prisoners. We started getting a few really hard cases in the last two years and they started really terrorizing the general population."

Alexia made it her mission in prison to attempt to make up for her own predations on other people as a Unitary Senator and her crooked dealings. She had used her Senate position to get ahead at the expense of countless others. After she got caught in a financial securities kickback scheme and became the scapegoat for several higher-ranking Senators, she realized what she has been doing all her political career and had a change of heart. Until I met her, I didn't think most politicians had a heart in the first place, let alone one that could change for the better. She was very resigned to her lot in life as a prisoner, so she used her skills to wheel and deal to get herself and those around her extra benefits, privileges and protections. Many times it cost her personally, just to help keep the other, mostly male, predators in the prison away from those that would normally be just another nameless victim.

"These new tough guys had one particular leader who managed to convince several of the other toughs to join him to establish a new order, and succeeded when Warden Harper decided to start favoring

210

him instead of me. I guess she got tired of her girl toy and wanted a new boy toy. Not much later, I find I'm the target of a new investigation for something I supposedly did back as a Senator. That was enough to keep me in prison past my release date. Things got rough and I started getting word that my gang and I would be taken out with the Warden's informal blessing. At that point I started trading in every favor I could and bribing guards to arrange getting us out. I always had ways to get information smuggled into the prison, that's how I found out about you having a ship." I kinda look away as she mentions that and she catches my chin. "Don't you fret none! I know you couldn't have come and gotten me or my crew out of there! Hell, I'm not stupid, I know you couldn't just come to bust us out with guns blazing and to be honest, I really wasn't ready to leave. Strange as it sounds, I was at least happy, feeling like I was doing some real good for once in my life. Anyway, now that I look on it, I think just about everything was a setup from the word go to get to you and I'm sorry for that."

"Don't be. If I knew it was a setup I'd still have tried to find a way to get you guys out." Not sure if I could have but I would have tried at least.

"Well we're here now. Thanks for doing this on nearly blind faith. Now I'm in your hands."

"I've got a good crew and a good ship. I'll get us out of this." Somehow.

"Marlene, can you do me one more small favor?" This seems to be the day for calling them in.

"Sure, what?"

"Can you please get us some new clothes?! I've been wearing the same damn prison uniform for years! I'd like something baggy and warm for once. And real underwear and socks, too!" The prison uniform is a one piece singlet from neck to bottom with no arms or leggings and made of a durable spandex type of material. Prisoners were only issued one lime green uniform and slippers and had to wash them when they took showers. Hard to hide weapons and the like from guards when you have nowhere to hide them on your person that wasn't uncomfortable.

"Let me get you guys to my ship's quartermaster. We'll get you all set up and get you some quarters as well." I help Alexia hobble off the hanger deck to the ship's stores for some new clothes.

******

Surprisingly, we're not in as bad a shape as I feared. After a few hours of damage assessment, we've lost plenty of armor and most of the point defense guns topside, but the rear thrusters are all back at one hundred percent, our plasma cannons are all operational, torpedo and missile launchers are working and I've got my rail guns. I love my rail guns. The options those babies give me are just not available to most captains of ships the size of the Bootlegger. Of course, most ships in the Bootlegger's class have more armor and plasma cannons than we do, so we generally don't stand up well in a straight up fight. So, I avoid getting us into straight up fights in the first place. Like now. The Uni's did pretty much as I expected and now a half a day later, two ships show up. Two USN destroyers. USN destroyer-class ships are already bigger than we are and most have twice the guns, but thankfully none have rail guns retrofitted along their ventral spine like ours are. But they do have nuclear warheads for their torpedoes. They folded in on Goree 1's poles, one on the planetary north and the other south. They know we have to use the planet's gravity well to fold out of the system, so they've covered the planet top and bottom and set up MEGS satellites to look for our approach. For us to fold away we need to be at a relative stop compared to the planet's gravity well to make a fold envelope. Of course if we decelerate to the relative zero velocity around the planet, as needed for a fold, both of the ships will quickly maneuver toward us. They'll either demand our surrender, if we're really lucky, or just pound us so hard they'll make a nice tiny little Bootlegger diamond for the squadron leader to put on his lapel. If we make a standard approach to the planet, even with the stealth systems the Bootlegger was made with and the other systems I've added since then, at some point they will detect us. As we slow down to approach

Goree 1, they can be in position hours before we're in a position to get close enough to fold away.

Yup. It seems we're in a might sticky situation. May not survive it at all. We can all either be captured, tried and executed - or die a horrible fiery death in a glorious but futile fight to the last man or woman.

Or I can get creative.

*****

"Captain, we'll be in firing position in 1 minute."

"Thank you, Ms. Haggerty."

I invited Alexia to the bridge so she can have a front seat to the 'show' that is about to begin, but I didn't tell her my plans. Most of the crew know their parts, but once we engage, there are still a lot of ways that things can go wrong to kill us all. That's just the fun of it.

She looks over at me from Mr. Samuel's normal bridge chair which he so gentlemanly offered to Alexia, "So, looking out at your main view-screen, if I'm reading the display correctly, we're viewing what's directly in front of us right now?"

"That is correct." I smile at her.

"And I'm no navigator nor any real sort of space faring type, but don't we have to be pointing the other way to decelerate the ship to slow down?"

"Oh, no. Our thrusters have full forward ports as well as rear. Nice design in this class of ship."

"Oh, okay. Any reason though that we're NOT decelerating? Seems like that planet is coming up awfully fast in the last few minutes."

"Oh we will. Don't worry. Just not until the last second."

"Won't it take us a few hours of deceleration?"

"Normally yes. We did some deceleration earlier."

"Yes, but don't we have to be at a relative stop to fold? We're still moving awfully fast it seems to me.

"We're in position." My helms-woman calls out.

"Chief Green, proceed with the railgun salvos."

"Aye aye, Captain! Helm! Nose up sixty degrees from our current vector! All hands prepare for multiple rail gun salvo power loss! Bridge to weps! Once you have a final targeting solution, fire salvo one."

"Solution ready...shot." Weps calls out. The lights dim just a touch as the Bootlegger's two spinal-mounted railguns fire a round each at the northern destroyer's thrusters. We're at a sixty degree angle of attack to their nose position as they were set up for an incoming vector from the prison. I had us come in on the elliptical orbit vs. the direct line from the station. Slightly longer route but it gave me a different angle of attack on the planet. I can't fathom why they didn't take orbital positions with the destroyers each taking 180 degree orbital paths. That way they could stay moving and expend power keeping polar cover positions. But they kept their north and south pole emergence positions and pointed themselves directly at the station. Don't look a gift horse in the mouth I suppose.

"Helm!" Chief Green continues coordinating the bridge, "Re-orient one hundred and twenty degrees down from our current long axis for a firing vector for target two."

"Aye, aye Chief."

Alexia pipes up to me again "So you're shooting out their engines?"

"Yes. We're not really shooting them out, as their armor and the angle of attack we're coming from won't obliterate them, but it will damage them enough to cripple them for a short time. At least long enough for us to get away." I hope.

"Oriented for target two Chief." the helm pipes up.

"Bridge to weps! Once you have a targeting solution, fire at target two." Chief Green is as precise as a old Swiss watch.

Again the power and lights dim. "Shot." replies weps.

"Helm! Reorient back to a thirty degree nose up from our current movement vector. Give us belly approach to the planet."

"Aye aye, Chief."

"Ma'am" the chief addresses me directly, "two rail gun salvos fired and we're reoriented

My guest taps my shoulder to get my attention, "In any event, won't they see us approaching the planet?"

"Yup, they will, eventually."

"Marlene..." she glowers at me.

"Alright. Alright. When I acquired this ship it was apparently an experimental stealth vessel. It was converted by the Unis from a standard Corsair interceptor ship. With the materials they used and the hull design changes, we're pretty hard to see as long as our engines and maneuvering thrusters aren't lit up. Add in the stealth systems and our angle of approach from the elliptic vs from the station; we positioned ourselves on the elliptic vector before they arrived so they never saw us maneuver. And on top of all that, I planned on us burning extra hard during our initial run up away from the station, so we made our trip back in less than eight days, so we're a bit earlier than they expected."

"It was years ago when I last made this trip and I was going the other direction. I have no clue how long it should have taken. I'm confused however. You just made some maneuvers. Won't they see that?"

"Nope. That's because my chief engineer modified our maneuvering thrusters so they can switch modes and just emit hydrogen, un-fused into helium plasma, essentially making them just a sprayer. Much slower to maneuver and only small corrections can be made but nearly undetectable as there is no energy signature. It's actually an old pirate trick boarding shuttles use that he applied to a much larger scale. He says they are a bitch to keep maintained converted that way but it's worth it."

"Ma'am, they are also a bitch to maneuver with accurately." Susan pipes up from the helm.

"Yes they are. That's why I have you."

"Yes ma'am." she beams back. She really is good, better than me at helm control - and I was the best I knew at helm control for ships of the line until I got her.

"So," Alexia tries to get my attention back, "how soon will they see us?"

"Well we did emit a gravity energy signature when the guns fired, but no baryonic energy radiated that they can interpret easily. Detecting dark energy flow by its gravity effect in such a localized area as a rail gun like ours is much harder to do than a simple fold emergence or the large flow into a planetary body which creates it's gravitational field."

"Huh? Okay you lost me there. Remember, I was a politician not a physicist."

I laugh out loud at that, stellar mechanics isn't easy to understand if you don't have to live and die by it everyday. "Alright, short form, they won't see us until its almost too late for them to do anything about it, in about oh, ten seconds. I hope the rail gun rounds help give us that extra time we need. "

"And if the rail guns don't give you your extra few minutes?"

"God help us all."

"Captain, this is weps. We have two solid impacts on the northern destroyer's rearward hull section. Looks like there's hydrogen venting, we must have hit a feeder line or a tank. That's gonna leave a mark. And... rails three and four also hit their mark. The southern pole destroyer is hit square on as well. No hydrogen venting but she is listing quite a bit."

"Good job weps." I toggle the 1MC ship-wide virtual circuit to address the whole crew. "Good job, everyone! Here's where it gets tough. We're in for a very rough ride and I'll need everyone on their toes to help keep this ship together, but when we get back to Tortuga the drinks are on me!" I hear a cheer from the entire bridge crew with echos from around parts of the ship nearest the bridge.

I switch off the broadcast and turn towards my chief of the ship. "Nate, sound General Quarters. With exception of bridge, weapons, and engineering crews, all else should be at primary damage control stations."

"General Quarters! General Quarters! Damage control..."I tune out Nate for a minute while I focus on my AR display of the Bootlegger's position. Helm has us right in the pipe, headed straight for the gas giant's upper atmosphere.

"Marlene? While I'm not a physicist, I do remember that we still need to be stopped in the planet's gravity well to make a fold out of here."

"Yes we do. We're about to take care of that, however."

"Yeah , you said that earlier. How?"

"Like this. Helm! Maximum reverse thrust! Rotate us so our belly is towards the planet and give us a 45 degree nose up to the tangent of the atmosphere. Keep us there until we complete a full orbit."

"Aye Captain!"

"We're doing an orbital and atmospheric braking maneuver to slow us down. We came in with a high enough velocity so we would minimize our visual exposure to the destroyers, but we gotta slow down somehow."

"Um, Marlene, isn't this dangerous for a ship this size?"

"Very much so." and just as I speak the ship begins to buckle and shake and the braking forces jar the ship more than the gravity systems can keep up with.

The Present:

Chaos erupts all at once. The damage alarms start blaring, and everyone on the bridge is talking to someone for some needed information, adding to the noisy chaos. My chief of the ship grabs my attention while we're being shaken about "Captain, I'm getting automated damage reports from all over the ship! Hull stress warnings going way beyond original design tolerances! We've got ventral hull breaches! We're not going to hold together for much longer!"

"Captain, engineering! The lower thrusters are overloading! The heat from the atmo is roasting the engines more than they can take!"

"How much longer will they last, Chief!?"

"I don't know, maybe a minute?! Maybe less?!"

"Alright! Shut them down! Shut them down! And just flood the hell out of those engines with whatever water we can spare. Keep those engines alive! We may need them last minute! Whatever you do, leave enough water for our fold out of here -- no water, no fold! Helm! You're gonna lose the lower engines any second now! Be ready to compensate!" Damn! While most of our braking is from the orbital swing and the atmosphere, losing the thrust from the lower engines does mean it will take just a bit longer to slow us down. How much, who knows. Seconds to a minute or so. No time to calculate it. But if we lose those engines for good, we lose half our main thrusters, and if we have to go into combat maneuvers after slowing down, we'll be really screwed.

Speaking of going into combat, "MEGS! How are our friends at the poles doing?"

"I can barely see around us, Captain! Trying to compensate as best as I can. I can't see anyone out there near us for all the flames! We're pretty much flying blind towards anything that's in our flight path!"

"Keep trying. You see anything, you sing out immediately!" I knew we'd be effectively blind trying this crazy maneuver, but it still makes me extra nervous not knowing where those other ships are.

"Conn, this is Bell. We've lost most of the belly guns and all the point defense systems. Those are gone until we get back to somewhere safe. No chance of getting them back right now. I've got the DC crews prepping new MEGS sensor pods as soon as things cool down around

218

here."

"Very good! Keep on it."

"Conn this is Finely. Lower engines are down. We're cooling them as fast and safely as we can. They're gonna be at reduced output but I think they are still functional."

Good news! "My compliments to your crews, Matt."

"Thanks, Cap't."

My helms-woman pipes up again, "Captain! We're about to complete a full orbit. We still haven't bled off enough velocity to get to a stand still."

"Chief Nate, talk to me."

"The belly is roasted good, we're out the lower engines until we get out of atmo, and we're blind. And I'm now getting reports from Bell on some hull breaches on the belly. We need to get out of atmo now."

"Helm, half forward thrust and nose up for just a few seconds to skip us out of the atmosphere." As soon as she pours on forward thrust we slip right out of the atmosphere and the flames all around us stop roasting the ship.

"Get us into a stable orbit and full reverse thrust. How soon until a complete stop?"

"With half our engines, and pulling out now ... revised time of ... five minutes forty five seconds." So close. "Nate, prep us for a fold."

"Ship, prepare for folding operations" chimes out Nate as he takes over the logistics of a fold.

"Signals, punch me up damage control group 2. Mr. Bell, get those MEGS sensor pods replaced as soon as you can. We need to see around us."

"Captain," Colmes, my MEGS operator pipes up, "every ventral sensor pod for the MEGS is fried. Would you rotate the ship so we can see around us?"

Damn, I should have already thought of that. "Helm, start rotating us starboard at a rate of two revolutions a minute please. Mr. Colmes, what have you got for me?" I'm watching his feed directly on my CIAR glasses. As we rotate towards the planet we can see the destroyer at the north pole in a holding pattern, but beginning to drift towards the planet. Good. They've launched some torpedoes at us, but they don't have an angle on us for effective plasma cannon fire.

"Weps, conn. You see the inbound torps?"

"Yes I do. I've only got two point defense guns left Captain, and they're topside. We have to stop spinning to get them." Of course we do.

"Contact!" Mr. Colmes shouts, "Off to ship starboard -it's the other destroyer! They've maneuvered away from the southern pole and are headed straight for us! Incoming missile barrage!"

"All hands brace for impact!" I hear over the ships speakers from Nate.

The smaller missiles from the second destroyer are much closer to us by the time we discover them. Weps manages to knock out half of the swarm by luck of our position, but the other half impacts onto our topside. We're all slammed around again as they hit, I can see smoke coming from behind me from somewhere on the bridge. That wouldn't have done as much damage had we not already been roasted in the atmosphere braking maneuver. We're in deep trouble.

"We just lost those point defense guns, Captain!" Nate tells me over the bridge fire alarm. I look over my shoulder and see Alexia with a fire extinguisher, putting out a fire with Johnny in the CIC area of the bridge.

Alexia sees me looking at her from my command chair and yells over the noise on the bridge, "Looks like were not gonna make it huh? Thanks for trying. I guess all my favors are finally used up."

I'm not giving up yet!

"Weps! Whatever you got left, throw it all at that destroyer! I don't care if they're spitballs! Get it out there! Helm! Get us back in the upper atmosphere, right now! Forty-five degree angle of attack, topside to the planet! Navigation! Have fold plot ready! We're folding from the upper atmosphere!"

"What?!" I hear from multiple voices on the bridge.

"Captain, what are you thinking?" Nate asks as I get up from my chair. Normally, a ship can't keep a stable fold envelope in any sort atmosphere. Too much dispersion of the fold energy field through the atmosphere, so a fold envelope won't hold the energy around the ship properly. We would only fold a part of the ship, like every third molecule. A very ugly way to die, that's why no one does it. Being a gas giant planet of mostly light density elements like hydrogen and helium, I'm hoping we can keep a stable enough fold envelope in its upper atmosphere to get out safely. I don't think anyone's ever been desperate enough to try what we're about to do.

When we hit the atmosphere we come to a violent dead stop. Finally. While folding in atmo is dangerous enough, folding while moving in relation to your gravity well anchor makes the fold calculations helleciouslly difficult.

"Captain! Those torps from the north pole are under a minute away!" My MEGS operator shouts out. Oh yeah, the first torps.

"Noted." I hope this works!

I quickly reach the helm station and quietly talk to my helms-woman, "Susan, you're relived. Sit in my chair, I've got this. And take notes, just in case we ever do this stupid stunt again." I put us in this mess, my responsibility to see it though. Although if we don't make it, I doubt I'll have to worry about the crew lynching me. We'll be dead pretty fast. "MEGS! Gimme a running countdown to impact!" I take Susan's place at the helm and spin us lengthwise in place fast and start the water spray which shoots water all around us further than normal all the while Mr. Colmes is counting down to impact. The difference is I'm holding the spray for much longer than normal trying to saturate the area around us as much as possible. In seconds, the water stops as we've used everything in our tanks. I just hope that the extra water stays with us long enough to fold.

221

"Navigation where's my!... " and of course as I'm shouting, Agit has already transferred the final numbers to the fold system.

"Five, four, three! Brace for impact!" I hear shouted on the bridge as the torpedoes reach us. I pull the fold engage switch.

The main view screen goes black.

Then brightens as the glow from Tortuga's sun glows from the dawn side of the planet. Thank the Lord, we made it!

*****

Chief Nate is holding down the ship in dock with a skeleton crew, while the rest of us are planet-side at Blue Oyster Bar and Grill in Tortuga's main city. While Nate can drink with the best of them, he isn't the type to get plastered anymore. I'm guessing it has to do with how he got drummed out of the Navy. However, I have a feeling this party is going to last a lot longer than a single ship's watch anyway. Everyone is having a great time. Other than Alexia's losses, we got away with few casualties ourselves and no one dead among them. Any time that happens it's celebration time.

I've invited a few local factors - including Morgan - to help line up some deals and maybe a bit of front money for a cruise. Really can't exclude Morgan on anything like this. It's his planet. Anyway, I need to get the Bootlegger in dry dock and once she's been refitted, I'm flat broke. Already paid the crew for the rescue job, at least. But we'll need something profitable really soon or I won't be able afford to keep her running for very long.

"Marlene, over here!" Alexia waves me to come over to the bar where she's got a small cluster of local factors. She told me she would help try to get some business deals for me, but I didn't think she'd get them done this fast.

"Hiya Marlene! I've just been chatting with Mr.'s Percy and Levin here and it seems they have some extra cases of some very exquisite wines from a Confederation colony that would sell very well inside EarthSpace planets."

"Is that so?" I question Alexia.

"Yes. Quite so, but with the high tariffs on imported alcohol and especially the ban on some goods from Confed worlds..."

"Like wine or other alcoholic beverages." I reply.

"Yes, yes... just so. I happen to know a buyer who would love some new wines to sell to his clientele, without all the hassles of tax stamps, special import permissions and the like. If you think you could get it to him, I think these gentlemen would see clear to cut you in for twenty five percent of the action."

"How much, when and where?"

Alexia grins at me, "Enough to fill all your holds, sometime roughly two months from now when the wine is ready and to Mars, Sol system."

"Thirty five percent, I've got expenses to cover getting into Sol system." I fire back automatically.

Percy pipes up now. "Thirty percent, and we'll toss in an extra pallet for you and your crew personally."

"Done." I shake hands with both of the men and Alexia to seal the deal.

Now Levin speaks up, "Well very good. Please excuse us as we have other business to attend to. It was very good to meet you Alexia. I'll comm you in two weeks to start working out the details and to hold you to dinner." Both men leave the bar and the party.

"Wait. You introduced yourself to him as Alexia? Not Alex? What about your notion of separating yourself from your past?"

Yeah well, if I did that I wouldn't be here, now would I? My past is just as big a part of me as the present. Time I recognized that. Thank you again." She proceeds to grab me and give me the biggest bear hug she could manage.

I begin to cry on her shoulder as she hugs me. "Dammit, I'm so sorry about not coming for you before. I should have tried something.

You wouldn't have had to rot in that prison hell-hole for so long if I hadn't been so selfish thinking about my situation for so long."

"Stop that right now! We covered this already. I wanted to be there. Needed to. Not just for me, but others that were sent there that I looked after. You remember Jalaine? Two years after you left she was attacked by some of the other thugs in the prison and I managed to help save her from being raped and beaten to death. Convinced Warden Harper to give her some good behavior time off and got her out of there a year early. You on the other hand have your own gang to look after. Look all around you here. I've counted over twelve toasts to the Captain of the Bootlegger at various tables. They followed you willingly to help you break a friend out of prison for no prize money and only some extra pay from their captain." She grabs my face between her hands and forces me to stare her down. "You have over a hundred and fifty people dependent on you aboard your ship and from what I've heard from them, they would follow into hell for the Devil's own toothbrush if you ordered it, no questions asked. That's damn rare anywhere. You've taken good care of your people, and that means not going on some fool rescue unless the circumstances were such that it wasn't going to be a suicide mission."

"If you're gonna put it that way..." as I sniff. She's right of course. I have a responsibility to my crew and ship. We risk our lives for prize money and possible riches, but I'm ultimately responsible for them all. Funny how they never really taught that part of command back at the Academy. They used to once upon a time, I think, but not now. It's just follow orders and back deal or back stab to get ahead. "Thanks Alexia. I probably needed to hear that."

"Hey, what are friends for? Speaking of, you haven't introduced me to Henry Morgan yet."

"Ex-Captain Morgan. Of Morgan's Spirits pirate fleet and now the owner and governor of this planet." I stand up and motion Alexia to do the same as I point out Morgan across the party room.

"Yeah, that sounds familiar. Wasn't his ship named after some drink? Bottle of something?"

"Yes, that's him. He runs this place now. I have a feeling the two of you are going to do very well together."

Patrick A. Waldoch

The Favor

Patrick A. Waldoch is a Computer System-Network BOfH *(look it up) with too many expensive hobbies. Between motorcycle track days (when he can scrounge up the cash for track fees), practical shooting sports (when he can scrounge up the cash for ammunition) and his newly minted fiancée (when he can scrounge up the cash for dinners and sparkly things for her. - Just kidding she's the best!) he also plays RPG's regularly with the other authors from this volume. At Gencon you might know him as one of the dwarves from Bad Apple Inc,- Grumpy.*

Afterward:
On Writing My Story

Matthew J. Kolell

Matthew J. Kolell

Afterward: On Writing My Story

It all started many years ago in the sixth grade. She strolled past my desk wearing those tight fitting dress pants and a tight fitting pink sweater. When she turned around her hair did that flip and she flashed a dazzling smile like something out of a movie. She was the student teacher. Younger than any of our mothers and older than the girls in our school, with curves in all the right places. She wasn't even from the U.S. She was from someplace exotic like Canada. I would have done anything for her. Get her food, run to the post office, knee my best friend in the crotch, she named it, I would have done it.

She didn't ask me for anything but she did say I should read more and said I might enjoy <u>The Hobbit</u>. The next day I had my mom pick me up from school instead of taking the bus and take me to the library. When I finished the book, I excitedly told her the next day at school. She gave me an underwhelming, "I'm glad you enjoyed it," but I was already hooked.

I started reading on a regular basis, other fantasy, adventure or any book that had an interesting cover. Then I found the endless quest books. They were fun and gave the reader a chance to make choices that altered the outcome of the story. You usually wouldn't read the entire book even if you reread them two or three times because of the different variables but then there was this one book <u>Return to Brookmere</u>. I kept re-reading it going over possible choices, because I hated the way it ended. You got lost in this one cave and came across trolls or goblins or some other such baddie. The point of the book was to escape alive to warn of the danger they posed. You could get caught or escape, while I wanted to be the hero and destroy them all or at least kill something. The main problem was that I never felt like my character was in danger while reading it.

That led to my first foray into writing. I could write a better story than that so I thought awhile about the plot and decided to start the book. I dug out the family typewriter and some paper and set out to write my first book. After completing a couple paragraphs on a half page of paper, I called it a day, to pick up again tomorrow. The next day came but the story was abandoned. Even though I never finished it or didn't even write another word, it was something I always wanted to do. I'd still recall that book into my teens and college years and think I could do better.

***

I'm not sure if I was too young to appreciate the danger of that endless quest book or not, but eventually getting into role-playing-games, I was able to appreciate a sense of foreboding.

Before the game even started, the gamemaster let on that aliens might be involved in the adventure and our characters could die. So the investigation of the underwater facility with only one way of escape, led to in-depth searching and a sense of paranoia. As soon as we came across an actual sighting of an alien, we hightailed it towards an exit, but we ended up in a fight with one of them on the way. Even though we managed to take it out, we were so paranoid as players that we decided to get out of the facility with our lives, even though we had only explored half of one of the three levels and also putting in jeopardy any payment we might get for not exploring further. But because of the danger aspect it was one of the funnest adventures I had while gaming.

Fast-forward some years, I continued to want to write and thought up whole stories but never actually sat down to write them. Sure I wrote some poetry but nothing very long or time consuming. Then one day after work while taking the elevator down, she stepped through the doors. I don't remember much of what she looked like except that she was attractive. So as I glanced down to see what her legs looked like, and I spotted the most amazing thing. She was carrying a purse made out of Matthew McConaughey. Not his flesh or hair or any such gruesome thing but pictures of him put on some type of material that made up the entire purse. I'm not sure if she saw my face or not but my eyes were glued onto the purse from the moment I saw it until she walked out through the doors. At first I was shocked and unsure if I was seeing right when I noticed Matthew and then slowly my mouth opened in amazement that either she or someone else had taken the time to make the purse and then openly carry it in public.

It wasn't the stalker-ish aspect of it, it was that it was of Matthew McConaughey. Sure he may be attractive and have some sex appeal, but there are better looking guys out there and he can't act. Running through my mind while looking at that purse, there has to be some men out there who are just as handsome, if not more so, who actually have acting talent. But then how many of those guys actually pursue acting and then those that do still have to get a break somewhere. Even though some may be great actors and might even dream of it, they will never be one unless they put themselves out there and hone their talent.

So with that realization in place, I came across some people who are also trying to start writing and encourage each other. So with two stories already written, I sit here with this message before me: "PJW- Remember 3/31? Need help desperately, not much time left. Please, you're the only one! 2713311869101001 You know what to do. - Alex," and I don't know what to write. I have some ideas but am not sure how to make the message mysterious or bring out mystery and a sense of urgency to the story. I could go back to the first story and write a spinoff of how Balt finds a dead soldier outside after the explosion. He sees the note in his hand and then sets off on an exploration into trying to find out the meaning of the message. Or I could have it set in the future where a young boy in the slums gets the message and sets off to help his sister. Still another possibility, a husband gets the message from his wife. He rushes out of work and embarks on an errand where he needs pick up an item and get to his wife before its too late. The story would be filled with intrigue and excitement as he hurries through town avoiding those who would stop him. It ends with him giving the bra to his wife which was the stock number she needed because the one she had wouldn't work with the new outfit she would wear for her first appearance as spokesperson for the new hotel opening on the strip.

With all these ideas going around in my head, I think I need to take a lesson from Matthew. Even if you're not that talented, you'll never know unless you actually put yourself out there. And who knows, maybe there is greatness there or you could get that lucky break even if you're only as good as Matthew is at acting. Maybe if I just pick an idea and start writing, and work on the story, some more will come to me.

It all started many years ago...

If you read writing blogs, watch podcasts, attend workshops, and talk to authors – it becomes pretty clear that writing is far more often a skill learned through study, hard work, and practice, rather than simply a natural-born talent possessed by all authors.

AuthorsRising.com is a place for up-and-coming authors to come together and collaborate on stories, learn from each other, and hone their skills. Authors Rising, LLC publishes collections of those stories, on behalf of the authors involved.

If you'd like to be a part of one of our books, and are willing to work hard, meet deadlines, and take & give honest, well-intentioned feedback from your fellow authors, come check us out.

We'd love to have you be a part of the community.

Premeditated or heat-of-the-moment, accidental or under orders, a matter of pure survival, or pure evil...

Your first kill changes you, defines you. Your reaction reveals who you are, and sets the path for who you become.

Casanova is a rising star in his shady Organization, "Matt" is fighting to keep his sanity... will both become the monsters others believe them to be? In wars of the future and past, will Urzzt and Junior, two reluctant soldiers, go against their natures in the heat of battle? Can Swan, trained to just observe, take action to turn the tables on her hunter? Can training prepare Ship's Officer Danny Garrett for the trauma of his first kill, and allow him to continue on when lives are at stake? What will become of Whisper and Daniel after the "accidental" deaths of those they love most? What happens to Dave and his killer now?

Join Authors Rising as we share in nine very different characters' stories, and explore how they and their lives are affected by their FIRST KILLS.

Get <u>You Never Forget Your First</u> at authorsrising.com!

Take a seat at the table, ante up, and get ready to "read" your fellow players...

In four stories about poker and the sometimes unusual players that make it so interesting, Authors Rising takes us on a tour of the game, from Mars to Milwaukee.

Will Earth's first contact with an alien intelligence still leave time to finish a crucial hand? Will a mid-level enforcer be able to stay in the game, or be forced out by a jealous madam? Will a captain's winnings be enough to save her ship once the shooting starts? Will Lady Luck unravel the bonds of a merc unit's brotherhood?

Read these exciting new stories by our up-and-coming authors to find out!

Get <u>Read 'Em & Weep</u> now at authorsrising.com!

www.ingramcontent.com/pod-product-compliance
Lightning Source LLC
Chambersburg PA
CBHW050508260626
47157CB00004B/1237